VIOL

FIRES

CW00641433

GHOST SQUADRON
5

AUDEAMUS

ERIC THOMSON

Violent Fires

Copyright 2024 Eric Thomson
First paperback printing November 2024

All rights reserved.
This book, or parts thereof, may not be reproduced in any form without permission.

This is a work of fiction. Names, characters, places, and incidents either are the product of the author's imagination or are used fictiously. Any resemblance to actual persons, living, or dead, business establishments, events, or locales is entirely coincidental.

No generative artificial intelligence (AI) was used in the writing of this work. The author expressly prohibits any entity from using this publication to train AI technologies to generate text, including, without limitation, technologies capable of generating works in the same style or genre as this publication. The author reserves all rights to license uses of this work for generative AI training and development of machine learning language models.

Published in Canada
By Sanddiver Books Inc.
ISBN: 978-1-998167-11-1

Sanddiver
Books

— One —

Falen Senesca would die in fifteen minutes, although he didn't know it. The head of the Senesca Ranching Corporation was doing his last round of the main ranch compound before going to bed. He alone remained awake at this time of night, but the habit was so ingrained he couldn't sleep unless he visited every building and checked the doors. Finally, at oh-one-hundred hours, Senesca entered the sprawling single-story residence at the heart of the ranch and headed for his bedroom.

That was the signal the attackers waited for. They'd not only observed the ranch for several nights running but had also infiltrated a few of theirs as casual labor now that it was harvest time. Some deportees from Celeste, generally referred to as deps, sought seasonal work to supplement the government benefits that kept them idle for the rest of the year, making it common to find them engaged in legitimate, albeit menial, jobs.

Invisible to the naked eye, dark shadows crept through the fields around the compound, closing in on it beneath a sky heavy with clouds and short on the natural illumination usually provided by Garonne's moons and the stars. The scent of rain hung heavily in the air, yet it held off so far, save for a few droplets here and there. The attackers would have preferred a torrential downpour to further mask their approach, but humanity still hadn't gained control of the weather on Garonne or any other human-occupied world.

But it didn't matter. Security on this ranch, like on others in the area, was virtually non-existent. They were too far from the nearest city, Tianjin, to attract any dep riffraff looking for items they could steal and resell. Deps, by and large, were opportunists whose high time preference and low impulse control made them undesirables on Celeste. And so, the mother world had deported them to its colony, Garonne, while it still held sway. They mainly were petty criminals, those with a propensity for violence, the unemployable, the lazy, the ones with subnormal intelligence, and the troublemakers. They preferred preying on each other and those living in the cities rather than traveling out into the deep countryside looking for victims.

Until this night.

As they neared the compound, they coalesced into groups, one for each occupied structure. Two per team moved ahead of the others and pulled out spray cans. They crept up on sensors attached to the sides of the buildings and encased them in rapidly setting foam, effectively rendering them useless. Everyone froze, listening for alarms, but they heard nothing. The compound remained as still as before.

Then, more shadows detached themselves from each group and placed small explosive charges on the door locks while the teams got ready to rush inside their assigned targets. Immediately after they confirmed their readiness through radio communication, the charges exploded in unison, producing subdued, muffled thuds as the attackers' leader remotely set off their detonators.

The doors were blown open, and they silently entered, weapons at the ready.

In the laborers' bunkhouse, the deps who'd infiltrated the ranch had already begun cutting throats by the time the team assigned to it entered the first of four sleeping bays. The team leader quickly dispatched his people to the others, and two dozen men and women died in their sleep, blood pooling on the floor beneath their beds. Then, he led his team back out into the open and had them take up a defensive arc facing the sole road connecting the Senesca ranch to the rest of Garonne.

Things didn't go quite as smoothly in the two-story apartment building housing the ranch's permanent employees, and firefights broke out inside, killing four attackers. The rest withdrew after tossing high-powered incendiaries into the ground floor units and then picking off those who tried to escape the subsequent blaze.

But the attack almost unraveled in the main house, where the extended Senesca family lived. Falen, the patriarch, woke immediately at the sound of the lock being blown, even though it made no more noise than a book falling on the floor. He was out of bed within moments, hand reaching for the blaster he kept in his night table drawer, and then he glanced through the window.

"What the hell?" He muttered, seeing black shadows move around outside. Then, he noticed windows in the apartment building briefly lighting up multiple times and recognized it as plasma fire due to his experience in the Marines four decades ago.

"Alarm!" He shouted, rushing into the hallway. "We're under attack."

He opened the door to his wife's bedroom and, when he saw she was stirring, said, "Arm yourself and get the grandkids into the basement, love."

Falen Senesca then rushed to his eldest son's room and found him already up and brandishing a gun while his daughter-in-law was hastily pulling on a pair of trousers.

"Come on. I'm sure they blew the front door lock."

His youngest son erupted through a door, also armed.

"What the hell is going on, Dad?"

"There are a lot of people outside, and they're shooting up the apartments. I have no doubt they're even now entering this house."

With Falen in the lead, they headed for the living room and came face-to-face with a dozen figures dressed in black. Falen instinctively double-tapped the first one while his eldest son shot the second. The three backed up around a corner as the intruders returned fire, winging the youngest son, who barely suppressed a gasp of pain.

"I've called the police," Falen's wife shouted behind them.

"They'll take at least what? Twenty minutes? We're on our own, love," Falen said over his shoulder.

A small black cylinder flew through the air and rolled to the bend in the corridor. Before any of the men could react, it burst into flames, momentarily blinding them, and drove them back.

"Incendiary," Falen said, shielding his eyes with his left forearm. "That stuff will burn until it's good and done, and it'll be done when everything is ashes. We have to get out of the house."

As if to underscore his words, wall hangings began to burn, as did the wooden floor, and they turned.

"Get the grands, love. We're escaping through the back door."

"And what if the bad guys are waiting for us there?"

"Then we'll fight our way through." Falen Senesca sounded determined, but he felt panic gnaw at his gut, the sort he'd never experienced before. He was nothing if not a realist and knew their chances of escape were dwindling rapidly.

Still, Senesca led them through the house, picking up both sons' wives and the five grandchildren, varying in age from five to sixteen along the way while flames grew behind them. Just as he reached the back door, he heard a muffled thump, and it swung open, revealing two black-clad figures who hosed the hallway with plasma fired from military-style carbines.

Falen Senesca died first. His sons a few seconds later, followed by the rest of the family. One attacker tossed an incendiary device through the door, and then both turned on their heels and vanished into the night, leaving the flames to consume the Senesca family's bodies.

Within minutes, two of the buildings were aflame, lighting the night, but no one remained to watch them burn — the intruders were gone, leaving nothing but dead bodies behind, including those of their own fallen.

The quick reaction group from the 27th Federation Constabulary Regiment's Tianjin Battalion arrived twenty minutes later aboard armored aircars bearing the Constabulary's scales of justice balanced on a downward-pointing arrow insignia. By then, any trace of the attacking force had faded as they dispersed to the four winds aboard ground vehicles.

"No life signs, sir," the sensor tech said, glancing over his shoulder at Inspector Mando Trenor, who was in charge of the QRG and sat behind him in the command aircar.

"Damn." Trenor's face hardened as he contemplated what he'd find once they got there. They'd seen the burning buildings from a fair distance and feared the worst. "All units, this is QRG Leader, land at the center of the compound."

The six aircars settled, dropped aft ramps, and disgorged armored constables carrying plasma weapons. They quickly dispersed under their sergeants to check out the various structures.

"QRG Leader, this is QRG Two," one of them said a few moments after entering the bunkhouse. "You need to come and see this."

Inspector Trenor hurried over, and the moment he entered, he felt bile rising in his throat. Pools of blood were coagulating on the floor beneath the cooling bodies whose heads lay at unnatural angles.

"There's two dozen of them, sir, dead with their windpipes sliced through." The sergeant's tone, though soft, mixed horror with anger. "And another six beds that were in use but their occupants have vanished."

"Horrible." Trenor shook his head in dismay. "Begin collecting their IDs and DNA samples, but leave them in place until we've recorded every square centimeter of this building."

"Yes, sir."

Trenor exited the bunkhouse and hurried to where another of his squads had deployed a firefighting hose they'd found in the small structure housing the wellhead and water pump and were spraying down the staff apartment block. But it seemed like a vain effort. The entire building was on fire, and as he watched, he saw the second floor collapse, sending sparks everywhere.

"Any idea how many people died in there?" He asked the sensor tech who'd been following him around, recording the actions taken by the QRG for Trenor's report.

"Based on the information available, seventy-two individuals resided on the ranch. Of these, thirty were in the bunkhouse, and eleven were Senesca family members.

Therefore, if our records are accurate, it means that thirty-one people lived in the apartment block. From the bodies surrounding the doors, it can be concluded that none of them escaped alive. That leaves the six unaccounted for from the bunkhouse, who may have infiltrated the ranch on behalf of the attackers and left with them."

"Sixty-six innocents murdered in cold blood." Trenor shook his head again. "How the hell is that possible in this day and age? It's a massacre."

Just then, the radio came to life. "Tianjin QRG Leader, this is Niner. I'm headed your way. Status report, over."

Trenor groaned inwardly at hearing the voice of Chief Superintendent Kyra Bain, the 27th Constabulary Regiment's commanding officer. It figured she'd be up at oh-one-hundred hours and coming to see the mess that was the Senesca ranch for herself. Bain, newly promoted to command the 27th, still liked to be at the center of the action instead of letting her subordinates deal with matters themselves. She wasn't a bad CO, but often got in the way.

"Niner, Tianjin QRG Leader here. We're at the Senesca ranch. No life signs. Twenty-four bodies in the bunkhouse, throats slit. Staff apartment block and main house on fire, burning beyond any hope of control. We suspect that sixty-six out of the seventy-two individuals living here have been killed. The other six appear to have vanished."

Silence filled the air as Bain processed the information. Then, in a more subdued tone, she said, "Thanks, QRG Leader. I'll be there in ten minutes. Niner, out."

— TWO —

"This is one hell of a mess." Mike Verrill, president of soon-to-be fully sovereign Garonne, kicked a piece of charred wood as he studied the Senesca family home or, rather, its ruins. The sun had barely risen when he'd shown up in his official aircar, escorted by a squad of officers from the Iskellian Police Service. The bodyguards had become necessary in recent times because of an upsurge in terrorist activities. Or so the Iskellian police chief thought. Verrill, tall, powerfully built, with a salt-and-pepper beard framing a square face, wore the clothes of an ordinary laborer and would easily have been mistaken as such. But anyone looking into his eyes would have seen steely determination and hints of a veteran insurgent's ten-thousand-meter stare.

"It is that, sir," Chief Superintendent Bain, standing beside him, replied. Stocky, with short black hair and deep-set, watchful brown eyes framing a strong nose, she wore the Constabulary's gray working uniform with her rank insignia, two diamonds, and an oak leaf wreath on the collar. "I don't even know how to begin dealing with it.

The satellite surveillance showed a dozen ground vehicles, old junk without registration beacons, leaving the area, mostly heading for Tianjin. We have constables looking for them, but I don't hold up much hope. The perpetrators would have hidden or discarded the vehicles by now and dispersed. As for the bodies of the permanent employees and family, we'll be lucky to recover anything identifiable. Preliminary investigation indicates they used incendiary devices, and those burn hot enough to cremate human beings."

"But why attack a peaceful ranch?" Verrill turned to glance at Bain, incomprehension evident on his rugged face.

She shrugged.

"Because it's isolated and far from the nearest law enforcement in Tianjin. Or at least far enough to act before the QRG makes it out of the barn."

"I meant, why shift away from targeting government facilities? So far, that's everything they - whoever they may be - have done. But now they escalated drastically by committing something that I can only qualify as a massacre. Sixty-six civilians murdered in the space of minutes, with the ones whose bodies weren't burned beyond any recognition having their throats slit as they lay in their beds."

Bain mentally scoffed. The situation was glaringly obvious, and she was well aware that Verrill had once led a group of guerrillas more than a decade ago in a rebellion against Celeste's colonial government. He even achieved partial success by obtaining home rule for the colony after a nasty insurrection, so he should be well acquainted with the techniques involved. Perhaps he'd forgotten. Or, more likely, he'd never targeted civilians in his day, only government officials and militia personnel. An ethical revolutionary, so to speak.

But she merely said, "The insurgents, terrorists — call them what you like — are deliberately upping the ante, sir. If they hit one ranch, they can hit any of the hundreds on Garonne, and that'll spread fear like wildfire, threaten the food supply, and stretch my and the local police resources past the breaking limit. We still don't know who they are, except a portion of them are obviously deps skilled at disappearing among the wider dep population."

Verrill snorted angrily.

"Ah, yes. The damned deps. Celeste's revenge for having to grant us home rule. That decision by the Commonwealth Supreme Court gave us the worst possible outcome back then. No full independence, no more Celeste-funded militia to keep order, and no way to stop Celeste from dumping even more of their undesirables on us. We're well rid of the corrupt lot, even though their actions will still bedevil us for a long time."

"At least the flow stopped once Garonne seceded along with the rest of the Federation two years ago, leaving Celeste behind, sir."

"No doubt, but they sent us enough of them in the years immediately before secession to ensure we'll be dealing with deps and all the problems they cause for generations.

And now that we've declared we won't provide them with benefits to remain idle all day long once Garonne achieves full sovereignty and takes charge of its internal matters, the troublemakers are becoming more than just vocal." Verrill let out a bitter bark of laughter. "That's probably what triggered the attack on this place, come to think of it. Keep the bennies flowing, and we'll stop cutting throats."

"Maybe," Bain admitted. "We'd better put out a communique telling every citizen of this attack and warning farmers and ranchers, especially those in outlying areas, that they're now vulnerable. Will you do it, or should I?"

"I'll do so," Verrill replied. "But I'll run the text by you first."

Bain nodded once.

"Done. When you write it, keep in mind that the 27th Constabulary is already stretched to the limit since we're still only at half-strength, so make no promises of protection on our part. What with the deps becoming more active, our investigating this," she made a sweeping gesture with her arm, "and our regular policing tasks, we don't have enough constables or hours in the day. The ranchers and farmers need to protect themselves, at least until a QRF can respond."

"Let's hope this was a one-off."

"We must expect more attacks, sir. That's almost guaranteed after the complete success of this one. Our only option is to hope that the next raid will be less lethal as people will be more vigilant.

"How many of the scum do you think did this?" He nodded at the burned-out house.

A shrug.

"Hard to tell. Whatever surveillance sensors they had, the control center with its recordings is somewhere under those ashes, probably melted into an unrecognizable blob. But I'd say there was a fair number of them. Perhaps as many as forty or fifty. Maybe even more. A dozen ground cars could easily carry up to seventy."

"And many of the farms and ranches have twenty or fewer people, not all of them armed." Verrill sighed. "I wish I knew who the driving force behind the deps was. They certainly didn't organize themselves into a large raiding force on their own, that's for sure. Off-worlders must be involved."

"Agreed, and we'll look for that driving force, but again, don't hold your breath. We're simply too underpowered for those sorts of investigations." Bain hesitated for a few seconds. "You could always ask the Fleet to provide aid to civil authority. I think the situation is such that they would send Marines to backstop us and the local police forces. After all, Garonne is technically still a Federation colony, even though you're almost independent."

"Ask the Fleet or the Federation government on Wyvern?"

"The government, via the Minister of Defense, who's empowered to authorize aid to civil authority under the Federation's constitution. But send a copy of the request to the Grand Admiral at the same time. It'll speed things up."

Bain paused again. "Sir, getting a battalion of Marines would make a world of difference. They could institute the sort of patrols that might discourage the insurgents from attacking isolated farmsteads."

"Very well. I shall make the appeal. But if you're right, a lot more people will die before the Marines get here."

And she was. Three nights later, attackers targeted a farm in the Holback region, located three hundred and fifty kilometers south of Iskellian, the capital. Even though the thirty inhabitants were ready, warned by President Verrill's message, they all perished, but not before taking a dozen assailants with them. The attackers torched the farm itself, as well as the surrounding fields.

Then, a company of the 27th Constabulary, based on a tip they'd find evidence concerning the fatal attack on the Senesca ranch, attempted to raid a notorious dep stronghold in Tianjin's no-go quarter but were bloodily repulsed with six casualties among the constables. It quickly became clear that the so-called informant was in the opposition's pay, and the company was lured into a deadly ambush.

The running gun battle between heavily armed deps and the Constabulary turned into a rout for the latter because their rules of engagement prohibited them from risking the lives of bystanders. The deps had no such rules and caught a dozen civilians in the crossfire.

Verrill considered declaring Tianjin to be in a state of insurrection. But Bain convinced him otherwise. The authorities simply didn't have the strength to deal with it, and any declaration would have been an empty gesture ripe for mockery.

Within days of making the request for aid to civil authority, Verrill received a reply from Wyvern. The Federation government had issued orders to Fleet HQ. It would send a force capable of stopping the depredations as fast as possible.

— Three —

Brigadier General Zachary Thomas Decker, Deputy Commander - Operations of the 1st Special Forces Division, smiled at the memories resurfacing as he read the order from SOFCOM to deploy an SF squadron to Garonne. He and his spouse, Rear Admiral Hera Talyn — she'd been a commander and he a chief warrant officer at the time — had worked with Verrill's insurgents to overthrow the colonial government a decade earlier. What he wouldn't give to be a lieutenant colonel again and revisit the place at the head of Ghost Squadron to put the damned deps and their enablers out of business for good.

But those sorts of black ops were for younger people, and Decker found his current duties rather enjoyable despite himself. He was the man who dispatched SF companies and squadrons around the Federation and beyond its borders on secret missions. And he knew all there was to know about each of them, making him SOFCOM's closest thing to an omniscient officer. It also meant that he couldn't leave Caledonia except by special permission and that he had to keep SOFCOM informed of all his movements in case the opposition ever targeted him for kidnapping or elimination. Not that anyone attempting to get at the information stored in his capacious brain would be successful. Decker was fully conditioned against interrogation and would die before revealing a single bit of data.

He didn't have to look up where the division's squadrons were on the road to high readiness and which were already deployed — he also had that information in his head. And as luck would have it, across the three SF regiments, his old unit, Ghost Squadron, was the only one fully reconstituted and within days of being declared ready for further operations. Considering the by now nasty and swiftly deteriorating situation on Garonne, he couldn't have asked for better than humanity's premier black ops outfit.

Decker glanced at the time and decided he'd go up to Fort Arnhem and personally brief Curtis Delgado, Ghost Squadron's new commanding officer. It had been several weeks since he last visited the Special Forces home station, and he needed to breathe in its pure air to regenerate himself. Even though he no longer wore the winged dagger insignia on his beret but that of general officers — crossed swords over a starburst — he would remain an SF trooper until the day he died.

After calling the Joint Base Sanctum motor pool for an aircar, he promptly switched into battledress, anticipating that Delgado would likely be out in the field performing the last validation exercises.

Decker always kept a complete set of uniforms in his office closet and didn't need to visit his quarters. Then, he left a note for his spouse and SOFCOM saying he was driving himself to Fort Arnhem and would return by seventeen hundred hours.

Hera called him just before he was about to leave his office.

"Off to the Fort, are you? Does that have anything to do with the situation on Garonne?"

"As a matter of fact, it does. Ghost Squadron is next up on the high readiness roster, and I'm going to brief Curtis myself on the mission, considering our history with the place."

"Would you like to have Miko accompany them? She's available, and, as you might recall, she played a significant role during our last visit to Garonne."

Chief Warrant Officer Miko Steiger, Federation Marine Corps, detailed to Naval Intelligence's Special Operations Division, which Hera Talyn commanded, had become one of the most skilled and deadliest undercover agents in special ops, as good as Decker and Talyn were in their day.

"You have to ask? Of course, I'd like Miko in on it. She's ideal to infiltrate the deportees behind the latest outrages."

"That's what I thought. Hang on for half an hour, and I'll have her join you on your visit upcountry."

"Alright, it's a deal. Make sure she's wearing battledress. We may have to visit Curtis in the field."

Less than twenty minutes later, a tall, muscular blond wearing a chief warrant officer's four silver bars on her battledress collar and a beret with a military intelligence cap badge appeared in the doorway to Decker's office and saluted.

"CWO Steiger reporting to the general as ordered."

Decker, who sat behind his desk, momentarily stiffened to attention and nodded since he was bareheaded.

"How are you, Miko?"

"Growing tired of doing analysis work instead of excelling in my strengths."

Decker smiled at her.

"You can't always be out in the field. Otherwise, you lose your edge, which doesn't help an agent's long-term survival. Hera and I also did office stints between outings when we were field operatives."

She sighed theatrically.

"I am aware of that. Am I correct in thinking you have a mission in mind for Ghost Squadron?"

"Yep, on one of our old stomping grounds, Garonne. You must have seen the most recent intelligence reports."

Steiger nodded.

"Looks like it's getting rough out there."

"President Verrill — remember him — he's still running the place. He requested aid to civil authority, and we drew the job, which means the situation there is already beyond a regular Marine battalion's abilities."

"And that's saying a lot."

Decker climbed to his feet and picked up his beret.

"The aircar should be waiting for us outside."

They found it in one of the visitor spots in front of SOCOM's entrance to the giant Fleet HQ building, and it unlocked at their approach. Decker climbed behind the controls.

"Shouldn't I be doing that, Zack?" Steiger asked in an amused tone once she sat in the passenger seat. "As in, generals ride while warrant officers drive."

Decker gave her a mock glare.

"The Almighty forbid. I've seen you fly aircars before, Miko."

"And what's wrong with my technique?"

"In bed, nothing. Otherwise, plenty." Decker lit up the power plant and drove it through the Joint Base Sanctum main gate. Once on the ring highway, he switched on the antigrav and the thrusters, sending the car into the air under Sanctum central traffic control's oversight, accelerating until they reached four hundred kilometers an hour at five hundred meters altitude above the ground. Decker put the car in autopilot and turned to face Steiger.

"So, what's Hera been having you do lately?"

"Analyzing the reports from other undercover agents in the field. Looking for stress points, things that are off, mistakes — the subtle signs they've been compromised."

"I recall that being interesting, especially during the Black Sword debacle."

"Oh, for sure it is. But I prefer being out there, bamboozling senior Commonwealth officials, cutting throats — you know, doing fun stuff."

Decker grimaced.

"I hear you. If I had my druthers, I'd strap on my Pathfinder knife and return to Garonne in person."

Steiger winked at him.

"Surely, you mean your fatal blade, Zack."

They set down on the road leading up to Fort Arnhem's main gate and stopped at the security post, where they presented their credentials.

"Welcome back, General," the private who stood guard snapped off a salute as he opened the barrier. Decker returned the salute and drove through, heading for the 1st SF Regiment's HQ.

There, he parked in the VIP slot, climbed out, and stretched.

"We'll say hi to Josh before we find Curtis."

"Of course."

The guard must have called ahead because Colonel Josh Bayliss, the 1st SF Regiment's commanding officer, popped through the HQ building's front doors, a welcoming smile pasted on his craggy face. He saluted as he walked toward them.

"Good morning, General. And how are they hanging on this fine day?" Bayliss asked in his deep voice.

"One lower than the other, Josh."

"And how are you, Chief Warrant Officer Steiger?"

"Stuck behind a desk and bored."

"To what do I owe the honor of your visit? Since you brought Miko, it has to be a mission for Ghost Squadron." Bayliss gestured toward the door. "Do you have a few minutes for a coffee and a brief chat?"

"Of course, Josh. Lead on."

When they settled in Bayliss' office, coffee mugs in hand, Decker asked, "What do you know about the current situation on Garonne?"

"Not much. My attention has been on regimental matters lately."

Bayliss' face took on a serious expression as Decker explained about the deportee raids on ranches and farms and the fact that someone was organizing them. Yet, they were unaware of the individuals involved and the reasons behind it.

"I guess it must be serious if President Verrill sent up the red flag," he said when Decker was done.

"Probably on the suggestion of the 27th Constabulary Regiment's CO. They're overwhelmed and taking casualties. That's how bad it is. Mind you, they're still understrength but as good as any gray-leg outfit."

"I'm sure Curtis will be delighted to visit the site of one of your former glories for his first mission as Ghost Squadron's CO. He's doing really well, by the way."

"As we expected, hence his early promotion to lieutenant colonel. What's he up to right now?"

"Finishing off field problems with the 1st Marine Light Infantry as opfor. It's a mere formality. As far as I'm concerned, Ghost Squadron is at high readiness status already."

"Good. The sooner they leave for Garonne, the better."

"What ship?"

"*Iolanthe.* She's the only Q ship currently in the Caledonia system. Since I expect some wet work to deal with the deps and their enablers, the mission needs plausible deniability, meaning it'll be a black op. Hence Miko being part of it."

"Understood. And how are things with you at HQ?"

"Good. Jimmy Martinson is still as easygoing as ever and stays out of my way while running interference for me with SOCOM and the Grand Admiral."

"How's Kal?"

"Having the time of his life as head of the Grand Admiral's Political Planning and Analysis Division. He's spending a lot of time on Wyvern, and I suspect our Kal is gently guiding the Federation president and her government in the right direction. I tell you, Kal hides a political streak a parsec wide under that ironic smile and those Pathfinder wings."

A twinkle appeared in Bayliss' eyes. "And Saga?"

Decker grinned at his old friend. "Doing splendidly as one of Kal's political analysts, but she's going to be some pissed at me for sending Curtis away for the Almighty knows for how long right after he comes out of high readiness testing."

"Ah, young love. They'll either find a way to make it work across the stars, or they'll end up being ships passing each other in hyperspace."

"Saga and Curtis?" Steiger asked with an air of surprise. "When did that happen?"

Decker shrugged.

"About a year ago. They never said how it developed and have kept things low-key, but Hera and I have hosted both for supper at our residence a few times now." The grin returned. "And they're so cute together."

"You'd accept Curtis Delgado as a son-in-law?"

"He's in my top ten list of candidates. At least we have many interests in common. But don't let them know that. They must decide for themselves."

Steiger smirked.

"I'll bet. I can just see the two of you swapping war stories over a glass of whiskey late at night while Saga and Hera commiserate about husbands whose first love is the Marine Corps."

"Laugh as much as you want, but Curtis is an exceptional officer and a fine human being."

"Oh, without a doubt. I'm just having a tough time picturing you with grandkids."

"Whoa. Let's not get ahead of ourselves." Decker drained the coffee mug. "And now, Josh, if you could get us to where we can talk with Curtis, we'll get out of your hair. Or at least what's left of it."

Decker winked at his oldest friend as the latter let out a low mock growl at the jab.

"My hair is just fine, General, sir."

— Four —

Lieutenant Colonel Curtis Delgado stiffened to attention when he spied the single silver star on his visitor's collar. A fraction of a second later, so did Chief Warrant Officer Metellus Testo, the squadron's operations officer. Both were in a field command post established beneath layers of cammo cloth, which made it almost invisible from the ground and undetectable from the air. They were standing by a map projection of the Fort Arnhem training area with tiny blue and red markers.

"General, sir. To what do we owe the honor?" Delgado smiled broadly. "Wait. Don't tell me. If that's Miko right behind you, I'm going to guess you've got a mission for the squadron."

Decker glanced over his shoulder at Steiger.

"Can't hide anything from the lad, can we?"

"Nope. He's as smart as he is handsome."

Then Decker stuck out his hand, and they shook. "How are you, Curtis?"

"Just grand, sir. I never figured I'd get to command Ghost Squadron. Hell, I didn't think I'd get beyond major."

"You earned it fair and square." Decker turned to Testo. "And how's the Warrant doing this morning?"

Testo grinned as he took Decker's hand.

"Keeping the colonel out of trouble, as usual, sir."

"Where's Emery?" Decker asked, referring to Squadron Sergeant Major Hak.

"He's out having fun with the MLI."

"You mean he's acting like a one-man wrecking crew just for shits and giggles."

Delgado gave Decker a half-shrug.

"Yeah, that about sums it up. In his defense, he was getting bored in the command post once the companies deployed for the final field problem."

"You have about thirty minutes to spare for me?"

"Sure, sir. Metellus can oversee the rest of the exercise. Shall we leave him to it?" He gestured at the command post's opening, beyond which dense vegetation in all directions cut the horizon down to a few paces. They exited and sat on fallen logs under a gray sky threatening an imminent drenching.

"So, what's the mission?" Delgado asked.

"You're taking Ghost Squadron to an old stomping ground of mine, Hera's and Miko's — Garonne, in the Rim Sector."

Delgado nodded but said nothing. He knew Decker would tell him everything in his own way.

"Garonne has a particular problem with deportees from Celeste which owned the place until the Federation seceded. It resettled countless thousands of undesirables, petty criminals, and troublemakers on Garonne during the fifteen or so years leading up to secession, with most resettled in the final five years. We — Miko, Hera, and I — helped Garonne win home rule while a petition for sovereign star system status wound its way through the courts. The Supreme Court of the Commonwealth rejected the request and kicked the decision back to the Senate, which sat on it. But Celeste's anger led them to increase the number of deportees shipped to Garonne and insert violent criminals into the mix. This was done so they could both empty their own prisons and destabilize the Garonne government. Secession ended that, but by then, the minor troubles caused by the deportees were growing into colossal problems."

Decker paused for a few heartbeats.

"Now, it seems someone is organizing them. They've graduated from mere criminality to small-time terrorist attacks over the last six months and recently took it several notches higher." Decker went on to recount the assault on the ranches, farms, and the Constabulary. "The Garonne government has asked for aid to civil authority and you're it."

"I assume the fact you're sending Ghost Squadron means you want the problem solved permanently without creating a big splash?" Delgado asked, tilting his head in question.

Decker tapped the side of his nose with an extended index finger.

"Find out who's organizing them and ensure they'll never do it again. Take out the leaders and the most violent among the deportees, definitely anyone involved in the large-scale massacres."

Delgado nodded once.

"Got it."

"Of course, that means it's a blacker-than-black operation. The squadron is going in as an undercover mercenary outfit. You and a few of your senior folks can identify yourselves to President Verrill and Chief Superintendent Bain, the CO of the 27th Constabulary because some coordination will be required. But no one will know the squadron's size nor how you deploy it. And you'll definitely not take visible credit for any successes, not even with Verrill and Bain."

"Understood. When are we leaving, and on what ship?"

"Monday, aboard *Iolanthe*. That'll give you three days to sort yourselves out and then take the weekend off." Decker pulled a memory chip from his tunic pocket and handed it to Delgado. "Everything you need is on here. Call me directly if you have any questions after reading this, even after hours, if necessary. Even better, come to Sanctum on Friday after work. Hera and I will treat you to supper, and we can discuss any issues you might see."

A lazy grin appeared on Delgado's face.

"Will Captain Decker be there, sir?"

"Unless she's called to join General Ryent on Wyvern between now and then, I suppose I can invite her too," Decker said in a dubious tone as he climbed to his feet.

"Oh, and Josh asked me to pass something along." Decker grinned at the younger man. "Endex. You're now officially at high readiness and available for immediate deployment. Pack 'em up and head back to the barn."

"Yes, sir."

Delgado jumped up and snapped off a salute.

"Warrant Testo," he called out. "Endex. Have the companies head to their pickup points and warn Major Tesser so he can send the transports. And tell the 1st MLI thanks for playing."

"We got a mission, sir?"

"Yep. If the general would be kind enough to take me back to the base with him, I'll leave now and digest the information he handed over. Let's have a command group meeting at fifteen hundred hours."

Testo stuck his face through the command post opening.

"Will do, sir. Where are we going?"

"Garonne, in the Rim."

"Nice. I've never been there."

Decker clapped Delgado on the shoulder.

"Of course, I'll give you a lift. Grab your gear."

Delgado returned to the command post and emerged again with a pack, helmet, and carbine.

"Ready, sir."

They walked out of the command post hide to where Decker had parked the all-terrain ground car borrowed from regimental HQ beneath a dense canopy of trees bordering a rutted dirt track of the sort common in the Fort Arnhem training area. Delgado tossed his pack and helmet into the back and climbed in beside Decker, while Steiger sat behind them.

"Still driving yourself, sir?"

Decker jerked a thumb over his shoulder.

"It's safer than the alternative."

Delgado chuckled.

"You're a braver man than I am to disrespect Chief Warrant Officer Steiger, General. Her body count must be astronomical by now."

"You do remember who I married, *n'est-ce-pas*? One of the greatest assassins of our time."

A wince.

"Right. Never mind."

When they were back at the main base, Decker and Steiger joined Josh Bayliss for lunch in the Pegasus Club. Delgado said he would munch on a sandwich while going through the memory chip and organizing his thoughts for the command conference. After eating, the two visitors made their farewells and returned to Sanctum.

"Ever thought of applying for a commission, Miko?" Decker asked once they were airborne and headed down the Nestor Valley toward the capital. "As a chief warrant officer, you could become an instant major, like I did."

"Nah. If I become a field grade officer, they'll expect more bullshit from me, like leading a team, and I'm a loner by inclination. My grade school reports consistently mentioned my inability to play well with others. Besides, the pay is almost the same, so why take on more grief?"

"True."

"I have no ambitions to rise any further. Heck, if it weren't for you, I'd still be a happy freelancer selling my services to those with both scruples and money."

"Of which there are very few, if any, in the galaxy. I've found money and scruples have an inverse relationship. Besides, admit it, you're a lot happier back in the Service doing good for humanity."

Steiger blew him a kiss.

"You know me so well, Zack."

"Flattery will get you everywhere, sweetheart, except back in my bed."

She gave him a sly smile.

"I wouldn't even dare try. Your wife is a lot scarier than anyone else I've ever met."

Decker burst out laughing.

"And coming from you, that says a lot."

— Five —

Delgado opened the door to Captain Saga Decker's unit in one of Joint Base Sanctum's junior officers' apartment blocks, having been added to the permission list months earlier.

"Honey, I'm home!"

When he got no answer, Delgado poked his head into every room and realized Saga hadn't returned yet, and a smile spread across his face as he contemplated the options he had to greet her. Such as reclining on the sofa in the altogether.

Nevertheless, the front door opening and Saga Decker walking in put an end to any nascent plan. She stopped the moment she spotted him and broke into a broad smile.

Decker was tall, with shoulder-length blond hair framing a strong yet finely chiseled face dominated by the intensely blue eyes she'd inherited from her father. Seeing her for the first time after they'd been apart always made Delgado's heart skip a beat.

"You're early," she said in a mock accusatory tone.

"I took the regular shuttle from Fort Arnhem, which means I'm on time, and you're late." He walked over to where she stood and took her in his arms. "But you can make it up to me."

Saga returned his embrace but then broke away and smiled seductively.

"We're due at Dad's and Hera's place in half an hour, Curtis, and I'd rather take my time with you, especially since you're going off-world for a few months. I'll make it up to you once we're back after supper."

"Ah, you heard about my little trip."

"There's little I don't hear as one of General Ryent's intelligence analysts. But I got it from Dad. He wanted to ensure I made the most of my weekend with you."

Delgado grinned back at her.

"Well, what do you know? The old man is playing Cupid."

"He really likes you, Curtis. You remind him of what he could have been if he hadn't screwed up by the numbers when he was a command sergeant."

"And yet he still made general."

"Sure, but it cost him more than most men could bear to get back in the game. And no, I won't tell you. Those are his stories, and he'll either share them with you someday or not. Be aware that he has no objection to having you as his son-in-law. "Not that it's a marriage proposal," she hastily added when she saw the glint in Delgado's eyes.

"Aw, damn." He put on an air of massive disappointment.

Saga let out a delighted peal of laughter.

"Making big puppy eyes at me won't help your case. Now, let me change into civilian clothes. Yes, you can watch if you like," she said, noticing the lecherous look that replaced his earlier expression. She headed for her bedroom. "Follow me and get an eyeful. Maybe it'll prime you for later and make things that much more passionate."

"I don't see how they could. It's the pinnacle of pleasure every time with you."

"So that's the only thing you want from me — sex?"

Delgado stuck his tongue out at Saga as she unbuttoned her tunic.

"You know I'm eager for the entire package."

She slapped her bum.

"You mean this package?"

"Well, yeah, that part of it too. Are you sure we don't have time?"

"No." Saga finished stripping off her uniform and slipped on khaki slacks, a short-sleeved green blouse, and loafers. "We're heading to Dad's place, and although I'm aware of how quick you can be, I'm nowhere near as fast, and I want to enjoy myself."

"You're a hard woman."

She winked at him.

"Just as long as you're a hard man later."

They walked across Joint Base Sanctum's residential area to flag officers' row under a late afternoon sun, chatting about their respective work weeks. The Decker-Talyn residence was under the latter's name since she outranked her husband and, therefore, slightly larger and more luxurious than a brigadier general's would have been.

As they climbed the steps to the front door, it opened, and Zack Decker appeared, wearing an obnoxiously loud shirt of the sort he enjoyed shocking people with, tan slacks, and a big smile.

"Saga, Curtis, come in, come in."

"How are you this evening, sir?" Delgado asked as he shook hands with Decker after the latter embraced his daughter.

"What have I repeatedly told you about that?" Decker growled. "Seeing as you're in our home and wearing civvies."

"Sorry — Zack." Delgado gave him an apologetic grin. "It's hard to shake the habit."

"I'll bet it is." Decker turned on his heels and led them through the house to the covered patio at the back.

Rear Admiral Hera Talyn, Commissioner Caelin Morrow, who headed the Federation Constabulary's Anti-Corruption Unit 12, and Chief Warrant Officer Miko Steiger, all wearing relaxed civilian clothes, were already seated in wicker chairs, holding tall glasses in their hands.

"Hello Saga, hello Curtis." Talyn stood to greet them properly, Saga with a kiss on the cheek, and Curtis with a handshake. "How are you?"

"Just grand," Delgado replied, smiling. He turned to the other two. "Commissioner, nice to see you again, and you, Miko, even though we met earlier this week."

"Caelin, please, Curtis. And it's good to see you again as well. Hello, Saga."

Steiger watched them with an ironic look pasted on her face.

"What?" Delgado asked her.

She smirked. "Just watching the larger family reunite. It's rather touching."

Decker pressed drinks into their hands, and they joined the circle by taking the last two chairs.

"Your health, everyone," Decker raised his glass. "And to another week in hell done."

"Hell?" Delgado guffawed. "Is that what you call Fleet HQ?"

Talyn snorted.

"That's just Zack's way of bemoaning the fact he'll never be in the field again. It always comes out whenever he's had a — shall we say, challenging week."

"And what was the challenge this time?" Caelin Morrow asked. "Or should I avoid the subject?"

"Oh," Decker made a dismissive hand gesture, "dealing with the regular Navy's less than stellar intellects concerning sustainment of deployed Special Forces units. They clearly don't grasp that SF operates at its own pace, and sadly, employing explosive methods to rouse them is frowned upon for some reason I can't fathom."

"And now we come to the nub of the problem," Miko Steiger said, smiling mischievously. "Zack can't use explosives to solve his problems anymore, and that's making him testy."

Decker grimaced at her.

"Laugh as much as you please, funny woman, but unless you've experienced some of the fools at HQ, you haven't truly understood the agony of dealing with them."

"And that's precisely why I don't want to take a commission."

"I hear you. Some days, I wish I'd stayed a chief warrant officer myself. Anyway, I figure we ought to get business out of the way first. Caelin, what can you tell us about the 27th Constabulary Regiment and its CO, Chief Superintendent Bain?"

"I reached out to my sources immediately after you called me on Tuesday, as I am not familiar with either, and received responses this morning. Bain recently got promoted and assumed control of the 27th a few months ago. She's from Cascadia, and it's her first time on Garonne, so she's still adapting. No blemishes on her career, but no outstanding notations either. Her superiors consider her solid, dependable, and intelligent, and she will likely make at least commissioner. As an aside, the Professional Compliance Bureau vets all nominees for regimental commander positions, so her career will have come under the microscope. Her appointment indicates that there are no dark secrets in her past. Whether Curtis will find her cooperative, I don't know. I couldn't very well ask my sources if she'd have any qualms about working with Special Forces troopers operating undercover."

Morrow paused to take a sip of her gin and tonic.

"The 27th Constabulary Regiment has been in existence for only two years and is still quite understaffed, with only half of its positions filled. Just like in any other regiment, the quality of the personnel varies, but it is considered effective and has successfully passed the latest efficiency evaluations. However, the latest events and the casualties the 27th took have alarmed Constabulary HQ. If the Garonne government hadn't asked for aid to civil authority from the Fleet, the Chief Constable would have. And that's it. No hidden surprises. Now the policing situation on Garonne is a different story. From what I gathered, things in the major cities — Iskellian, Tianjin, Holback, and Oshin — have been getting worse in the last six or seven months, not that they were great during the previous eight or nine years."

"The deportees from Celeste," Delgado said in a flat tone.

Morrow nodded.

"Just so. The biggest concentration of deportees is in Tianjin, which is rapidly turning into a wild frontier town. Criminality and gang violence are overwhelming the local police as well as the Constabulary half battalion stationed in Tianjin. Some parts of the city have become no-go zones in recent times where the law is simply inoperative. Civilians cower in fear, at least those who haven't left yet, and are forced to support the deportee gangs. Iskellian, the capital, is rapidly deteriorating as deportees from outlying cities and towns congregate there, but the police and Constabulary still control most of it."

Delgado nodded.

"That tallies with the intelligence reports the general — sorry, I mean Zack — gave me. Thanks, Caelin."

"My pleasure."

Decker turned to Steiger.

"Miko?"

"I'll be infiltrating the deps in Tianjin. I wish I could leave before Ghost Squadron and already be on the inside by the time you get there, Curtis, but traveling with you in *Iolanthe* is my only option. There's no aviso available to take me there. That means I must transform myself into a slovenly dep before we get there, land ahead of you in Iskellian, and head to Tianjin before your troopers disembark. Since it's a given the deps don't all know each other, someone from Iskellian will likely be accepted, especially if she acts like a crazed sociopath looking to kill Garonne citizens in revenge for the government cutting off benefits or whatever motivates the psychos these days."

"That shouldn't be a stretch for you," Delgado replied, winking at her.

She quickly stuck out her tongue at him.

"Just as long as your people remember I'm one of you when it comes down to the wire."

"No danger of them forgetting, not after you travel with us to Garonne. They'll have you imprinted on their brains."

Decker clapped his hands once and said, "That takes care of business unless you have last-minute questions, Curtis."

"No. I'm good."

"Excellent. Now, drink up. I'm serving appetizers in the dining room shortly."

— Six —

"Had a good weekend in Sanctum, Curtis?"

Delgado and Sergeant Major Hak stiffened as they heard Colonel Josh Bayliss' voice behind him.

"Most excellent, sir."

"And how is Captain Decker?"

A smile appeared unbidden. "Doing well. She sends her love."

Bayliss stopped beside Delgado and Hak at the edge of Fort Arnhem's main parade ground and let his eyes roam over the members of Ghost Squadron. All wore the sort of unmarked, black armor typically used by mercenaries and other private sector fighters, complete with visored helmets. They carried carbines and other weapons available on the open market and generally looked like anything but a Marine Corps Special Forces unit. They could have belonged to any of the hundreds of private military corporations active in the Federation.

Standing by troops and companies in three ranks, their bags and packs in front of them, they stared straight ahead while their command sergeants carried out the final checks. Collective gear, extra ammunition, and ration containers were neatly stacked behind each troop.

Soon, the command sergeants reported to the company first sergeants, who in turn reported to the company commanders. Judging by what they saw, Delgado and Hak figured everything was in order and the squadron ready to depart, which the company commanders confirmed with a thumbs up directed at them. And not a moment too soon.

The faint whine of shuttle thrusters reached their ears, and both looked up into the brilliantly blue morning sky. They eventually made out fourteen of the small craft coming down in a tight formation.

"Right on time," Delgado said after glancing at the time display inside his helmet's visor. Then, movement to one side of the parade square attracted his attention.

"And there's Miko."

Steiger climbed out of a staff car's passenger seat and pulled a duffel bag from the rear compartment. She wore street clothes and Delgado knew she had several weapons hidden on her. But she did have visible piercings and tattoos, as well as a strange haircut which saw the sides of her head extremely short but the top a crest of longish hair running from her forehead down to the nape of her neck.

"And she's already looking like a dep," Delgado added.

"Colonels, Sergeant Major," Steiger said, waving her right hand near her brow in an approximation of a salute as she walked over to where they stood. "I guess I made it right on time."

"Only just." Delgado pointed upward.

"Ah. Well, I'm here before the shuttles, so it counts."

"Nice appearance."

Steiger mock preened, fluttering her eyes. It looked ridiculous coming from a tall, muscular woman like her, as she intended.

"You like? It's the latest in deportee chic."

"It certainly scares me," Hak said, chuckling. "I hope you can remove those tattoos."

"Restoring everything to its original configuration can be done in a matter of hours, except for the hair. It'll just have to regrow on its own."

"I kind of like the hair, though," Delgado said. "You remind me of a Viking warrior."

Steiger gave him a wink.

"That's precisely the effect I was going for."

The whine of shuttle thrusters increased to the point where further conversation was pointless, and they simply watched the unmarked craft come down and land in unison.

"Impressive coordination," Steiger said once the noise abated. "Or were they just showing off?"

Delgado gave her a sideways glance.

"A bit of both, I suspect."

Aft ramps dropped, and Steiger let out a soft grunt.

"They seem pretty old and dinged."

"Camouflage. Inside, they're state-of-the-art. Same for *Iolanthe*, the second of that name. She looks like an old bulk freighter, but no more than five or six years have elapsed since her launch, and she's armed like a cruiser beneath hidden hull plates. Welcome to the Q ship universe, where nothing is what it seems. Ah, here we go."

Ghost Squadron climbed aboard, one troop and some company HQ elements per shuttle until only Major Washburn Tesser, the squadron's second in command, stood on the parade square. He turned to face Delgado.

"Squadron is loaded, sir. Your shuttle is there." He pointed at one of the two sitting ahead of the rest. "Mine is the other."

"Then we're all set." Delgado and Hak came to attention, and the former raised his hand in salute. "With your permission, Colonel?"

Bayliss returned the compliment.

"Go and rid Garonne of her infestation, Curtis. Good hunting."

With that, they turned on their heels, picked up their bags, and headed for their shuttle, Steiger in tow. Bayliss remained at the edge of the parade square and watched them lift off. Then he returned to his office and the eternal fight with administrivia that had become the bane of his existence. Life had been so much easier when he was the Pathfinder School's sergeant major before taking his commission.

The shuttles landed on *Iolanthe*'s hangar deck thirty minutes later, and when the space doors closed, Commander Keever Ardross, the Q ship's captain, came through the inner airlock to greet Delgado. Stocky, bald, with hooded eyes and a silver goatee, he, like the rest of his crew, wore a merchant uniform and rank insignia, indistinguishable from those worn by employees of the major shipping lines.

"Welcome aboard, Curtis." Ardross smiled when Delgado headed for him, hand outstretched.

"Keever, you old pirate. Good to see you again." They shook.

"Ghost Squadron looks in fine fettle," Ardross said, nodding at the troopers forming by company in the center of the hangar.

"We've been on the road to high readiness for the last seven months, so they're impatient for some actual work. How have you been, and how's *Iolanthe* or whatever her cover name is this time around?"

"I've been just grand. She's *Freya* these days and has recently come out of a minor refit, meaning my crew is raring to get real as well."

"A match made in heaven, then."

Ardross caught sight of Miko Steiger disembarking with Sergeant Major Hak, and his eyes widened.

"Who the hell is that?" He asked in a low tone.

When she got near, Delgado said, "Commander Keever Ardross, meet Chief Warrant Officer Miko Steiger, Federation Marine Corps. She works for Naval Intelligence's Special Operations Division."

The two of them shook hands as Ardross studied her adornments.

"Let me guess," he said. "You're going to infiltrate the deportees on Garonne."

"Can't put anything past you, Captain," Steiger replied, grinning. "I will indeed be doing that while Curtis and his troopers find, fix, and strike the enemy."

"And what's the mission? I haven't received any instructions apart from picking up Ghost Squadron on Monday morning, transporting them to Garonne, and remaining as orbital support, all of it covert." Ardross gestured toward the inner airlock. "Let me see you to your quarters and you can tell me along the way."

Delgado explained everything about the operation as they walked toward the Marine barracks, leaving Ardross to shake his head.

"It'll be interesting to see who you find behind the deportees. I agree someone is organizing them."

"That's a definite, Captain," Steiger said. "And it's my job to uncover whoever that is for Curtis so he can eliminate them with extreme prejudice. I might even take a hand in it. There's no way we can leave folks who massacre civilians among the living."

"Glad you're on our side, Warrant!" Ardross directed an amused gaze at her.

"Every single one of us is," Delgado said as Ardross guided him into a small, private cabin labeled Commanding Officer, Embarked Troops. He looked around. It held a bunk, a desk, a chair, and cupboards; through the inner door, he could see private heads with a shower. Everything looked shiny and new. "Nice. Did you guys spruce the barracks up?"

"The yard did a bit of updating during the mini refit. Now, since there's some urgency in getting you to Garonne, I'll head up to the bridge and get us underway. We can chat about the mission in the wardroom over lunch."

"Sounds good."

Delgado stuck his head out into the passageway after Ardross left and watched his officers, warrant officers, Miko Steiger included, and the squadron sergeant major find their cabins near his, and within moments, signs above the doors lit up, identifying the occupants.

Moments later, the public address system came alive with the notification that *Iolanthe* would break out of orbit in five minutes. Delgado stripped off his armor and stowed it securely, along with his carbine and blaster, then unpacked the things he'd need during the trip. Once he was done, Delgado wandered off to the wardroom for a cup of coffee and a pastry, knowing he'd find both in abundance mid-morning aboard a Navy starship, even one operating undercover.

— Seven —

"Looks peaceful from up here," Commander Ardross said as *Iolanthe* entered Garonne orbit. He, Curtis Delgado, and Miko Steiger were on the ship's bridge, the latter two having been given free access.

"Every single one of the inhabitable worlds does, including those wracked by storms powerful enough to threaten human survival," responded Miko Steiger.

"Let alone those beset by human conflict," Delgado added. "At least according to today's standards. I doubt the scars of the Migration Wars were invisible from orbit."

"No orbitals other than standard satellites, sir," the sensor chief reported. "And not that many of them, either."

"Good. The less there is to snoop around on us, the better, especially since we're staying for the duration. When did you want to speak with the good people of Garonne?"

"I think I'll contact Chief Superintendent Bain from here first. No point in showing up at her doorstep when she doesn't know me from Adam. Especially not in civvies, which is all I brought. She can introduce me to President Verrill."

"Now?"

"Sure. Why not? It's what? Approximately eleven hundred hours in Iskellian? She should be reachable."

Ardross nodded and gestured at his signals petty officer.

"Open a link with the 27th Constabulary Regiment's HQ on the encrypted military emergency channel. Identify us as the merchant ship *Freya* and tell them we have someone who needs to speak with Chief Superintendent Bain over governmental secure means. They should twig that we're official."

"Aye, aye, sir."

While the petty officer busied himself, Ardross turned his eyes back on the bridge's primary display.

"It looks so placid, yet there's so much dying. Why do we keep on killing each other, Curtis?" He asked in a soft tone. "You'd think after the horrors of the Migration Wars we'd have a snootful of death."

Delgado shrugged.

"Humans have been at each other's throats forever. As a species, we're inherently violent. Sure, a thin veneer of civilization barely keeps our brutality and inhumanity in check. But that veneer will crack at the slightest provocation, and it's not something that will change anytime soon. I'm afraid we're stuck with our current disposition as controlled barbarians."

"A bleak assessment, my friend."

"Maybe, but I have witnessed firsthand how frequently we harm each other, Keever. It makes me despair that we'll ever become peaceful. Then, I remind myself that the universe is so inherently hostile to any form of life that we're better off keeping a spark of the old fighting instinct alive lest we get wiped out. But finding the right balance between that instinct and peacefulness is the insoluble problem every generation faces."

Ardross chuckled.

"I'd never figured you for a philosopher."

"You either continually seek wisdom or your thought processes ossify. I much prefer the former. Most people don't, and it's part of our problem as a species — too many are stuck in modes of thought harkening back to the dawn of humanity."

"Deep, very deep." Ardross nodded slowly as he digested the meaning behind Delgado's words.

"Sir." The signals petty officer raised his hand. "I have Chief Superintendent Kyra Bain, Commanding Officer, 27th Constabulary Regiment, on a secure link."

Ardross gestured at Steiger.

"It would be better if you weren't within range of the video pickup, Chief Warrant Officer."

"Of course." Steiger moved over to a vacant workstation.

"Put it on the primary, Signals."

The face of a tired-looking woman in her late forties wearing a gray uniform with the oak leaf wreath and twin diamonds of her rank on the collar replaced the view of Garonne.

"I'm Bain."

"Thank you for taking our call, Chief Superintendent. I'm Commander Keever Ardross of the Federation Navy ship *Freya*. Standing beside me is Lieutenant Colonel Curtis Delgado, Federation Marine Corps. He's the mission commander and the one who wants to speak with you."

Delgado dipped his head.

"Chief Superintendent, I'm the commander of A Squadron, 1st Special Forces Regiment. I understand Garonne has a serious infestation problem and needs specialized help."

Bain stared at both of them in disbelief for several heartbeats.

"Pardon me for saying so, gentlemen, but neither of you is in proper uniform, nor do you look like members of the Federation Armed Forces. The only thing that hints at your legitimacy is you being able to generate a secure military link."

A smile appeared on Delgado's face.

"We work for Special Operations Command, and they have designated our mission to help you and the Garonne government as a black op. That's why my Navy colleagues wear merchant uniforms and drive a Q ship while my troopers and I wear mercenary outfits."

"We were expecting a battalion of Marines, not a Special Forces unit."

"The Fleet deemed the situation on Garonne to be beyond the capabilities of a single battalion. It was either a full brigade, possibly even a division, or a Special Forces squadron whose orders are to terminate the problem with extreme prejudice."

Bain frowned.

"Terminate the problem? What do you mean?"

"We make sure the doers can harm no one ever again."

"Whoa!" Bain reared up. "If you mean kill every single one of them, then I object." They should face the full penalty of the law, and if that means death, then a court will decide, not a Marine Corps lieutenant colonel."

"Sorry, Chief Superintendent, but that's no longer your call. You face a situation that is, for all intents and purposes, an insurrection by forces hostile to the Garonne government and by inference to the Federation itself. The legal niceties of arresting and charging people don't apply to insurgents. We either terminate them or transport them to Parth for life."

Bain shook her head ruefully.

"Hence the black op designation. Your actions are intended to breach the laws of armed conflict and, at the same time, be deniable."

Delgado nodded.

"Just so. The people committing the massacres of innocent civilians have placed themselves beyond the protection of any laws, as have those organizing and arming them. But to maximize our effectiveness and minimize the time we spend hunting them, we need your help, Chief Superintendent."

"I will not have any member of the 27th Constabulary Regiment involved in your black op, Colonel.

"And they would be a hindrance, if I may be frank. We will take care of the problem on the ground by ourselves. But we could very much use every bit of intelligence you have on the deps involved and their putative backers because they didn't just wake up one morning and decide to terrorize the countryside. And, of course, stay out of our way. Will your scruples allow you to do at least that much?"

Bain let out a heartfelt sigh.

"Alright. This is me talking now, not the senior Constabulary officer and regimental CO whose sworn duty is to uphold the law by whatever legal means necessary." She paused as she met Delgado's eyes. "I'll do whatever I can to help you eradicate the people who've committed these atrocities. I've witnessed the aftermath too many times, including the deaths of my own constables, and whenever I think about the doers, I feel a burning rage building inside me."

"Have there been more attacks in the last two weeks?"

A look of disgust spread across Bain's face.

"Oh, yes. Four more farms and ranches burned down, but thankfully, not everyone in them died. And the farmers killed a dozen deps. Unfortunately, another five of my constables lost their lives, as well as sixteen Garonne police officers." She grimaced. "The deps have essentially taken over Tianjin. The police and my folks are under constant attack there and utterly unable to enforce the law. Honest citizens are taking shelter or evacuating the area completely."

"So, we're not only facing insurrection but also a terrorism campaign."

A nod. "That would be the long and short of it."

"And neither you nor the Garonne police can respond effectively because that would mean escalating matters beyond the boundaries of the law, seeing as how conditions are verging on anarchy."

"Unfortunately. No matter what happens, we're still bound by legislation and regulations, and quite frankly, we're being overwhelmed — not by accident, I might add."

"What do you think the people behind the rampaging deps have as an end goal?"

Bain gave him a weary shrug.

"I don't know, and neither do most of the deps, I suspect. They may be murderous bastards, but they can't expect to overthrow the Garonne government and take control, so it's not regime change."

"Do you have an intelligence section?"

"Yes, and they've been working flat out at uncovering whoever's stirring things up and why. Still, my people are used to working criminal intelligence, and this is much more in line with national security and military intelligence, so they're not having much success. Do you have assets that could help?"

"I brought some, but they won't be able to work with your lot directly, although we'll share any data we collect. You understand my assets aren't constrained like yours are and will do whatever is necessary to gather information about the opposition."

A wan smile appeared.

"The senior Constabulary officer in me doesn't want to know about it. Nevertheless, I'm hoping you'll figure things out." Bain took a deep breath and exhaled. "The deps and their enablers need to be stopped by any means necessary."

Delgado heard the anguish hidden by her flat tone and said, "We will. You can be sure of that. Would you mind sending us everything you have on the matter — incident reports, intelligence digests, suspect profiles, the whole lot?"

"Certainly. Give me a few hours to package everything. I assume you'd rather knowledge of your arrival not be broadcast?"

"If you could keep the people informed of our presence to a minimum, it would be helpful." Delgado grinned. "My unit's nickname is Ghost Squadron. Our unofficial motto is 'we strike without warning and vanish without a trace.' You should see the results of our actions without ever spotting us."

She let out a bark of laughter.

"The best way to maintain plausible deniability, no doubt?"

Delgado's grin widened.

"Just so. Do you think I need to meet with President Verrill, or can you tell him the Marines have arrived and will fix his problem?"

"Given that he made the request for aid to civil authority, it might be preferable if you spoke with him directly but allow me to connect you. There's no need to meet in person. Hang on. I'll try his office."

Bain's face vanished although the link remained open, and Ardross made a cutting gesture at the signals petty officer.

"Audio off, sir."

"The situation is worse than we expected," Miko Steiger said.

"So it seems." Delgado stroked his bearded chin, lost in his thoughts. "Especially with Tianjin, Garonne's second city, which has turned into a no-go zone as far as the authorities are concerned. We have our work cut out for us."

"I'll find the pricks egging the deps on, that I promise."

Delgado gave Steiger a quick smile. "I know."

Bain's face reappeared on the primary display, and Ardross gestured at the signals petty officer to reestablish audio.

"President Verrill is overjoyed at your arrival and is anxious to speak with you. Stand by while I link him in."

The image split and a man whose short salt-and-pepper beard framed a face lined by worry appeared.

"Mister President, I'm Lieutenant Colonel Curtis Delgado of the 1st Special Forces Regiment, Federation Marine Corps, and this is Commander Keever Ardross, captain of the Federation Navy ship *Freya*."

"I can hardly express how glad I am to see you, gentlemen."

— Eight —

"That is one distressed man," Miko Steiger said once both Verrill and Bain's faces faded from the bridge's primary display. "He hides it well, but you can tell the situation is getting to him."

"That's right. You know him from way back, don't you?" Delgado glanced at her.

"Yep. And he looks a lot older than he should."

"But at least he didn't show any qualms about our proposed approach to ridding Garonne of its infestation, unlike Bain."

Steiger let out a humorless bark of laughter.

"That's because, at heart, he's still the revolutionary who almost broke Garonne free from Celeste. If he had achieved complete independence a decade ago, the individuals who died at the hands of the deps would still be alive as deportations would have ceased instead of escalating.

"One more crime we can lay at the feet of the Commonwealth government and its tame, centralist Supreme Court," Ardross said with a faint air of loathing.

60

Delgado shrugged.

"They'll get their full comeuppance in due course, Keever. You don't think the Federation will allow the old Commonwealth to fester at its heart for very long, do you? The capital of empire has already passed from Geneva to Draconis on Wyvern. Give it another twenty years or so, and we'll have absorbed the Home Worlds on our terms."

Ardross gave Delgado a quizzical look.

"What do you mean, capital of empire?"

"Since the late twentieth or early twenty-first centuries, a theory has been floating around that suggests an imperial capital has ruled the core of humanity since the beginning of recorded history. Call it the epicenter of economic and political power that holds sway over a large portion of our species at any given time, if you like. Whenever an old empire dies, meaning it loses its overweening economic and political influence over human affairs, a new one replaces it, and the capital of empire shifts.

"Ah. I see. The Commonwealth is the dying empire while the Federation is the new one."

Delgado nodded.

"Yes. And for the first time in history, the capital of empire has shifted from Earth to another world. It will probably never return to humanity's planet of origin because Earth will become ever more insignificant in human affairs as time goes by."

Ardross shook his head.

"You've got some strange notions, Curtis."

"Heh. You ain't heard nothing yet, buddy." Delgado grinned at him. "It's what happens when you make history your primary focus of study. Well, that, and challenging the Command and Staff College examinations."

He clapped Ardross on the shoulder.

"And now, I'll head back to my quarters so I can begin planning while I wait for the data package from Bain."

***

"You've read the information provided by the CO of the 27th Constabulary Regiment?" Delgado looked around the table at his command team and saw confirmatory nods.

"It's nastier than we expected," Sergeant Major Hak said in a somber tone. "Whoever figured sending the worst of Celeste scum to Garonne would be a fine idea deserves to be hung by the balls until they rip off."

Grunts of approval greeted Hak's pronouncement.

Delgado shrugged.

"Celeste wasn't the only one doing so before the OutWorlds seceded. Besides, getting rid of undesirables by shipping them off to your colonies has been going on since well before the first starship left Earth. But it's undeniable that Celeste increased deportee shipments to Garonne by a significant margin out of sheer malice after the Senate granted Garonne home rule at the Supreme Court's urging. Any comments on the package?"

"Looks like Tianjin is the epicenter of the deportee revolt," Major Washburn Tesser said.

Miko Steiger nodded. "That's why I'll be heading straight there the moment I land in Iskellian."

"What'll your angle be?"

"Pissed off dep who got fired by her boss in Iskellian for bullshit reasons. But since she was employed under the table, like so many deps are, she has no recourse. So she's moving to Tianjin, where she hears the deps are running things and is looking to join in the fun."

Tesser grinned at her. "Simple, yet believable."

"And we'll try to get you on the ground as soon as possible," Delgado said. "We will deploy to Tianjin as well. Or at least Erinye and Moirae companies are. Keres Company will remain aboard *Iolanthe* as our rapid reaction force and reserve."

Captain Q.D. Vinn, officer commanding Keres Company, cocked an eyebrow. "Keeping me away from the pleasures of the sinful city, Skipper?"

"I'm sure you'll see plenty of action before this is over, QD. Now, the companies deploying won't go down at once." Delgado turned his eyes on Captain Rolf Painter, the officer commanding Erinye Company. "Rolf, you'll send one of your troops to Tianjin to recon the area. Find us somewhere quiet to set up. An abandoned warehouse or something like that."

Painter, who'd been commissioned and given the Erinyes when Delgado left the regiment to spend two years on the SOCOM staff, nodded once.

"Figure out where you want the troop to land and at what time of the day, but they must arrive in Tianjin unnoticed and stay that way until the rest of us join them. They go in fully armed but deniable and wearing civvies."

"Understood. It'll be D Troop. They're my most experienced in those sorts of shenanigans."

Miko Steiger raised her hand, and when Delgado gestured at her, she said, "I'd like to be in Tianjin at least twenty-four hours ahead of D Troop. That'll allow me to check things out and get back to you before they arrive. Besides, there will be less of a chance I, as a new arrival, will be linked to D Troop, should anyone notice the sudden influx of twenty-five physically fit, watchful people carrying hidden weapons."

"Right." Delgado nodded. "It's late afternoon in the main settlement area. We can arrange to insert you in a few hours once it's dark. Do you still wish to land in Iskellian and travel to Tianjin via train, or should the shuttle drop you off at oh-dark-thirty a few klicks outside Tianjin? Time is of the essence. We have no idea when the deps are planning another hit."

"It would be better if I traveled by train, Colonel. That way, people will see me getting off at the Tianjin station, which will reinforce my story."

"Iskellian it is, then. You'll carry a communicator?"

"Yes." She produced a cheap-looking, scuffed civilian model and held it up. "Don't let the looks fool you. This is fully encrypted and military-grade beneath the skin, and only I can use it. Try to avoid contacting me unless it's truly an emergency. Wait for my calls instead. That way, I won't be interrupted while pretending to be a bloodthirsty killer."

A few chuckles greeted her words. The Ghost Squadron command team knew Steiger well enough by now. There would be no pretense in her case.

"All right. We'll insert D Troop tomorrow night. That should give Chief Warrant Officer Steiger enough time."

"Come to think of it," Painter said, "how about we drop D Troop off in Iskellian and have them travel by train as well, but twenty-four hours after Miko?"

"Sure."

— Nine —

"Nice. A little tattered, but better than a squat in the slums." Siana Bailo looked around her as she inspected Arnis Sprax's new digs. Dark, short, and bland, Bailo had the sort of face no one ever remembered. Sprax, on the other hand, was as memorable as they came — purple hair in a ridge going from front to back, tattoos climbing up his neck and down his arms, and piercings in his eyebrows, nostrils, and lips.

Sprax gave her a broad grin, revealing sharpened teeth, and said, in a gravelly voice, "A man's gotta look the part. Besides, the former owners felt a sudden urge to move, if you know what I mean."

"And left you with the house and the contents."

"Can't help myself if I'm persuasive. Last I heard, they hightailed it all the way to Iskellian." He chuckled, a sound more menacing than merry. "But it was mighty nice of them to give me everything."

They stood the living room of a small house in Tianjin's older quarter, which was now controlled by the

Deportee Action Committee — a recently created organization to act as focus for the insurgents — and was a no-go zone for the police.

Arnis Sprax was the head of the DAC. Not that he'd been elected or otherwise nominated by his peers.

Sprax had merely emerged as the most depraved and psychotic of leaders among the deps, one who inspired fear among his followers and absolute terror in his victims. In turn, Bailo, whose orders were creating political chaos on Garonne, had selected Sprax as one of her puppets, albeit the most important among them.

Tianjin, the second largest city on the planet and its center of agriculture, was currently the focus of her activities and the base from which she encouraged the spread of the insurgency. Iskellian would come later once they'd exhausted the government's forces and driven them to abandon the outlying towns and cities.

A young woman's face poked through the kitchen door. She, like Sprax, had the dep hairstyle and wore plenty of ironmongery on her face.

"Hey, Arnis, you want me to bring you and Miz Bailo beers? They're good and cold."

"No thanks, Marina," Bailo said. "But you go ahead and have some, Arnis."

"Yeah. Don't mind if I do." Sprax gestured at the worn but clean sofa. "Sit, Siana, sit."

Sprax was the only one among the deps who dared use Bailo's first name. She tolerated it from him mainly because any objection, any attempt to make him feel subordinate to her, might trigger a homicidal outburst she wasn't sure she could fend off. He was as physically powerful as he was prone to using violence, and he was cunning as well. It made him the perfect tool to carry out her mission of spreading mayhem on Garonne, but one fraught with inherent peril. As she'd learned over the last few months, Arnis Sprax was the epitome of unpredictability.

Bailo sat on the sofa and crossed her legs, eyes studying Sprax as he accepted a beer bulb from Marina, popped it open, and took a big gulp. He burped and smiled as he took the easy chair across from her.

"The beer came with the house. So did the wine and booze. Really nice people, the former owners. A couple of my friends also found houses freshly abandoned around here. Things are looking up." He took another healthy swig of beer.

"So…" He drawled as his crafty, soulless eyes met hers. "What can I do for you?"

"I think it's time for a direct attack on the Tianjin central police station, my friend, so we can send them running to Iskellian as well."

Sprax frowned.

"Gonna cost us a lot of casualties."

"Not really. We'll equip you with building busters. I should have an inbound shipment any day now. You destroy the station first, then shoot anyone left alive. Piece of cake. Besides, you got more troops than you know what to do with." She paused for a few heartbeats. "Same deal as before. We provide the weapons and the training. You don't say anything about the target until the night of the attack."

"When?"

"Three days after the next weapons shipment comes in. Training and organization will be the night before. That way, there's less chance of the police suspecting they're the target."

"You got it." Sprax drained his beer bulb and sighed contentedly. "I'll be real happy when we own this entire shithole town."

***

Miko Steiger, wearing a dep's black, fake leather pants, boots, and cutoff jacket and carrying a small bag slung over her shoulder, got off the train at the Tianjin station and looked around. A few obvious deps were loitering in the shadows of the platform, watching the few people emerge from the passenger wagons. A larger contingent, many carrying big bags, climbed aboard for the return trip to Iskellian. Most looked either scared, sad, or angry and Steiger figured they were citizens of Tianjin fleeing the dep paradise expanding throughout the city like a malignant tumor.

If she'd had her druthers, she'd have spent a few days in Iskellian, evaluating the situation there before heading to Tianjin, but time was of the essence. Chief Superintendent Bain's data prompted Ghost Squadron's intelligence officer to anticipate a more significant attack soon, heightening the importance of moving fast to prevent it.

Almost at once, Steiger attracted the attention of several dep watchers, and one of them headed for her as she made her way through the terminal. Steiger pretended not to see the man and let him catch up with her long strides.

"Oi." The man grabbed her upper arm from behind.

Steiger shook it off as she swirled around, snarling.

"What the fuck do you want, asshole? And don't fucking touch me."

The man held up both hands in surrender.

"Hey, no disrespect intended. It's just that you're new here, and we got orders to intercept newbies."

"How do you know I'm new?"

He grinned and tapped the side of his head. "I've been here for almost ten years and would remember someone like you."

"Oh yeah? Say, you wouldn't know where a girl can find some colonist-bashing action, do you?"

"Nope. But if you head for the Old Quarter, you'll find it owned by our sort, and there's always a meal and a bed available for those who want to be useful."

"Thanks, buddy."

Steiger clapped the man on the shoulder hard enough to make him wince in pain.

As she walked through the terminal's front door and out onto the street, Steiger figured she'd better warn Ghost Squadron that the station was under surveillance by the deps. Twenty-five healthy, if scruffy-looking men arriving all at once might trigger alarms.

Once she was out of sight from the station, Steiger fished her communicator from a jacket pocket and quickly thumbed in a simple line — *all arrivals at the station watched by deps.* Then she sent it up to the geostationary satellite *Iolanthe* had deployed to ensure the ship was always in contact with the surface, no matter where she was in her orbital period.

Steiger soon reached the old part of Tianjin, and the wary citizens she'd encountered along the way, moving aside for her, not making eye contact, gave way to strutting deps with various hairstyles, the ubiquitous fake leather clothing, lots of tattoos, and lots of piercings. They acted like they owned that part of the city, and the absence of any police or Constabulary personnel patrolling supported the impression.

Figuring the largest pub in the area might be a headquarters of sorts, she walked around until she found one with deps lounging in the morning sun outside its open windows. The sign hanging over the door — Tianjin Arms — had been defaced with the crudely applied words 'Under New Management by the DAC.'

Steiger walked past the deps and through the door into the pub's shadows, blinking a few times to let her eyes adjust to the relative darkness inside. The first thing she spotted was a big man holding court in a large corner booth by a window overlooking a lush backyard where more deps lounged around wooden tables. He gave off an aura of power, though his watchful, knowing eyes were dead, proof he didn't own a soul.

Her height and build attracted his attention, and he waved her over.

"Who are you?" He asked when she neared his table. "I've never seen you around."

"Evana Kor. Came in on the train from Iskellian this morning. And who might you be?" She said in lower class Celeste-accented Anglic.

The man grinned as he looked at the deps surrounding him.

"Who am I, she asks?" He replied in the same accent. "Who am I?"

As if on cue, the others chuckled with delight. Whether feigned or real, Steiger couldn't tell. She met the man's eyes and waited patiently.

He leaned forward.

"I'm Arnis Sprax, darling, and I own Tianjin."

Steiger smiled at him as she took a chair unbidden to the dirty looks of Sprax's entourage. But the man himself appeared fascinated by Steiger. Even beneath the dep disguise, or perhaps even because of it, she remained a striking woman — tall, muscular, with strong, even features and piercing eyes.

"A pleasure, Arnis." She adopted a relaxed posture, projecting quiet self-confidence. "So, tell me, how did you get to own Tianjin?"

His grin returned.

"By being the biggest, baddest bastard of all, darling. Now, what do you want in Tianjin?"

A shrug. "Have some fun, scrag a few colonists, and enjoy life."

"And why would you want to scrag colonists?"

"Assholes have fucked me around ever since I got sent to this planet of shitheads five years ago."

"They've fucked all of us around. Why, after five years, did you decide to leave Iskellian and come here?"

The hardening in Sprax's gaze told Steiger he was suspicious of her motives. Whether it was her manner, words, or on general principle, she couldn't tell.

"Colonist sonofabitch for who I was working tried getting into my pants. When I turned him down, he threw me out onto the street. Since I wasn't officially on his books, there was nothing I could do. Left him with a black eye and a few bruised ribs, though. But he couldn't go to the cops without admitting I worked for him as an undeclared employee. It was sort of the last straw if you like. I want to get my revenge on the damn colonists."

Sprax rubbed his square chin.

"Worker, eh? Living on bennies ain't enough for you?"

"Nope. Besides, I don't like being an idle bum, and I got my pride. Bennies are going away anyhow."

A humorless bark of laughter escaped Sprax's throat.

"We'll see about the bennies. Where you from back on Celeste?"

"Angelique, the lower town if you want to get precise. Got rounded up during one of the cleansing operations the government ran in the slums and sent here." Another shrug. "I like this place a lot better than Celeste. The air is purer, and you can move around to your heart's content. I just don't like the arrogant colonist pricks."

"What's the name of the guy who tried to get in your pants?"

"Bill Morden. He runs a sweatshop making clothes called Morden's Fashions. I wasn't the only undocumented worker there."

Steiger held Sprax's gaze. Morden's Fashions actually existed and hired deps to work under the table. Chief Superintendent Bain had passed along the necessary information at her request, and Bill Morden did sport a black eye and bruised ribs thanks to a brief visit by Steiger to his workshop the previous evening. He'd been having sex with one of his employees in his back office, and she didn't look as if she enjoyed the act at all. In fact, the woman, another dep, had scurried out and vanished into the night when Steiger began whaling on Morden.

Sprax glanced sideways at one of his hangers-on and nodded at him. The man stood and disappeared into the back room. They were actually going to check her story out. A good thing she'd given Morden what he deserved. If their contacts in Iskellian were going to speak with him, he'd deny knowing her, but then they'd expect that.

"Well, Evana Kor, welcome to Tianjin," Sprax said, leaning back in his chair. He must finally have noticed something in her he liked because he added, "We can always use people who show some ambition and hate colonists. Tell me more about yourself and where you'd like to go."

And so, Miko Steiger spun him a tale of her woes and her villainy, one designed to catch and cement his interest in her.

—Ten—

"Looks like taking the train is out," Captain Rolf Painter said as he entered the compartment where D Troop, under Command Sergeant Faruq Saxer, was brainstorming its assignment. The twenty-five special operators variously sat or stood around a three-dimensional holographic projection of Tianjin covering most of the compartment's floor. Generated by *Iolanthe*'s recon AI based on images provided by surveillance satellites in low orbit, it was as close to a real-time view of the city as possible.

"How come?" Saxer looked up at his company commander.

"Miko sent a message saying the Tianjin station was under surveillance by the opposition. She wouldn't have bothered if she thought D Troop passing through tomorrow morning wasn't a problem."

Saxer shook his head.

"It seemed way too easy in any case. Okay, let's try this on for size. We rent a couple of transports, each big enough to carry a troop, and drive up from Iskellian. It's what? A six or seven-hour run upcountry. Show up at the rental place the moment it opens tomorrow morning. Better yet, let's try to get one vehicle from each of three rentals, so we're even less obvious."

"Sounds like a plan. I'll ask the Skipper to get in touch with Chief Superintendent Bain and see if she can canvass the likely places in Iskellian."

"Thanks, boss."

"Got any blinding insights yet?" Painter asked, gesturing at the projection.

"Other than the Old Quarter looks like it's a dep-only zone from up here? No. However, there are promising warehouses along the Yangtse River just downstream of Tianjin that look underused or outright abandoned. We'll be checking them for suitability straight off. And there's a pub in the heart of the Old Quarter, the Tianjin Arms, which looks like dep central from up here. The amount of sketchy people streaming in and out of the place, especially this early in the day, marks it as an HQ of sorts." Saxer gave Painter a faint smile. "We might even have seen Miko enter."

"All right, then." Painter clapped D Troop's leader on the shoulder. "I'll let you get back to it."

***

Miko Steiger, unsure whether Sprax had offered her a job, at least provisionally, perhaps one involving violence against cops and ranchers, stepped out into the sunshine that bathed the pub's walled back garden and looked around. Sprax had invited Steiger to take her ease there, presumably while his contacts in Iskellian checked her out.

A few deps lounged on wooden chairs beneath large umbrellas and gave her searching looks as she wandered around. They seemed fit or at least fitter than the average and exuded an aura of controlled violence. Sprax's enforcers, perhaps, waiting for an assignment? Did his sending her to join them mean anything? Or was she slated to be killed quietly, out of view of the masses, if he didn't like the answers from Iskellian?

Since none of the enforcers spoke with her, she ignored them as she took a vacant chair in the shade near the door, leaned back, and closed her eyes, entering into a light meditative trance while her ears picked up sounds from near and far. She heard the breeze rustling tree leaves, the sounds of the city beyond the walls — ground cars passing, a distant train whistle, the muted ripple of voices, and a shuttle far overhead. Steiger also caught bits of conversation coming from inside the pub, Sprax's powerful voice dominating them.

"So she's my type. What the fuck does that have to do with anything?"

A soft mumbling Steiger couldn't make out answered Sprax's words.

"I'm telling you I see something of myself in her — ruthless, hard, out for blood."

Another unintelligible response.

"Look, Jett, I've got the best instincts for people on the entire fucking planet. And they tell me she's not only genuine but likely to be a hell of an asset."

Steiger smiled inwardly. Her approach with Sprax was already paying dividends. Of course, over the years, she'd discovered that she had a talent for manipulating people, almost like a Sister of the Void, if the stories were to be believed. Still, not bad for a morning's work.

"I'm not debating this anymore. We wait for confirmation from Iskellian. If she checks out, she's in. As a probie, sure, like everyone. Does that satisfy you?"

A final mumble and she heard chair legs rubbing against the wooden floor as someone pushed away from the table.

Steiger spent the next two hours motionless, to the growing amazement of the deps in the backyard. When the aroma of cooking food began wafting through the open windows and door, her eyelids snapped open, and she straightened in her chair. At that moment, Jett Khan, dark-haired, dark-complexioned, and with a somber mien, popped his head through the door and pointed at her, then jerked his thumb.

"Kor — get in here."

"Sure." She smiled at him and stood with the sort of fluid grace that attracted attention, even from Khan, judging by the brief appreciative glint in his eyes. Steiger figured that with their appetites so close to the surface, she could have a lot of fun teasing them.

She followed Khan back to Sprax's table — the man didn't seem to have moved since she'd last seen him — and the latter indicated she should sit.

"My friends in Iskellian did some checking on your story, darling. Wanna know what they found?"

Steiger gave him a languid shrug.

"You're going to tell me whether or not I want to, so you might as well go ahead."

Sprax chuckled at her effrontery — a good sign.

"Bill Morden denies knowing anyone called Evana Kor, but he employs deps off the books and doesn't know their real names anyhow. However, someone blackened his right eye, and he moves like a man who has been repeatedly kicked in the ribs, probably sometime in the last twenty-four hours. He did mention a tall, muscular dep woman was responsible for his injuries." Sprax held out his hand over the table. "Welcome aboard. You'll be working as one of my enforcers — a probie to begin with, of course."

"Thanks, Arnis. Or do I call you Mister Sprax now?"

"Just Sprax will do fine. We don't stand on ceremony or first names around here, Kor. You'll live in this place, which, as you may have guessed, is my HQ. Someone will show you to your room where you can drop your things. Then, we'll eat lunch, and you'll be coming with me and the guys for my afternoon rounds so you can get the lay of the land."

That evening, she met the young woman with whom she'd share the room, Nettie Grach, who oversaw the pub's kitchen. Grach was plain, stocky, and sported an almost permanent sneer. However, when they turned in for the night, she made advances toward Steiger and was unhappy when she rejected her. It seemed Steiger's predecessor as roommate had been more forthcoming. Appetites close to the surface, indeed. And no future time orientation, as she expected from people deported to Garonne because they were primarily petty criminals, troublemakers, and undesirables.

They lived for today. Tomorrow would take care of itself.

Except for Arnis Sprax and a few others in his close entourage, who could see beyond the immediate and plan accordingly. Which was why they led the mostly amorphous deportee community. Still, she hadn't spotted any organized groups capable of coordinated attacks on civilian ranches and farms, let alone on police and Constabulary officers. But it was only her first day, and Sprax wouldn't let her see that part of his operation yet. Steiger still had to prove herself.

She slept lightly that night, yet Grach didn't press her case any further, no matter how disconsolate she might have felt at Steiger's refusal to go beyond shaking hands, though she snored quite a lot.

The next day, Sprax summoned Steiger and three of his cutthroats after breakfast. As they stood in a loose semi-circle in front of his favorite table in the pub, Sprax said, "We're seeing Volker this morning. He failed me for the last time when he didn't remit the creds from his sales last night and needs to become an example. Steiger, I'm bringing you in on this one because you need to learn how we deal with thieves. Eventually, you'll be doing stuff like this on your own."

She nodded once but didn't speak.

"All right. Let's go." Sprax climbed to his feet, surprisingly limber for a man of his bulk, and headed for the front door, followed by his people, Steiger included.

They went to a dilapidated quarter of Tianjin, a slum where three- and four-story buildings seemed ready to fall down in the slightest breeze. Garbage littered the streets and sidewalks, and hollowed-out shells of ancient ground cars sat haphazardly along the verges. A general aura of despair hung over the area, and people quickly vanished into darkened alleys or doorways as they approached, fearing violence from the big dep leader and his four equally large enforcers.

Sprax stopped in front of a tenement that appeared in even worse shape than the rest. He nodded at two of his men.

"Get Volker out here. We're doing this in public to warn everyone about what happens when you try to screw over Arnis Sprax."

The men vanished into the building's dark lobby and climbed the stairs. Steiger heard thumping from the open door, followed by a cry of anguish cut short after a muffled thud. Moments later, the men reappeared, half carrying, half dragging an emaciated, unshaven individual in his late twenties, another dep by his body modifications and clothing. They let him go in front of Sprax, and the man collapsed to his knees.

"Sprax, my man." Volker tried to smile, but it turned into a rictus of fear. His voice was tremulous, and he seemed on the verge of voiding his bowels. "How are you?"

"Get up, you fucking waste of skin." Sprax leaned down, grabbed him by the front of the jacket with his left hand, and hauled him to his feet. "You know why I'm here, don't you?"

"N-no. If it's about the creds, I'll have them for you by the end of the week."

"Meaning you pissed the money away and are now desperately looking for a source to make it up. But you're too late, my friend. The due date was yesterday, and you missed it. That was the third and final time. You know what happens to those who disappoint me once too often, right?"

A sudden stench reached Steiger's nostrils, and she knew the man had voided his bladder. Upon closer inspection, she noticed the red flecks in his eyes, a sign of drug abuse, and she understood Volker had been sampling the wares he was supposed to sell. In her experience, a dealer who did so generally died before the drugs put him on a mortuary slab.

Sprax's massive right hand clenched into a fist, which struck Volker's nose with a meaty thwack, and blood exploded from the nostrils. Steiger was suddenly conscious of many unseen eyes watching from behind polarized windows or curtains and from darkened alleys and doorways.

After that initial strike, Sprax began systematically beating a sobbing, screaming Volker. He broke teeth, then the jaw and cheekbones, before dropping him like a sack of wet rice. Sprax kicked him into unconsciousness and, eventually, death, leaving a broken, bloody carcass on the sidewalk.

"That's for being a thief and stealing from me," Sprax said in a booming voice that echoed off the building walls. "The moral of the story is don't take what isn't yours."

Steiger, who had witnessed Volker's gradual demise under Sprax's brutal treatment, felt sickened, although she maintained a stoic expression and impassive eyes. Volker was obviously not the first he'd beaten to death. How many more victims suffered the same fate? Only Sprax could tell, and she wasn't about to ask. Psychopaths of his sort were too unpredictable. Still, the irony of his words didn't escape her, considering Sprax had probably taken plenty that didn't belong to him over the course of his life.

As Sprax turned to leave, she asked, "What about the cops? Won't they home in on this?"

He laughed without humor.

"The cops don't come around here anymore. Besides, who's gonna testify against me?" He made an expansive gesture with his blood-flecked right hand. "I own everyone who lives within two kilometers of this place."

Once they were within hailing distance of the pub, Sprax turned to one of his men.

"Get me the kid."

"Will do," the man replied in a flat tone.

Sprax entered and immediately took the stairs. Steiger turned to another of the enforcers and feeling her heart sink, she asked, "What's that about?"

A faint look of disgust crossed his face.

"Whenever Sprax kills someone, he gets horny."

"And the kid?"

"Sprax sometimes wants little boys instead of grown women, especially when his blood is up." With that, the two heavies walked out into the back garden and sat in the shade of open umbrellas, stony expressions on their faces.

Steiger felt herself become physically ill as she joined the men in the garden and vowed she would definitely kill Sprax herself when the time came.

— Eleven —

Staff Sergeant Osmin Sberna, who led D Troop's 1st Section, shouldered the rickety wooden gate aside and stepped into a garbage-strewn yard overgrown with native ground cover that bordered a single-story building sporting tall, dirty windows and half-closed vehicle-sized doors.

As he'd expected from the orbital feed, it appeared that the rundown warehouse had been abandoned a long time ago.

He waved at the large, old civilian pattern cargo cube idling on the curb, carrying the rest of 1st Section, and it cautiously drove through the opening. Sberna pulled the gate shut and signaled for his people to disembark. Seven armed troopers, dressed in laborers' worn clothes and looking scruffy, climbed out of the vehicle. They carried their carbines loosely in their hands, and their eyes were everywhere, taking in the surroundings.

"Let's spread out and search the area. Martin, you and your guys will take the outside. I'll do inside with mine."

Sergeant Davros, 1st Section's second in command, nodded. "Wilco."

Sberna led his half of the section through one of the partially open vehicle doors. Almost immediately, a small creature shrieked and skittered deeper into the building. The Marines spread out and inspected the interior but found nothing more than scattered garbage and plenty of dust, nothing else — no pallets, no boxes, and no furniture in the offices lining one side — except the usual fixtures in the toilets, streaked with rust and bone dry.

"It's big enough for both companies," Corporal Leroy Taggart said once they regrouped near the door. "Heck, the entire squadron, if we want to get cozy. None too clean, though."

"But it's isolated. There isn't a single human life sign within a kilometer." Sberna looked around, then turned and headed for the van where Davros was waiting.

"And?"

"A two-meter-high wall, in good shape, goes around the warehouse. A few critters living here and there, but nothing to show anyone's been here in years. I say we set up."

Sberna nodded. "Right."

He pulled a communicator from his shirt pocket.

"One-four, this is one-four-alpha. The target area is suitable."

Moments later, Command Sergeant Faruq Saxer's voice came over the encrypted troop push.

"One-four understands the target area is good. On our way. Out."

Sberna nodded at Corporal Taggart to open the gate, then reached into the van and retrieved his duffel bag. Two more nondescript cube vans nosed into the compound a few minutes later and stopped beside Sberna's. One disgorged eight troopers, the other nine — including Saxer.

"Can't see your vehicle from outside the wall, Osmin," the latter said by way of greeting. "And the open area is big enough for at least three shuttles landing at the same time, which means this place is excellent for our purposes."

After a brief inspection of the compound and the building, Saxer ordered the three vans parked inside and selected a spot for his troop — and the rest of Erinye Company — to bed down. The troopers immediately got to work cleaning the space while two of them, with plumbing knowledge, looked for the main water valve. They found it within minutes and turned the wheel, sending rusty water to spray from the faucets and toilets in the bathroom. It cleared after a while, and one of them ran a sensor scan.

"We're good to use the water, Sarge. It's clean."

"Excellent. Osmin, how about you take your people on a stroll into town after lunch?"

Sberna grinned.

"Finally seeing some of those damned deps up close and personal will be a pleasure."

The Marines ate a reconstituted meal from the boxes they'd brought with them and, carrying no more than their Pathfinder daggers and handguns concealed beneath their loose shirts, One-Four-Alpha ambled along the main road between Tianjin and Iskellian until they reached the Old Quarter and began seeing idle deps sitting on front stoops, hanging around street corners in small groups, or passed out in doorways.

Many of the deps, in turn, watched them walk by in two and threes through eyes narrowed with suspicion. Understandably, since the Marines gave off a predatory aura even from under the scruffy looks, sunglasses, and old clothes, one other predators, like so many of the deps, could sense.

Their sunglasses, equipped with video cameras, captured everything they witnessed and every face they encountered, although the Special Forces operators were no slouches in the memory department. They eventually passed the pub that served as Sprax's HQ and Osmin Sberna glimpsed Miko Steiger through an open window. Whether she spotted him, he couldn't tell. But she knew they'd be in town by now.

A couple of deps lounging on the terrace in front of the pub stood as Sberna and his troopers ambled by, and one of them, a big, solidly built man, stepped forward, scowling.

"I think you're in the wrong part of town. Best you get going back to where you belong."

Sberna smiled pleasantly at the man as he raised both hands, palms facing outward.

"Sure thing, buddy."

Then, he picked up the pace and led his team back toward the Iskellian Road, but via a roundabout route that took them through a fair chunk of the old town before returning to the abandoned warehouse.

"So?" Saxer asked when Sberna entered. "How was it?"

"Depressing. Deps have overrun the Old Quarter. We hardly spotted any regular folk and no police at all. A big monster of a guy hustled us along as we passed what I figure is dep HQ. I got the sense several of them think something was off with us based on the looks we got. Like they sensed we were threats. Oh, and I observed Miko inside the HQ pub. Dunno if she noticed me. Give us a few minutes to download the video from our glasses, and you can witness it firsthand.

"Sure thing. I'm heading out with Jared's section after supper, just before it grows dark. It'll be good to get a street view of the area ahead of time."

***

Miko Steiger had, in fact, seen Osmin Sberna and a couple of his troopers walk past the pub, looking for all the world like tourists, and she'd overheard the man guarding the front door shoo them away. But she didn't have time to dwell on it.

Sprax had emerged from his room looking like the proverbial cat who'd swallowed a pigeon and ordered two of his enforcers — luckily not Steiger — to dispose of the boy's body. A red curtain dropped in front of Steiger's eyes for a few seconds, and she feared she might lose her composure from the intense anger and hatred she felt for the man. Fortunately, it passed in a flash, and Steiger made herself look as the two carried the lifeless, naked little body down and out the back door. Where they disposed of it, she didn't know and wasn't keen on finding out. He probably wasn't the first victim, but if Steiger had anything to say about it, he'd be the last.

***

"That's odd." *Iolanthe*'s sensor petty officer of the watch frowned as he stared at his workstation display.

"What is?" The CIC officer of the watch asked.

"A newly arrived ship, whose transponder identifies it as the *Zenobia*, just launched a shuttle, yet she's a single-handed lander according to the Lloyds Registry, and it's the middle of the night in the main settlement area."

The OOW called up a repeat of the petty officer's display on his screen and studied it for a few seconds. His experience supporting special ops missions had allowed him to develop an instinct for things that didn't seem quite right. And this one whispered, 'watch me.'

"Keep an eye on her and the shuttle. Let's observe where it lands and what it does.

"Aye, aye, sir."

There wasn't much to do during the gamma watch aboard *Iolanthe* — she was in a stable orbit, connected to her own satellite constellation, and waiting for things to develop on the ground. So the OOW stared at the shuttle as it descended, and it soon became clear the small spacecraft wasn't headed for any pinpricks of light marking towns and hamlets.

As it dropped below a thousand meters, the OOW and the petty officer simultaneously realized the shuttle was going to land in an open field by a dirt road where a trio of darkened trucks waited, their power plants shut off.

"Do you think they might be smugglers, PO?" The OOW asked, breaking the silence on the bridge.

"Sure looks like it, sir. I'll zoom in."

The image changed as the PO ordered the geostationary satellite covering the area to focus on the trucks, and six life signs appeared, two per vehicle.

"Interesting."

The OOW leaned forward as the shuttle's thrusters flared, lighting up the surroundings and revealing the trucks to be old, battered cubes, brown in color, and thoroughly unremarkable. The same make and model were likely abundant on Garonne, a Rim Sector world with limited ground vehicle manufacturing capabilities.

"You're recording this?"

"Yes, sir."

The shuttle settled on the short grassy surface, and any remaining light vanished as its thrusters spooled off. The greenish tinge of the night vision sensors took over again as they watched the aft ramp drop while the six in the trucks climbed out and headed for it. A figure appeared at the top of the ramp and raised a hand while speaking.

"Too bad we can't hear what they're saying."

Three of the six men — all of whom wore similar dark clothing — climbed aboard the shuttle one after the other and, a few moments later, reappeared dragging antigrav sleds loaded with large, unmarked boxes. They briefly opened one crate in each stack, not enough for the satellite camera to see inside, and checked the rest with what appeared to be a standard issue handheld battlefield sensor.

"Um, sir?" The PO turned toward the officer of the watch. "If I'm not mistaken, those look like standard arms cases, the sort we use to store and transport weapons in bulk."

The OOW's eyes narrowed as he studied the sleds being pulled toward the trucks as the second set of three men went up the shuttle's aft ramp. They, too, emerged a short while later, dragging antigrav sleds with the same sort of cases piled on them.

"Scan them."

"Wait one, sir." The PO busied himself, then said, "Can't get a clean reading from the satellite's altitude, but I wouldn't if they're ordnance crates. Those things are scan-proof unless you're right up against them."

A humorless smile appeared on the OOW's lips.

"What do you think, PO? That we got ourselves weapons smugglers, the sort who are arming deps?"

"I'd say so, sir."

As they watched, one of the men from the trucks handed something to the one standing on the shuttle's aft ramp. The latter disappeared as the other man climbed aboard his vehicle, and the ramp closed.

The OOW reached for the communicator embedded in the arm of the command chair and rang the captain's quarters while keeping his eyes on the display.

When Commander Ardross, still a little groggy from sleep, answered, the OOW gave him a rundown of the events. When he was done, Ardross said, sounding fully awake, "Get Colonel Delgado to join me in the CIC, and don't let those trucks get out of sensor range. We need to figure out where they go."

"What about the ship, sir?"

"Once the shuttle is back aboard, we'll detain it for inspection. To that end, unmask us when there's no one around who can observe us. We'll be the Federation Navy cruiser *Iolanthe* on patrol in the Garonne system. At least for a short while."

A few minutes later, Ardross, wearing his Navy uniform, entered the bridge and took the command chair vacated by the OOW. He'd barely had a chance to review the recording when Delgado joined him.

"I hear something unusual is going on?" The latter said, as he dropped into a vacant workstation next to Ardross. "What gives?"

— Twelve —

The OOW repeated the story, telling Delgado the same thing he'd told his captain.

"We're tracking the trucks, which appear to be headed for nowhere in particular."

Delgado nodded.

"If those cases are filled with weapons, they can only be destined for the deps, meaning they'll hide them somewhere well away from the police and Constabulary. I figure they've got themselves a little place in the foothills, well camouflaged, that serves as a training area and depot. Which really makes me wonder who's behind this. The deps didn't just decide one day to get themselves organized for military action. Not after being on Garonne for so long." Delgado turned to Ardross. "What's with the official duds, Keever?"

"If you heard rumblings a few minutes ago, it was us turning into the Federation Navy cruiser *Iolanthe*. I intend to detain the trader and board him once he's recovered his shuttle. For that, I need my uniform."

"Ah. Of course. On what grounds will you base your actions? I'm just curious, that's all. Command and Staff College drilled the importance of legality into my thick skull."

Ardross chuckled.

"You care about legality? Since when?"

"Humor me."

"Alright, then. I'll simply tell him I'm sending an inspection team that'll ensure *Zenobia* is adhering to the Federation's shipping regulations. Once aboard, we'll match the shuttle and the man flying it with the satellite recording. If they correspond, I'll say I'm detaining them on suspicion of smuggling weapons and impounding their log and navigation records. All legal actions."

Delgado's eyes twinkled with mischief as he asked, "And then?"

"Then I'll play it by ear. We'll interrogate them, of course, but I do believe I'll be seizing the ship and placing my crew aboard, at least until our current operation is over. Meanwhile, I'll report the situation to SOCOM and see what they have to say. I know I'm pushing the bounds of legality if we don't find any smuggled weapons aboard, but needs must. Satisfied, Curtis?"

Delgado grinned as he sketched a salute.

"Thank you, Captain Ardross, sir."

"Now shush and let the Navy do its thing."

Silent and deadly, *Iolanthe* slowly caught up with *Zenobia* and descended to her level, undetected by the small trader. The crew, working with quiet efficiency, watched *Zenobia* recover her shuttle, and before the hangar deck door even shut, *Iolanthe* lit up.

"Trader *Zenobia*, this is the Federation Navy cruiser *Iolanthe*. Heave to and prepare to be boarded by an inspection team for a routine compliance check."

Ardross had the message put on repeat on the civilian emergency channel and waited. Finally, a man's deep voice came through the speakers.

"This is *Zenobia*. I'm in a hurry and can assure you I comply with the applicable shipping regulations, so I will not be heaving to."

The sensor PO raised his hand.

"He's engaging his sublight drives."

"Oh no, you don't," Ardross said. "Signals, give me a link."

"On, sir."

"*Zenobia*, this is *Iolanthe*. If you're thinking of running, think again. Refusing to submit to a compliance inspection is a violation of the shipping regulations and can result in your registration and captain's ticket being withdrawn."

"He's breaking out of orbit."

The same voice as before sounded through the bridge speakers.

"For that, you'll have to catch me first, and I'm faster than any old Navy tub." Then the man laughed before cutting the link.

"XO," Ardross turned to the holographic image of his first officer, who'd taken her place on the bridge shortly after Delgado's arrival in the CIC. "Please enter the following in the ship's log. I suspect *Zenobia* of weapons trafficking, and the captain is refusing to comply with my orders. As a result, I find myself forced to fire one or more warning shots."

"So entered, Skipper," she said after a few seconds.

"Guns, fire a warning shot to pass on *Zenobia*'s port side."

The gunnery officer, who'd been listening to Ardross's conversation with the first officer, immediately replied, "Aye, aye, sir. Firing one warning shot to pass on the target's port side."

A second later, a massive plasma round erupted from one of *Iolanthe*'s main guns, caught up with the fleeing trader, and passed within a few meters of his port hyperdrive nacelle.

Ardross nodded.

"Close enough to scorch him." He turned to the signals PO again. "Is that link still open?"

"Yes, sir."

"*Zenobia*, this is Commander Keever Ardross of the Federation Navy cruiser *Iolanthe*. I trust you noted the warning shot. If you do not return to orbit and allow my inspection team aboard, the next shot will shear off your port side nacelle."

Within moments, the voice was back but sounding a lot less amused.

"Are you crazy, man? You could have hit me with that shot."

"My gunner is one of the best in the Fleet. He put it right where he intended to. And the next one will eliminate your ability to go FTL. It's your choice."

"Shooting at civilian ships is illegal." The indignation in the man's tone caused Ardross and Delgado to exchange amused glances.

"Not if they're suspected of landing smuggled weapons on Garonne and refuse to cooperate."

"Prove it."

"First, you will return to orbit and submit. Otherwise, I will fire again, and this time immobilize you." When the man didn't immediately reply, Ardross said, "Guns, target *Zenobia*'s port side hyperdrive nacelle. Stand by to fire on my order."

"Okay, okay. I'm sorry. Blame it on nerves, blame it on a case of what the fuck is a Navy ship suddenly doing here, blame it on whatever you want. I shouldn't have left like that. I'll return to orbit and allow your inspection. But I guarantee you will find nothing to link me with weapons smuggling."

"Thank you, *Zenobia*. I'm glad you saw reason. Insert yourself at my altitude, five kilometers directly ahead of me, then shut down your drives completely and await further orders."

A sigh. "Will do."

"*Iolanthe*, out."

Ardross winked at Delgado.

"And that's how we do it in the Navy. Legally speaking, that is."

"Suits me. So long as we get our hands on *Zenobia*'s captain and squeeze him dry. Bastard must know who's shipping weapons to the Garonne insurgents."

"You want the first crack at him?"

Delgado nodded.

"Between them, my Constabulary liaison, Aleksa Kine, and my intelligence officer, Jake Nunes, should get him to talk. Both are extremely persuasive, and Jake is a wizard with interrogation drugs."

"You want to bring him here or send them there?"

"Definitely bring him here so he's not in his natural environment. Being in an unknown place helps loosen tongues. Or at least increases the chances of the subject making mistakes and unconsciously revealing things."

"Will do. Once we've seized *Zenobia*, I'll have the boarding party bring everyone aboard back to *Iolanthe*."

***

"Milos Hextar, captain and sole crewmember of the free trader *Zenobia*." The tall, lean, dark-haired woman with prominent cheekbones said as she took a chair across the bare table from the bearded, stocky man wearing faded coveralls. "I am Chief Warrant Officer Aleksa Kine of the Federation Constabulary. With me is Chief Warrant Officer Jake Nunes of the Federation Marine Corps."

Kine nodded at the compact blond man with the short beard who sat beside her. They were in a small compartment hastily turned into an interrogation room aboard *Iolanthe* and it contained nothing but three chairs and the table. Since Hextar hadn't been arrested, they didn't shackle or otherwise restrain him.

Hextar raised a skeptical eyebrow at her.

"Neither of you are in proper uniform. Why should I believe you're who you pretend to be?"

Kine's mouth turned up on one side in a cynical half smile.

"Who else would we be aboard a Federation Navy ship?"

The boarding party had worn naval-issue spacesuits, and the people who escorted Hextar to the interrogation room were in proper shipboard uniforms. Kine and Nunes wore the tan mercenary uniforms, which were the only ones they'd brought, but with a chief warrant officer's four silver bars on their collars.

Hextar crossed his arms and tilted his head to one side as he considered her.

"What do you want, Chief Warrant Officer?"

"A few answers," Kine replied, still using a mild tone.

"And you had to take me off my ship for that?" Hextar cocked an aggressive eyebrow. "I could have answered them over the radio."

"Ah, but we have impounded your ship pending our investigation, and Navy regulations state that no crew members should remain aboard until we have finished and are ready to release it."

That wasn't the entire truth, but Hextar wouldn't know it. Few Navy officers were even aware of the obligations surrounding the custody of a civilian ship since most could spend their entire careers in space without ever facing such a situation.

"Yeah, well, I just hope your captain does what he intends and fast. Every day I spend sitting here costs me money. A trader who isn't carrying cargo isn't earning."

Nunes spoke for the first time, and his tone was much harsher than Kines's. "Look, Hextar. You're not going anywhere anytime soon, so lose the attitude."

Zenobia's captain gave Nunes a hard stare, which the latter returned until Hextar looked away.

"I'm going to play a recording made by one of our geostationary satellites a few hours ago. Tell me if you recognize anyone."

Nunes stood and touched a control embedded in the wall. Almost at once, a virtual display appeared, showing the shuttle landing.

"That, clearly, is your craft, Hextar. We can see the registration number."

A disdainful shrug. "So what? I can land a shuttle on Garonne without breaking the law."

"Keep watching."

The shuttle's thrusters shut down, and the aft ramp dropped. A few seconds later, a man appeared — Milos Hextar — and gestured at the approaching figures in black.

"Are we agreed that's you, Hextar?"

"Yeah. Again, so what?"

The first antigrav sled loaded with weapons cases appeared.

"And do you recognize the cargo coming out of your shuttle?"

A crafty look entered Hextar's eyes.

"I recognize the crates. What's in them? I have no idea. I was merely contracted to deliver them to Garonne."

"Is this the first time you've delivered cargo at that location?"

Hextar briefly glanced away. "Yes. And it's still no crime to drop off a bunch of cases, even at night in the middle of nowhere."

Kine studied him with renewed interest. Did his voice just waver a bit?

"Who hired you?" She asked.

"An anonymous shipper."

Nunes slapped his hand on the tabletop, creating a loud sound that reverberated off the metal bulkheads. He leaned over to bring his face within a few centimeters of Hextar's.

"Bullshit, Milos. Utter fucking bullshit. You know what's in those cases and who contracted you to bring them here." Again, Hextar looked away.

"Those are ordnance cases of the sort used by both the Commonwealth and the Federation Fleets," Kine said in a calm voice. "What else would they contain but weapons? Surely, you at least scanned them, if only out of sheer curiosity."

Nunes straightened but kept his eyes on Hextar.

"Oh, he scanned them alright, Aleksa. He knows exactly what's in those crates. Stuff from a Fleet armory somewhere, either in the Commonwealth or the

Federation." Nunes sat again. "If it's from a Federation depot, someone stole it," Nunes said, sitting again. If it's from the Commonwealth…" An icy smile spread across his face. "Perhaps someone deliberately sent the weapons here instead of them going missing on their own."

"What sort of weapons were in the cases, Captain?"

"How the hell should I know?" Hextar replied in an irritated tone that masked what Kine thought was growing dismay.

"Portable, I figure," Nunes said. "The deps are no more than irregular light infantry, which means heavy weapons are beyond them."

"Deps?" The question slipped out of Hextar's mouth before he had a chance to think.

"Deportees from Celeste, Captain, who are currently running an insurgency against the Garonne government, which makes the crime of smuggling guns to them a capital offense."

Again, Kine was stretching the truth. If convicted, Hextar would face a lengthy stay in a prison colony on Parth, which might make him regret not receiving a death sentence.

Hextar reared up. "What?"

"Of course, full cooperation will ensure you remain among the living, Captain."

— Thirteen —

"Those trucks stopped somewhere, sir, but bugger if I can figure it out." The CIC sensor chief glanced over his shoulder at Delgado. "One moment, they were on a track paralleling the Yangtze River. The next, they vanished beneath the trees, one after the other in quick succession, and didn't reappear. Took about fifteen seconds. Since then, nothing on visual, nor on the sensors."

Delgado rubbed his chin, eyes narrowed in thought.

"Could be a cavern. Lots of them carved out of the riverbanks in the foothills. Admiral Talyn and General Decker hid a small starship in one of them around the same area years ago. That would explain why they're no longer registering on sensors. Given thick enough rock cover, they wouldn't detect a damn thing." He climbed to his feet and stretched. "Okay, Chief. Keep an eye on the area and try pinging it hard with the sensors. I'm going to grab breakfast and think about our next steps."

"Aye, aye, sir."

When he got to the wardroom, Chief Warrant Officer Metellus Testo and Major Washburn Tesser sat at a table, coffee cups in hand, quietly chatting. Delgado grabbed a sandwich from the buffet table, filled a mug from the urn, and joined them.

Tesser turned a questioning gaze on him.

"What's new, Skipper?"

"You heard about the oh-dark-thirty delivery of what seems to be standard ordnance cases in an empty field far from anywhere?"

Both nodded, and Testo said, "Nothing stays a secret on this ship."

"I just watched the trucks disappear into what I think is a riverbank cavern on the Yangtze, in the foothills."

Tesser grimaced. "Definitely up to no good, are they?"

"Aha!" Testo's face brightened. "The game's afoot. You're now thinking of sending a few of our people down there to investigate."

"Yep. Who do you figure would be best?" Delgado took a bite of his sandwich and watched Testo.

"One or two troops from the Erinyes. I assume you'll want them to go in tonight rather than during daylight hours?"

Delgado nodded. "Affirmative. We can send shuttles up the river, flying below treetop height, and have the troops dropped just before the last bend. It's what? A kilometer or so from where the trucks vanished."

"I wouldn't know about that, sir. But give me half an hour, and I'll have a plan for you. In the meantime, I assume the ship will keep the zone under constant surveillance?"

"It will."

"Well then," Testo climbed to his feet. "I'll take a look at the recording and figure out an approach route."

He left the wardroom, and Delgado finished his sandwich.

"What do you figure, Skipper?"

"I don't think the people who took the shuttle's cargo were deps, Wash. We always figured there were folks behind the deps directing things. I believe we got our first glimpse of them a few hours ago. They looked professional — wearing identical dark clothing, without any spiked hair or visible body art, and working efficiently. Hell, just the fact that they received two dozen weapons crates from off-world in a dark field in the middle of the night means a degree of organization I'd put beyond the deps. I mean, first of all, where would the deps be getting those weapons from? And pay for them how?"

***

Captain Hextar chewed the inside of his lip as he thought about Kine's words. The latter and Chief Warrant Officer Nunes knew they had Hextar at a critical juncture and remained silent, watching him. He finally turned his eyes back on Kine and sighed again.

"I guess I'm screwed, ain't I?"

"You are, Captain. But full cooperation will go a long way."

Hextar shifted uneasily in his seat. "Listen, I need creds. Lots of them. Running *Zenobia* costs me more than I bring in because I've had a string of bad luck and no backers. So when I saw an advert in the Shipping Digest looking for a discrete vessel capable of landing small but valuable cargo in non-traditional places and offering well above prime rates, I applied. Someone — and I don't know who they are — vetted me and must have found a desperate man because they contacted me a few weeks later and offered a run to Garonne. Not this one. This was my third time. Payment every time was made upon delivery in unmarked cred chips."

"That would explain the considerable sum the boarding party found in your cabin safe."

A look of alarm replaced the earlier expression of defeat on Hextar's face.

"You opened my safe?"

"Yeah. But the money is still there. Please continue. Tell us about who contacted you to offer the shipping contract."

"I never saw them. They did everything anonymously. They didn't disclose the cargo but assured me it wasn't drugs or anything outright illegal like that. When I accepted, they sent me to Celeste, where I picked up the load one fine evening after dark on the edge of a small, dilapidated spaceport in the interior of Baune, well south of Angelique. The load had been stored in a disused hangar. For how long, I have no idea. And yes, they were military weapons crates. I recognized them immediately, seeing as how I did a hitch in the Navy long ago. The guys who loaded them aboard my shuttle wore masks and didn't speak. One of them handed me a data wafer and merely said the rest of the instructions were on it." Hextar licked his lips. "Could I get a glass of water?"

"Sure."

Kine nodded at Nunes, who left the room. He reappeared shortly after that with a bulb of water, which he handed to Hextar. The latter cracked it open and took a deep sip.

"Better?" When Hextar nodded, Kine asked, "What were the instructions?"

"Head to Garonne. Once in orbit, send a message to a numbered node giving a code word. About half an hour after I sent the code word, I got a time and ground coordinates from that node. As requested, I acknowledged and then the node dissolved, so it's pointless for you to ask me to remember the address. He took another gulp. "I landed. The same six men as tonight retrieved the cases, and one of them handed me my payment, saying that if I wanted to do this run again, I just needed to contact the address in the Shipping Digest."

"Did you scan the crates during your trip?"

Hextar grimaced.

"Yep. The first load was a hundred plasma carbines, seventy-five blasters, plenty of power packs, and ammo. It looked like Fleet issue ordnance, so I'd say you — or rather the Commonwealth — have stuff going walkabout. In any case, the payment did a lot to improve my solvency issues, but not quite enough, so I went back to offer my services again. I wouldn't get a better deal. Besides, the chances of me getting caught were tiny."

A cruel smile spread across Nunes' face.

"Third time unlucky, eh?"

Hextar shrugged.

"I reckon. And there was no Navy ship in orbit when I arrived. I checked."

"When did you deliver the first batch?" Kine asked.

"A couple of months ago." He thought, then gave her a date.

Kine and Nunes exchanged glances. It had been a few weeks before the attack on the Senesca spread.

"Tell me about your second run."

"Same deal as the first, Celeste again, except the pickup was from the Antibes spaceport. Another hundred carbines, a hundred blasters, and a lot more ammo and power packs."

"When did you deliver?"

"A few weeks after the first. The man at the receiving end told me I could make another delivery immediately if I wanted. The pickup was to be on Celeste again, but this time at the Angelique spaceport. Since a third run would make me flush, I accepted, and he gave me a data wafer with instructions."

"So you landed on a Commonwealth world capital's spaceport, one with a lot of traffic. How did that work?"

"Just like the other times. I was in and out within a few hours. No one gave me a second glance."

"Almost as if someone bribed the authorities to avert their gaze?"

Hextar shrugged. "It doesn't cost much to make them look elsewhere on a planet like Celeste."

"And what was your cargo this time?"

A faint smile twitched on Hextar's lips.

"Single shot, disposable high explosive missile launchers, with warheads in place. I figure they were M-147s."

Kine's eyebrows crept up.

"You're sure of that?"

"Yep. Told myself this would be the last run I did for them. Small arms are one thing. But M-147s can do a lot of damage. They're only good for war."

"Yet you still delivered them." Nunes' tone was flat.

"What can I say? The payment was considerable. It would have set me up for a long time." Hextar exhaled loudly. "I should have stopped after the second run."

Nunes scoffed. "You? Stop when the money's so good? It didn't even cross your mind."

"No, I guess not," the merchant captain admitted.

***

"They're about to escalate again," Delgado said when Kine and Nunes briefed him on their interrogation of Hextar. "But where and when?"

"Another question is, who's bankrolling it?" Kine grimaced. They were in *Iolanthe*'s wardroom, empty at this time of the morning. "Someone with extremely deep pockets is behind this, considering the amounts Hextar was paid and the value of black-market military ordnance."

"That he made his pickups on Celeste points to Commonwealth interference," Nunes said. "Official interference. And M-147s don't simply march out of a munitions depot on their own, not even in the Commonwealth."

Delgado nodded. "Very true, Warrant. We need to factor in enemy action."

"Enemy, sir?" Kine asked, looking interested more than anything else.

"The Commonwealth is institutionalizing hatred of the Federation, which split humanity into competing star nations. Every intelligence report we've seen indicates it. And that means we'll eventually clash openly rather than covertly. This little fracas on Garonne strikes me more and more like a small fire lit by the Commonwealth, which is hoping it'll turn into a violent conflagration. Doesn't that make them the enemy rather than the restive neighbor?"

Kine inclined her head.

"True. What happens to Captain Hextar now?"

"I'll have to ask Captain Ardross, but I suspect we'll hold him incommunicado in *Iolanthe* until the mission is over." Then, it'll be SOCOM's decision whether we turn him over to the law or let him climb back aboard his ship with a stern warning. Quite frankly, I don't care which it is.

Hextar is guilty of greed driven by desperation, not of supporting some destructive ideology or of a criminal bent. As far as I'm concerned, he could be freed to carry on his trade. Creds to crumbs, he'll never take mysterious cargoes to distant former colonies ever again."

Nunes grimaced.

"Perhaps not, sir. But he is an amoral bastard. Maybe the universe would be better off if he were clerking in some planet-bound shipping office with safeguards against corruption."

Delgado gave his intelligence officer a half smile.

"Could be. Let's keep him on ice until the current operation is over. If I had my druthers, I'd release him and his ship but on a very short leash so he can point us at other questionable contracts. Make him our auxiliary, so to speak."

"Never squander a chance to improve the business, eh, sir?"

The half smile turned into Delgado's trademark grin.

"You know me, Warrant. Waste not, want not. Where's Hextar now?"

"He's locked in one of the spare cabins with access only to the ship's entertainment library. I figure we bring over some of his clothes and personal effects and make him comfortable."

"Okay. Get me the written report with your evaluation of its veracity, and I'll forward it to SOCOM under my thumbprint. Then we'll have to let Hextar molder until this mission is over."

— Fourteen —

Three unmarked shuttles without position lights skimmed the surface of the Yangtze River in profound darkness, taking the curves and passing through canyons with the greatest of ease even though they were flying at three hundred kilometers an hour.

Invisible to anyone equipped with mere Mark I eyeballs, the only sign of their passage was the whine of thrusters. The pilots, however, saw their surroundings clearly, thanks to night vision pickups feeding the displays surrounding their consoles.

Soon, the selected landing zone appeared on the contour map display, and the pilots, petty officers from *Iolanthe*, slowed. The shuttles' sensors showed no human life signs or electronic emissions anywhere within range. It felt like they had stepped into unexplored territory. As if they were the first to set foot on this planet.

The shuttles slowed as they rose to treetop height, then popped over a thick fringe separating the makeshift road from the river and landed on it. Aft ramps dropped, and the seventy-five troopers from Erinye Company's A, B, and C Troops, as well as Captain Rolf Painter and First Sergeant Ejaz Bassam, quickly disembarked and scattered in the woods on either side, disappearing in the scrub. Ramps rose again, and the shuttles lifted off one by one and headed toward an inaccessible clearing a few kilometers away to wait for the extraction call from Captain Painter. The entire maneuver had taken less than a minute, and very quickly, the sounds of native night creatures reestablished themselves.

Within moments, a black, armored figure appeared on the road, followed by many more at regular intervals as A Troop cautiously made its way to where the trucks had vanished the previous night. One of the two Marines running point had a handheld battlefield sensor in his hand and continuously scanned ahead and to the sides. Once the last of A Troop was about to melt into the darkness, B Troop, along with Painter and Bassam, emerged from the brush and followed them. C Troop would stay behind and secure the landing zone.

After fifteen minutes without the sensor picking up anything, they came to where the road ducked under an overhang dripping with vegetation, and the Marines on point stopped and dropped to one knee. Immediately, Command Sergeant Bernie Rankin, the troop leader, moved up to join them, and they pointed at the black maw of a cavern as he knelt.

"It's the place where those trucks fell off the sensor grid," one of them said in a low whisper that didn't carry.

"Can you detect anything?"

"No. There's nothing within scanning range."

"NV won't work in there, so turn on IR."

"Wilco."

The three switched their helmet visors to infrared detection while the trooper with the sensor turned on his helmet-mounted IR light. Immediately, the vast, low entrance to the cavern became visible, and they noticed that it had likely been cut into the cliffside by the river eons ago. Every visible surface was worn smooth, but there was no sign of the trucks.

Rankin turned on the company push.

"One-niner, this is one-one."

"One-niner," Captain Painter replied.

"We're at the right spot, and there's indeed a cavern, but we're not seeing anything from the mouth. Nothing on sensors either."

"You're clear to enter."

"One-one understands clear to enter."

Rankin and the point men climbed to their feet. The latter, weapons at the ready, slowly moved through the opening, the IR light sweeping the cavern. Rankin briefly shut off his IR detector and the scene was plunged into complete darkness. He switched it on again, smiling at the reappearance of his troopers. One-one-alpha, the first section, passed him and followed the point men, and Rankin tagged along behind them.

The cavern was much deeper than he initially thought and certainly big enough for a dozen cube trucks, but not a single one was to be seen. Then, the point men rounded a bend and came to a stop.

"One-one, this is November-one-one-alpha," one of them said over the troop push. "We have a funny situation up here. You should definitely come and have a look."

Rankin made his way to the head of the troop, and as he came around that same bend, he skidded to a halt. The point men were standing in front of a rock wall blocking any further progress.

"What's the funny situation?" He asked.

Instead of replying, the one with the sensor handed him the small machine, and Rankin glanced at its readout.

"I'll be fracked," he murmured. "It looks like there's something unnatural on the other side."

"That's what I thought. It could be that those are our trucks. In any case, the wall isn't natural either, and it's pretty thin."

"Well, then, let's search for an opening mechanism."

Rankin pulled out his own handheld battlefield sensor and began scanning the fake obstruction from very close up. He found what he was looking for within moments — a latch on one edge, where it met the natural tunnel side.

"Got a locking mechanism here."

The point man with the sensor glanced at him, then checked the opposite edge.

"And another one here."

"Let's check how it works." Rankin studied the fake rock surface and noticed a hairline crack running in a rectangle above the locking mechanism his sensor had detected. He simply pushed on it and heard a satisfying, if faint, sound like that of a hasp popping open. The point man did the same, and both pushed on the wall. It swung upward effortlessly, revealing a continuation of the tunnel that lost itself in darkness beyond the range of the IR lights.

But most importantly, three battered old cube trucks sat one behind the other on the left side. The open cargo doors made it obvious that they were empty.

"One-niner, this is one-one. We found the trucks, but the weapons cases are gone."

***

"And we didn't witness anyone emerge from that cursed cavern?" Delgado frowned as he stared at the side display showing the area.

"No, sir. I had it set up so it would notify me the instant something moved there, but nothing," the CIC sensor chief said. "I'll review the recording of the last twenty-four hours in case it blipped, but I doubt it."

"Okay. Assuming nothing came out, the only answer is that they transported the cases deeper into the cave on their antigrav sleds."

The chief nodded.

"That would be my guess."

Delgado turned to the CIC signals petty officer.

"Please reopen the link with one-niner."

"You got it, sir."

"One-niner, this is Niner."

"Go ahead," Rolf Painter said through the CIC speakers.

"We're working under the assumption that nothing exited through the front door, indicating that the cases were moved further into the cave."

"That's what I figure."

"Go ahead and explore. But be extremely careful and watch for booby traps."

"Wilco."

"And since radio doesn't work too well through rock, please ensure you have a line of re-transmitters out to the open air."

"Will do."

"Niner, out."

Delgado took his by now accustomed spot to the left of the command chair where the CIC officer of the watch sat and tried not to fret. This was his first operation as squadron commander, and he being in orbit aboard a starship while his former company was on the ground, perhaps closing with the enemy, rankled. He told himself that his job was now giving his company commanders their missions, ensuring they had everything they needed, and providing additional direction as required. His days leading special ops troopers into action were over. But it still peeved him.

Delgado would have been amused to discover his mentor and the father of his beloved, Brigadier General Zachary Thomas Decker, had undergone the same painful adjustment a few years earlier.

***

Rolf Painter left B Troop to guard the cavern's entrance and followed A Troop as they proceeded further into the cave. The troopers moved with assurance through the complete darkness, thanks to the IR light and their visors turning the night into day.

The tunnel widened and narrowed without rhyme or reason, and then it abruptly ended at a smooth wall.

"Another fake, it has to be," one of the point men said over the A Troop push.

"Do a broad-base scan," Command Sergeant Rankin replied. "Let's try to determine what's on the other side."

A few minutes passed in silence, then, "Um, I'm detecting life sign readings, specifically six of them, and this wall appears to be around ten centimeters thick and composed of a lightweight polymer, similar to the other one."

"Did you find the latching mechanisms?"

"Yep."

Rankin switched to the company push. "One-niner, this is one-one."

"One-niner."

The A Troop leader passed along the information and asked what he should do next.

"Because if we open the fake wall, I expect we'll trigger some sort of alarm. The life signs appear prone and not moving, probably asleep, but they won't be for long if we walk right in."

"Wait one."

Rolf Painter briefly debated whether he should kick the decision to go any further upstairs to Delgado, but then he recalled his mission — to keep the insurgents from deploying the M-147s. The only way he was going to accomplish that would be to punch through that fake wall, take the six life signs, and search for the single-use HE missile launchers.

"Alright, one-one. You're cleared to go."

"Roger that."

Rankin moved the rest of his troop up to the fake barrier while the point men checked for hidden presents. When they didn't find any, he signaled at them to undog the hidden latches.

They did so, and an alarm siren came to life as they pushed the wall out of the way and burst into an immense room interspersed with stalagmites and stalactites. Light globes floating just below the ceiling cast a soft glow, and the troopers spread out, weapons at the ready as they shut off their IR detectors.

In one corner, six sleep-befuddled men sat up from their cots and stared at the menacing figures with faces hidden behind blank visors and wearing black armor. The troopers quickly jogged over as they struggled to get out of their sleeping bags while Rankin shouted at them to surrender.

When all six raised their hands above their heads, he said, "Good choice. The other option would have been death."

One of them growled, "We're not being paid enough to die, buddy. Can we at least get out of our fart sacks and get dressed?"

"Sure. But any wrong move…"

"No problems."

As Rankin watched them, he realized the man had used a term for sleeping bag common among soldiers and Marines. Perhaps he used to be one or the other.

"Sarge."

Rankin turned toward the voice and saw one of his troopers point at six antigrav sleds loaded with weapons cases tucked into a corner.

"Excellent."

Just then, Rolf Painter and his first sergeant entered the large space and headed for Rankin, who waved at him.

"What have we got here?"

"Not sure, boss. They could be mercs. They don't look like deps, and one of them referred to his sleeping bag as a fart sack."

"Did he, now. Which one?"

Rankin nodded at the man.

"Him."

Painter raised his visor and walked over to the individual in question.

"You in charge here?"

He nodded. "Who are you?"

"Captain Rolf Painter, 1st Special Forces Regiment, Federation Marine Corps."

The expression of astonishment followed by fear on the man's face almost caused Painter to burst out laughing.

"Oh, shit."

"Yep. You and your people are my prisoners. Try to escape, and we will shoot you. Disobey any order, and we will kill you. What's your name?"

Painter saw calculation enter the man's eyes as he evaluated his situation and decided whether to cooperate. His gaze briefly went around the space, noting the armored troopers before returning to Painter.

"Squad Leader Max Upton."

"You're a mercenary?"

Upton nodded. "Mahkteere Private Military Corporation."

— Fifteen —

"Never heard of it."

"I'm not surprised. We're small and specialized."

"If I examine the Federation's PMC registry, will I discover it listed?"

A moment of hesitation, then a shake of the head.

"We're registered in the Commonwealth."

By now, the other five men listened intently as if trying to divine their future.

"And therefore, operating illegally in the Federation."

Upton shrugged.

"I'm not the one who took the contract. What'll happen to us now?"

"You'll be held aboard our ship until this is over. After that, we'll likely hand you over to the Federation's PMC Adjudicating Authority, who will decide whether to charge you and under what items". Painter made a gesture at Rankin. "Have these men shackled, Bernie."

"Will do."

Within moments, the six mercenaries were sitting on the ground, hands bound behind their backs by plastic restraints and under the guard of a pair of troopers.

Painter and Bassam walked over to where a group of troopers were opening weapons cases, revealing M-147 missile launchers.

"As advertised, boss," Sergeant Greaves, who had one-one-alpha, said. "Four M-147s per case, twenty-four cases for a grand total of ninety-six. Enough to destroy half of downtown Tianjin, I reckon."

Painter glanced into an open crate and saw the missile launchers cradled in padding.

"Any way of booby-trapping them so they don't do what they're supposed to?" He asked. "Give the deps a nasty surprise instead of usable weapons?"

Greaves raised his helmet visor and grimaced.

"These things are soldier-proof, sir. I can't think of any way to make them go bang in the tube or not function at all. Which leaves setting up the cases to blow when they're opened, but it's not guaranteed they'll go, and after the first one, the enemy will expect the rest to be rigged as well."

"Then we'll have to take everything with us." A smile twitched on Painter's lips. "In fact, when I say everything, I mean everything — those cots, the lights, the rations, the water cans, even the trucks. Clean the place out and let the other mercs wonder what the hell happened."

Greaves grinned at him.

"And see if we can also take the fake cave walls. Leave the cave like they never were here."

"Excellent idea." Painter opened a link on the company push and told B Troop's Command Sergeant Singh to remove them. Then, he returned to where Rankin stood, supervising his troopers as they explored the vast space's far reaches.

"Bernie, we're clearing out the place and leaving it pristine, like the mercs and everything else mysteriously vanished."

Rankin snorted with amusement.

"Nice idea, boss. Causing confusion to the enemy is always a fine thing. I'll get it organized."

"Moses is looking at getting the fake walls taken down as well."

"Even nicer. What about the trucks?"

"I figure we'll simply dump 'em in the river. It should be deep enough to make them go under completely."

A shout came from the room's far end, and both men hurried over. The moment they turned the corner, they saw what caused it.

Another fake wall hung open, revealing a broad, open space beneath an overhang dripping with vegetation. Beyond it, widely spaced trees revealed a well-used track that would be invisible from above, leading away from the cave complex.

"Interesting. A second exit." Rankin studied the dark woods with his IR visor and projector switched back on, then looked closer. "I think they're using this spot to train people with weapons. Aren't those divots caused by plasma rounds?"

"Yep." Painter nodded. "The skipper did figure there would be a training area nearby."

"You want me to send a patrol along that path?"

"No, but have your people take this fake cave wall as well."

Half an hour later, a heavily laden A Troop headed back down the tunnel to the cavern by the river. After marching the prisoners away, B Troop drove the three trucks into the river one after the other, followed by the fake walls.

Once Painter and his team reached the pickup zone, the mercenaries and their gear had vanished from the cave complex.

An hour after that, the three shuttles landed on *Iolanthe*'s hangar deck, and as soon as the space doors closed, Curtis Delgado stepped through the inner airlock, an air of contentment on his face. Rolf Painter had given him a verbal report during their flight back. Therefore, it didn't surprise him to see six prisoners and six antigrav pallets loaded high with weapons cases and sundry items emerging from the shuttles along with the Erinyes.

"Excellent job, Rolf." Delgado stuck out his hand, and they shook as he grinned at Painter.

"The only thing is now the opposition will know there's another player on the planet, one who's gunning for them."

Delgado shrugged.

"We couldn't let the M-147s get into dep hands. The damage they'd have done would have been incalculable. At least your solution creates a mystery for the tangos, one bound to unnerve them. And disconcerted people make more mistakes."

They watched as four bosun's mates escorted the mercenaries off the hangar deck and to the ship's brig. Kine and Nunes would interrogate them in a few hours.

"You know, if we keep on taking prisoners, *Iolanthe* is going to run out of cells to hold them," Painter remarked.

"Then, the crew will simply turn spare compartments into additional space. Can't very well shoot folks who surrender, not even if they're raving lunatic deps with severe body odor issues."

"No, I suppose not. What do we do with the M-147s and the mercs' gear?"

"Leave it on the hangar deck. Captain Ardross' people will take care of the lot. You do your hot wash, grab some chow, and hit the rack. QD's company is now high readiness. Oh, and by the way, the Mahkteere Private Military Corporation is registered with the Commonwealth Adjudication Authority. Or at least it was at the time we seceded. Prosecuting its employees for operating illegally in the Federation will make an interesting piece of jurisprudence, seeing as how we don't have treaties with the Commonwealth on anything, let alone PMCs, nor any laws yet governing the use of foreign PMCs in Federation space."

"No doubt, sir." Painter came to attention as he watched his troopers leave the hangar deck. "With your permission?"

"Go, Rolf."

***

"We interrogated them separately, and they've been held in isolation since they arrived aboard *Iolanthe*," Chief Warrant Officer Kine reported a few hours later. "So they didn't have any chance of coordinating their stories, but they told us pretty much the same thing, which gives us a high degree of confidence. They gave us their names and positions in the organization and said they were here to train and equip insurgents. They've been with the Mahkteere Private Military Corporation for at least five years, and they're veterans of various National Guards in what were the Home Worlds before we split off from the Commonwealth. Three of them are veterans of the Celeste National Guard, and Celeste is where the PMC is headquartered."

Delgado frowned.

"Celeste was Garonne's former colonial overlord. I wonder if there's a connection."

"Not that we'll find out from these six," Chief Warrant Officer Nunes said. "They're foot soldiers who know nothing more than what they've been told by their commanding officer, a Siana Bailo. But they're vaguely aware that their activities are illegal, so they spoke freely to lessen any penalty the Federation government will impose."

"And," Kine gave Delgado a wintry smile, "they still have the reflex of bowing to regular military forces as demanded by the Adjudicating Authority lest the PMC loses its license, even though they're Commonwealth and we're Federation. It probably hasn't registered yet that the Commonwealth's Authority, who issued the license, doesn't care what they do in a foreign star nation. In any case, they say there are forty-three Mahkteere mercs on Garonne in total, that they're not involved in the attacks — those were carried out by the deps only — and they have no idea who's behind this or what they intend to achieve. The six we have in custody state their role is equipping and training the deps, full stop, and they do that in the cave system where Rolf's people found them."

"They're not sure whether the others do more than that," Nunes added, "but suspect they also recce targets and develop assault plans for the deps. All of them show a marked disgust for the deportees they deal with, calling them psychos, sociopaths, scum, that sort of thing. Those feelings are almost certainly genuine. None of them appears to be a good enough actor to fake them. And they state they regret taking on this contract because the folks they work with are utterly objectionable, and getting involved in an insurgency against a legitimate government goes beyond anything they've done before."

Delgado chuckled.

"They would say that, now that we've nicked them. Did you ask when they expected a visit from their boss or colleagues?"

"Yes." Kine's smile turned predatory. "Siana Bailo is supposed to come by and inspect the new ordnance this afternoon."

"Excellent. That means we won't need to wait for a reaction. Did they say where the rest of the mercs hole up?"

Nunes nodded.

"We've passed the information to the CIC, and they're looking for the safe house as we speak.

"Well done. Do up your full interrogation report, and I'll send it off to SOCOM.

"Sir."

Both chief warrant officers stood, came to attention, and filed out of Delgado's small cabin, leaving Delgado to contemplate his next move. Capturing *Zenobia* had been a genuine stroke of luck. Now, he only needed a plan that could capitalize on it.

— Sixteen —

Siana Bailo, manager of the Garonne operation, slowed her ancient ground car as it approached the entrance to the cavern by the Yangtze River. She was impatient to see the M-147 miniature missile launchers and find out from Upton whether they were all in firing condition.

She pulled off the road and entered the cavern, stopping in her usual spot just before the bend where the first door hung, deep enough inside to be invisible from anyone passing on the road, not that it was much traveled. There used to be a vineyard a few kilometers higher in the foothills, but it faced financial ruin years ago, and the only visitors were occasional hikers headed upcountry.

Still, Bailo locked her car before heading deeper into the cave, carrying a powerful flashlight. But after a few dozen meters, she stopped, nonplussed. The first hidden door was no longer there, nor were the ancient trucks that were usually parked behind it. She frowned as her flashlight showed nothing but rock.

A sense of urgency suddenly seized her, and she almost ran down the tunnel before stepping off at a more cautious pace, loosening the blaster in her shoulder holster. Bailo reached the spot where the second fake tunnel wall should have been but saw nothing more than darkness beyond.

She burst into the vast chamber that had housed the equipment and training team and saw nothing. No glow globes, no cots, no piles of weapons cases, no garbage. Nothing. Not even the hidden door to the other end of the cave system, which gave onto the shooting gallery and the woodland trails, remained. It was as if the team had never existed, and Bailo felt a cold shiver run up her spine.

But how was that possible? She's been here two days ago to give the team its orders, those requiring them to take the M-147s from the shuttle to this place. And yet, the men, weapons, trucks, and even camouflage plates that blocked the tunnels were nowhere to be found.

She stopped spinning in place, illuminating the far corners of the large room with her flashlight, and tried to think.

This was the right place. This was where the weapons training team lived. She quickly made her way to the other exit and saw the divots from plasma fire, confirming it.

Yet they were gone. They had vanished completely, leaving no evidence of their existence behind.

This meant another player had just joined the game, one capable of making her people disappear without a trace. And taking the M-147s, which she'd hoped the deps would use to eliminate the police in Tianjin, with them.

"Shit." She closed her eyes. "Shit, shit, shit."

But when she reopened them, the cavernous room was as empty as before. Bailo hurriedly returned to her car and drove back to the isolated safe house outside Tianjin that she used as her headquarters. It was a simple but sizable two-story structure surrounded by a curtain of trees that rendered it invisible to passersby at ground level. Most of her team lived there at least part of the time.

She parked her car beside two other, bigger vehicles, climbed out, and hurried up the front steps. Once inside, she found four of her people playing cards at the dining room table and her second in command, Skyron Enneb, reading a book in the living room.

"We have a serious problem, folks," Bailo said in a loud voice. When everyone was assembled, she gave them a grim look. "There are new players in town, and they don't fuck around. Upton and his squad, along with the M-147s, the trucks, the fake tunnel walls, and everything — and I mean everything — in the cave complex has disappeared."

"What?" A look of astonishment appeared on Enneb's thin, bearded face. "You mean someone cleaned out the cave?"

"Yep." Bailo nodded.

"Any idea who did it?"

"Has to be Federation Marines. We know Verrill asked for help from the Fleet a few weeks ago."

Enneb frowned.

"That changes everything. We can't go up against regulars."

"Ya think?" Bailo replied with a hint of sarcasm. "Of course we can't. Never mind the corporation might jeopardize its license. We'll get creamed. Whoever cleared out the cave system isn't a bit player. I wouldn't be surprised if we faced more than just simple Marines."

"You mean Special Forces?"

"Yeah. I wonder how they found out about the caves."

Enneb grimaced.

"They must have set up their own satellite constellation and probably have a ship in orbit." He snapped his fingers. "I'll bet they spotted *Zenobia*'s shuttle landing and tracked the trucks."

"Crap. That means if a Federation Navy ship is in orbit, they'll have impounded *Zenobia* and questioned Hextar."

"Let's not panic," Enneb said, though he didn't sound convincing. "Hextar knows nothing about us. Sure, he might have indirectly led them to the caves and Upton, but that's it."

Then, it suddenly dawned on him, and he blanched. Bailo noticed, giving Enneb a grim nod.

"Yep — Upton and his squad know everything, and they'll talk."

"Meaning this place is no longer safe." Enneb glanced at the others. "Time to pack up, folks. Wake the rest of the team."

Bailo chewed on the inside of her lip as she thought. "Where will we go?"

"To the Iskellian safe house, I'd say. Upton and his crew don't know where that one is."

"But the primary action remains in and around Tianjin." Her eyes narrowed. "Hmm. Since the attack on the Tianjin police station is off, we'll hit the next target, Grayson Enterprises. I'll take Ivalice with me, and we'll bunk at Sprax's HQ. You and the rest go to Iskellian. I want us out of here in half an hour. I'll take the car. You take both vans."

"You gonna warn Upari?"

Bailo made a face.

"Do I have a choice? He'll be unhappy as hell, that's for sure. I'll contact him when we're out of here." Then, a thought struck her. "No, you'd better do it in person once you get to Iskellian. I'd rather not risk the opposition catching my transmission."

"Roger that."

***

"We appear to have found the place Siana Bailo uses as headquarters, sir, but there are no visible life signs," the CIC sensor chief reported.

Delgado looked up from his tablet and frowned. "Did you confirm the sighting with the detainees?"

"Warrant Kine just did, sir, and they corroborate."

"No life signs." Delgado stared at his cabin's bulkhead, then glanced back at the small display showing the chief's face. "I guess Bailo visited the caves, found them empty, and drew the right conclusions. Good for her. Not so good for us. I'll send a troop to verify anyway."

"Yes, sir. That was it."

"Delgado, out."

He climbed to his feet and headed for Captain QD Vinn's cabin so he could alert him to have a troop ready on the hangar deck in half an hour, then contacted Captain Ardross to ask for a shuttle. It took less than thirty minutes for the shuttle, loaded with Command Sergeant Ranit Favero's E Troop, to pass through the force field keeping the atmosphere in when the space doors were open and head down.

An hour later, Favero confirmed that the place was empty, but someone occupied it shortly before their arrival. The review of satellite imagery revealed that the former occupants left and got lost in the traffic on the road in Tianjin. As a result, the thread leading to the rest of the mercenaries and potentially resolving the deportee insurgency quickly was definitely broken.

But Delgado hadn't expected it to be easy. Otherwise, the Fleet would have sent a regular Marine unit, not the best special operators in the known galaxy.

***

Siana Bailo parked the car in front of the pub serving as Sprax's HQ and climbed out, followed by her winger. She figured that at this time of the day, the dep leader would hold court instead of drinking beer in the nearby house he'd liberated.

The deps lounging in the shade outside the door gave Bailo and her winger the once-over, but since she'd been a familiar fixture around Sprax for a long time now, none challenged her. She stepped into the cool room, eyes adjusting to the darker surroundings after being out in the morning sunshine, and looked around.

Sprax sat at his usual table, in deep conversation with another dep, while his enforcers, sitting or leaning against the wall around him, stared at her. One, in particular, caught Bailo's eye — a tall, hard-looking, muscular woman she'd never seen before. The woman was studying Bailo and her companion with an intensity she found just a bit unnerving. Sprax looked up and frowned.

"Bailo," he boomed. "What brings you here so unexpectedly? Did new weapons arrive?"

The dep who'd been speaking with Sprax climbed to his feet and stepped aside, leaving his chair for the mercenary commander.

"We have a problem, my friend," Bailo said as she sat.

Sprax cocked a questioning eyebrow at her.

"Oh? What sort of problem?"

"The new weapons were delivered two nights ago. This morning, I visited the place in the foothills to check on them and the training crew. Everything and everyone was gone, vanished without a trace, including the masking doors to the tunnels."

Sprax's eyes widened in surprise, and Bailo noticed the woman move forward as if she didn't want to miss a single word.

"What the hell happened?"

"I figure someone in orbit spotted the delivery and went after it. That someone now has Upton and his squad and probably the delivery ship's captain as well."

"Fuck." An air of anger suffused Sprax's face, and his fists clenched.

"Oh, it gets worse. I think we have a plague of Federation Marines on our hands. President Verrill did ask the Fleet for help a few weeks ago. But not just any Marines. It's more than likely the Fleet sent a special ops unit. Making the training team, the weapons, and everything else in that cave system disappear is something they'd do for shits and giggles to mess with us."

"So what now?" Sprax asked in a voice tinged with menace.

"We forget the target you and I discussed and move on to the next one, but I figure our time is limited." We have no idea who these people are, how long they've been here, or how deeply they've infiltrated the area. Assume anyone new you see could be the enemy." Bailo briefly glanced at the tall woman again. "For example, you have a new enforcer. How did you come to hire her?"

"You mean Kor? She showed up the other day, looking to join the fun. I checked out her background, so no worries. But now that you mention it, some of the guys saw small groups of newcomers wandering around recently. Fit-looking folks with eyes hidden behind sunglasses."

Bailo grimaced.

"That's bad news, Sprax. Those could well have been Special Forces Marines doing a reconnaissance of your area, which means they already have a good idea of where you're operating from and what sort of people you have."

"Well, thanks for letting me know."

"The reason I came to see you is because we've left the safe house. With Upton and his people prisoners of the Marines, they'll have been interrogated, and they know about it. I sent most of my folks off to another location Upton doesn't know about, but it's too far away from here. So me and my winger need a place to lie low until the next job."

"Sure. No problems. You can stay right here. There are enough rooms upstairs for you."

One of the men standing behind Sprax leaned over and whispered in his ear. Sprax turned to him.

"Then clear a few of the idlers out. Bailo and her man have priority."

"Yes, Sprax."

— Seventeen —

"So, what's your story?" Siana Bailo placed a full plate on the long table and sat on the bench beside Miko Steiger, who was already halfway through her evening meal. "Kor, is it?"

Steiger nodded as she gave Bailo a suspicious sideways glance. "Yep. Evana Kor. And what's your name?"

"Siana Bailo."

"Pleasure. What do you do for Sprax?" Steiger shoved a chunk of meat in her mouth and chewed on it as she turned her head to look directly at Bailo. Their eyes met, and Steiger saw suspicion reflected in Bailo's.

"I help him with training, planning, equipment, that sort of thing."

"Meaning you're the one behind the fun."

"Fun?"

Steiger gave Bailo a wolfish grin.

"Stuff like killing damned colonists and burning their farms."

Bailo gave her a noncommittal shrug.

"What Sprax does after we've helped him organize is none of my business."

"Sure." Steiger winked at Bailo, who returned it with a stony stare.

"Like I already asked, what's your story, Kor?"

Her voice had taken on what Steiger thought of as the tone of command, and she wondered whether Bailo was a former senior noncom or officer.

"It's a small tale filled with woe. I'm an Angelique girl, born and bred. You know where that is, right?"

"Yeah. I'm from Celeste, too."

Bailo was probably a former Celeste National Guard member. She probably did her twenty or twenty-five, then joined the private sector. She looked the right age.

"I got picked up during a slum clearing operation five years ago and shipped here. Been in Iskellian until a few days ago. Came here after my former boss, who employs deps under the table, tried to get me over one. I clocked him good and lit out before he could call the cops on me."

"Who was he?"

"Bill Morden of Morden's Fashions. Runs a sweatshop in the bad part of town. Likes to do his female employees. I figure I'm the first who turned him down. Weak little man, really. And you, what's your story?"

"I don't have one."

"Sorry to hear that. Your life must have been boring."

"I cope."

Steiger finished her meal and stood.

"If you want to talk later, around a glass of whiskey — or perhaps do a little more," Steiger gave Bailo a knowing smile, "I'll be in the back garden, enjoying the evening."

Bailo watched Steiger leave the dining room, intrigued by the tall, tattooed woman with the intense gaze despite herself. If Steiger had seen the look in Bailo's eyes at that moment, she would have been pleased — her impromptu plan to get close to the mercenary leader might actually succeed. She wasn't Steiger's usual type. Even so, anything to help her mission…

She sat under a leafy tree in a corner of the yard and closed her eyes as she fell into a semi-meditative trance. Working for Sprax was taking a toll on her nerves and she knew only too well what her fate would be if ever he or anyone else found out she was Fleet. Bailo, in particular, worried her. She was no amateur like the deps and clearly suspected her recent arrival in Tianjin might not be a coincidence, considering a shadowy unit had just relieved her of weapons and people.

After a while, she felt someone approach her, and her eyes opened a crack. It was Bailo, studying her as she came near. Steiger's eyes fully opened, and she smiled as she indicated the chair beside hers. The sun had dropped below the horizon by then, triggering a gentle Garonne twilight, and the sound of partying deps moving along the Old Quarter's streets was growing beyond the garden's confines.

"Join me, Bailo."

The latter turned the chair so she could face Steiger and sat, crossing her legs at the knee.

"So you used to be an Angelique slumster? What section of town?"

"Lavelle."

Bailo nodded. Lavelle was a notoriously dangerous part of Angelique's lower city, where the police rarely went except to round up people for deportation to the colonies.

"And you were unlucky to get caught in a sweep."

Steiger grinned.

"More like I didn't have enough creds to bribe my way through the police cordon when they rounded me up with a bunch of others." She shrugged. "In a way, I'm better off in this place than I ever was back home. At least here, I'm not stuck in a dark, dank, and crowded city quarter. Even Iskellian's worst neighborhood is full of fresh air compared to Lavelle. And now I even have a shot at some fun."

Her grin turned wolfish as she winked at Bailo.

"Well, you certainly exhibit the accent and manners of a Lavelle girl."

"You know a lot of us? Funny, I'd have made you for someone from the upper city based on your speech, and your sort doesn't mix with ours."

A bitter smile split Bailo's face.

"Let's just say I've met a few, and funnily enough, something about you is off, but I can't quite put my finger on it."

Steiger's eyes narrowed in amusement as she half smirked.

"In that case, you want to put your finger on something else?"

"Not until whatever's bothering me stops." She examined Steiger again. "Your tats, they're gang or wannabe?"

"Gang."

"Meaning you weren't just picked up at random for deportation, and bribing the cops wouldn't have worked."

"So?"

"Show me your ID tat."

Steiger cocked an arrogant eyebrow at Bailo. "And why the hell should I do that? It's in my past. My old *compères* aren't here."

"Humor me. If you satisfy my curiosity, I might satisfy yours."

Steiger shrugged off her leather jacket and undid the front of her shirt. She pulled the left side away, revealing the small brown and black tattoo of a half man half wolf above her breast.

Bailo let out a low whistle.

"*Loup Garou.* The biggest gang in Angelique. I'm surprised you didn't find more of your fellow werewolves on Garonne."

"We keep our former gang affiliations quiet around here. There's only one group that matters — the deps."

"Okay. Fair enough."

Steiger's eyes met Bailo's, and she asked, "And where on Celeste are you from?"

Bailo didn't immediately reply but then said, in a reluctant tone, "Havre de Grâce."

"Aha. A coastal girl. And what did you do back home?"

"Celeste National Guard. Twenty-five years," Bailo replied grudgingly.

"You were in the Green Grunts?" Steiger used the common, if slightly pejorative, term for the Celestan Guard. "What rank?"

"I finished as a major."

Steiger snapped off an ironic — and sloppy — salute.

"Got tired of it, or did they put you out to pasture?"

Bailo glanced away, a sign she didn't really want to answer the question, meaning she was probably separated from the service after her twenty-five under the services no longer required item or whatever the Celestans used in their regulations and orders. It might explain why she turned mercenary — she wasn't ready to try another field of employment yet.

"None of your business." Bailo's gruff tone seemed to indicate she regretted revealing even this little of herself to Steiger.

"Okay." Steiger raised both hands, palms facing outward in surrender. Understood. Can I ask what brought you to Garonne? Other than a starship, I mean."

The quip earned her a fleetingly brief hint of a smile.

"No, you can't."

Steiger made a moue.

"Not that I dislike dark and mysterious. On the contrary. But I am curious about your role with Sprax's organization."

And just like that, the hard suspicion was back in Bailo's eyes, and Steiger realized she'd gone too far. Bailo was obviously not the trusting type but someone who looked over her shoulder constantly.

"Question withdrawn." Steiger gave her a rueful smile. "How about you join me for a glass of whiskey somewhere more private, where we can become better acquainted?"

A humorless bark of laughter escaped Bailo's throat.

"If that was a proposition, forget it. You're not my type at all."

Steiger's face took on an air that was at once sly and coy.

"Not into women, are you?"

"I'm not into former gangbangers with *loup garou* tats." Bailo stood. "And there's still something about you that just doesn't add up."

Steiger watched the mercenary re-enter the pub and wondered what she did that made Bailo look at her with distrust. Or perhaps Bailo simply had a more developed sixth sense than most and could feel something wasn't right. Then again, since Steiger had never set foot on Celeste, let alone lived among the Lavelle underworld, and Bailo was a Celestan, it could be any number of things that set off her bullshit detectors.

She'd just have to take greater care around her and be ready to abscond at a moment's notice should Bailo decide she was an infiltrator. Still, it was an interesting turn of events for the experienced agent who'd learned to take on any identity necessary for her mission and never get caught. But there was always the first time. A shame it might happen on one of her most perilous missions to date.

Later that evening, finding herself alone in the room she shared with the pub's cook, Steiger sent a brief message to Delgado:

Siana Bailo, who I suspect is the leader of the mercenaries controlling the deps, has taken refuge with Arnis Sprax, head dep for Tianjin, after your op taking out their weapons cache. She said the loss of the weapons scratched a planned attack, and they'll go to the next one on the list. She also said she's sure a Fleet spec ops unit is already here and scouting the Tianjin area. She suspects me of not being who I pretend to be, and I might need to get out of here fast. Please send the location of D Troop.

Less than ten minutes later, coordinates flashed on her communicator's screen with a single word — *Thanks.* She called up a map and memorized the route to the abandoned warehouse, then deleted the coordinates before falling into a light sleep.

— Eighteen —

"Seems like our spotting the M-147 delivery was both a blessing and a curse," Delgado said as he took his seat at the head of the table the following day. "The tangos now know we're here."

As he relayed Steiger's message, most of Ghost Squadron's command team grimaced.

"But we had no choice, Skipper," Captain Rolf Painter said. "Who knows what the deps would have done with them?"

"Any ideas?"

Painter rubbed his bearded chin, eyes unfocused as he thought. Then, "Obviously hardened targets, like the Tianjin Central Police Station or the Constabulary's barracks next door. Aren't they proof against small arms, incendiaries, and the like?"

Chief Warrant Officer Testo nodded.

"Built like strong points and capable of shrugging off anything less than high explosives."

Delgado exhaled loudly.

"Seems logical. Eliminate the police and complete the takeover of Tianjin."

"Thank the Almighty we prevented that," Sergeant Major Hak said. "Besides, they would have become aware of us the moment we made a move against them."

"I'm worried about Miko, though. She's not the type to run, but something has her spooked."

Major Tesser frowned as he leaned forward, elbows on the table.

"Maybe she caught a glimpse of how this dep leader, Sprax, deals with people who disappoint him. We know the buggers are one step down from barbarians and more vicious than the Confederacy of the Howling Stars at their worst. With her alone among them, pretending to be a Celestan dep when she never set foot on that world, it could be dicier than the usual missions she carries out."

"True. Still, the fact that Miko overheard the mercenary speak with Sprax implies she's become close to him in record time."

Tesser chuckled.

"Miko has an uncanny ability to worm herself into someone's confidence without them even noticing."

"That she does." Delgado looked at Painter. "Rolf, once you're down there with the rest of your company joining D Troop tonight, you must be ready to move within thirty minutes. Hopefully, Miko will discover the deps' target early enough for us to intercept them before they can kill any more civilians, but we'll need to be ready to react if not."

"Got it, Skipper. I've already identified an isolated landing zone for the shuttles outside Tianjin. D Troop will pick us up in their vans."

"And since the tangos already suspect we're here, no more ground recons of Tianjin. I ran Siana Bailo's name through our database, and someone by that name showed up as a major in the Celestan National Guard with an assignment to their Special Forces. Or at least she was two years ago when we obtained our last update on Home World guards before secession. It means we could be dealing with a professional rather than your average mercenary."

"That might be why she's not liking Miko as a dep," Tesser said. "Maybe she can sense a fellow pro but isn't reconciling that feeling with Miko's appearance and demeanor."

"More reasons we should be ready to extract her at a moment's notice."

"Yep. But she'll tell us when, and knowing her, it's likely to be at the last minute."

***

Miko Steiger avoided Siana Bailo the next morning, suspecting her reservations about the tall, tattooed woman supposedly from Angelique's underworld might have increased after a night's sleep. She, along with the other enforcers, accompanied Sprax during his daily round of Tianjin's Old Quarter. But upon returning to the dep HQ,

Bailo was waiting for Sprax and, after giving Steiger a long, emotionless look, led him into a back room alone.

Both emerged half an hour later, and Sprax frowned at Steiger for a moment before following Bailo out to her ground car. They sped off, destination unknown, leaving Sprax's enforcers and Bailo's mercenaries behind. Steiger quickly surmised that she had been a topic of conversation in private, but since she continued to move about without restraint, Bailo likely only expressed her uncertainties.

They returned a few hours later, both seemingly deep in thought, and closeted themselves in the back room again. Steiger somehow knew they were discussing the next murderous attack on innocent civilians. She had to find out where the target was and warn Delgado. Otherwise, her infiltrating the deps would be for naught.

"I figure we got some fun coming up," Steiger said to one of the other enforcers sitting with her in a corner of the pub.

"Yep." The man grinned at her, showing discolored, crooked teeth. "Whenever Bailo shows up, it means action is on the way."

"When do we get told who we're scragging?"

The man cackled.

"When we get there. If we're lucky. Mostly, we just show up, have at it, and leave without ever knowing who it was."

Which would be too late for the next victims. And since Bailo had obviously spoken to Sprax about her, asking him nicely about the target wouldn't do anything other than see her dead. She would need to turn her communicator into a beacon and hope that Delgado's people could deduce the target's location based on their direction and arrive there before Sprax's murderous goons. If, of course, he took her along. If he didn't, Steiger could only hope her warning would suffice. And as the old saying went, hope was not a valid course of action.

That evening, while Captain Painter was preparing the rest of Erinye Company to join D Troop in Tianjin, Steiger sent another message to Delgado, warning him that an attack was imminent. But she wouldn't know where until they reached the place. Thus, from now on, he should watch the frequency she would use when she turned her communicator into a beacon once they were on their way.

When Delgado briefed Painter on the hangar deck, just before he was about to embark, he told him to monitor the frequency as well via the geostationary satellite and get on the deps' ass the moment Steiger's beacon activated. Delgado would also send Keres Company and hopefully figure out the target before the deps arrived so they could land and ambush them. It wasn't ideal, but they would make the most of the circumstances.

An hour later, in an isolated clearing south of Tianjin, the Erinyes, wearing mercenary-style armor with rucksacks on their backs and carbines in their hands, walked down the shuttles' aft ramps and climbed aboard the vans driven by D Troop. They then headed for the abandoned warehouse, meeting no other vehicle along the way, it being the middle of the night.

"How are tricks, boss?" Command Sergeant Saxer asked when Painter climbed out of the lead van.

"Tricky." Painter looked around at the cavernous place, cleaner now that D Troop had gone through it with brooms. "Nice. Plenty of room, not that we'll need it for very long. Miko says an attack by the deps is imminent but won't find out anything about the target until she gets there. She'll be activating a beacon the moment the deps are in motion, so we'll be checking the appropriate frequency. Since it hasn't happened yet tonight, I figure we're good until tomorrow evening. Or rather this evening, considering we're already tomorrow. We're at thirty minutes' notice to move until sundown, then we'll be at two minutes, so have your people crash but stay ready once daylight hits because, after that, they'll be sitting around fully kitted."

"Understood."

A, B, and C Troops quickly settled in their assigned zones and removed their armor while D Troop began watching for the beacon on one of the high-powered communicators they carried. Soon, the warehouse quieted as most of Erinye Company's special ops troopers fell asleep or sat on their bedrolls reading and waiting.

***

The following day, an electric atmosphere filled the air as Steiger and the enforcers accompanied Sprax around Tianjin's Old Quarter. He spoke privately with several underbosses, the first time he'd done so since she arrived, and she assumed he was warning them to be ready.

Siana Bailo gave her speculative looks when she, Sprax, and the other goons returned to the pub just before lunch, but Steiger ignored her. The last thing she needed was to feed the woman's suspicions just as the deps were preparing another massacre. Steiger ate her meal with the enforcers, joshing and joking and roaring with laughter as if she didn't have a care in the world.

When the sun disappeared below the horizon, Sprax instructed his team to prepare and departed for his nearby house. He returned wearing black leathers and a rolled-up balaclava. His triggermen also came down from their rooms dressed the same, and one looked Steiger over. She always wore black as a matter of course.

"You need a 'clava, Kor. Got one?"

"Nope. Do you have a spare?"

"Hang on." The man made his way back upstairs and returned moments later, tossing a small bundle of fabric at her. She rolled it and pulled it over her head.

"Better?"

"Yep. We roll it down just before going in. Scares the marks if they don't see faces."

"Come on." Sprax gestured toward the door. "Let's start moving."

He led them along several side streets to the back of a boarded-up store. A door opened at his approach, and a black-clad dep stuck his head out.

"Everything is ready, boss," he said, stepping aside to let them in. "Vraka Platoon is here and waiting."

"Good."

They entered, and Steiger found herself in a vast room containing four battered vans. Approximately thirty deps — Vraka Platoon, no doubt — sat on old crates or leaned against the vehicles with plasma carbines slung over their shoulders. All were dressed in the same way as Sprax, but contrary to their leader's impassive demeanor, most seemed excited, with shiny eyes and smiles both fierce and hungry.

An open inner door gave into what looked like an armory, with various power weapons stored in racks. Sprax walked over, and the armorer handed him a pair of blasters and dual holsters while the other enforcers took carbines. When Steiger stepped up, Sprax glanced at the man and shook his head.

"No gun for her this time. Give her a combat knife." He turned to Steiger. "Can't risk you shooting our own people by mistake, Kor. I'll make sure you're trained before the next one. You just stick with me and observe. If you get a chance to use the pig sticker, go ahead and enjoy."

Steiger took a knife whose blade was almost long enough to qualify it as a small sword, but it was well-balanced and sharp enough to slide between ribs and puncture a heart without effort.

"Sure, Sprax." She nodded at the assembled deps as she strapped the sheathed knife to her left hip. "Is this it, or are more coming?"

The man smiled.

"Two more platoons coming from different assembly areas will join us on the road."

He turned toward the assembled deps, now watching him closely, and shouted, "Climb aboard your vans, you scum of the earth and let's go get us some fucking colonists."

A roar of approval greeted his words, and as Steiger followed Sprax to his vehicle, she reached into her jacket pocket with one hand and switched on her communicator's beacon function. She now emitted a coherent signal readable by anyone with the right frequency.

— Nineteen —

The beacon lit up on D Troop and *Iolanthe*'s surveillance screens almost simultaneously. Command Sergeant Saxer, who'd been standing watch, climbed to his feet.

"We're on, folks. Climb aboard."

The fully armored and armed troopers who'd been lounging around the vehicles immediately sprang into action. At the same time, members of A Troop opened the warehouse doors and ran outside to open the gates. Since they didn't know what would happen, the Erinyes were taking everything with them in case they didn't return and had sterilized the area, removing every last trace of their occupation.

The A Troop van was the last to leave, picking up their gate openers along the way. D Troop, with Sergeant Saxer sitting beside the driver, was in the lead, and he guided them out of the warehouse warren and onto the main road between Iskellian and Tianjin. By that time, the beacon had begun to move north, away from the Old Quarter, so he directed the driver to take the ring road rather than pass through town.

Up in orbit, meanwhile, Colonel Delgado had watched Keres Company launch from the hangar deck aboard *Iolanthe*'s unmarked shuttles, headed for the beacon until they could estimate a target from its direction. The moment the space doors closed behind them, he returned to the CIC. The sensor chief briefly glanced back at him when he entered, then concentrated on his readout again.

Delgado took his accustomed workstation and turned the chair so he could face forward after nodding at the CIC officer of the watch and studied the main display. It showed the beacon headed north on a secondary road.

He repressed another surge of irritation at being stuck aboard a starship in orbit rather than racing for the surface with his troopers. But he knew his time with the operators on the ground was mostly over. His job was coordinating the various pieces of the operation from on high.

"There, Colonel." The sensor chief pointed at the display. "We can finally make out the vehicle in which Chief Warrant Officer Steiger is riding."

He zoomed in on the visual, and a red dot representing Miko Steiger's beacon appeared on top of a small van. Three more followed it, and as they watched, another three peeled out of a side street and joined the little convoy. A few minutes later, three more appeared and tailed onto it.

"What do you think the carrying capacity of those vehicles is, Chief?"

"Hard to say, sir. A dozen unarmored adults, maybe."

"Meaning that's probably a full company down there. Serious numbers."

"For an attack on defenseless civilians, sir? Overkill," the chief replied with a vague tone of disgust. Then, "They're passing the city limits now."

The ten vehicles, traveling in surprisingly good convoy discipline with five meters between each, ran dark, meaning the drivers either wore night vision devices or navigated thanks to an array of displays fed by night vision cameras. Either showed a greater degree of organization than Delgado had expected.

"We're getting voice from the communicator used as a beacon, sir," the signals petty officer said with a hint of astonishment.

Delgado swiveled his chair toward the man's workstation. "Put it on speakers."

"…but why?" Miko Steiger asked.

"Because you're a security risk. Bailo is right. I can't afford to keep you around," a man's rough voice replied. "You could be Fleet for all I know, seeing as how you showed up around the same time as those unknown operators."

"That's why I got a big knife instead of a power gun."

"Yep. Although I'll take that from you now. The cops will find your body among those of the Grayson family and their employees in the morning."

"Pretty cold-blooded, Sprax. What can I do to reassure you I am who I say?"

"Not a thing, darling. And if we weren't going on a raid, the boys and I would spend some quality time with you before we put you away. Quality for us, that is. Not you. But since we have the opportunity to leave your body at the scene of the crime, so to speak, that'll serve as a warning for your buddies."

Delgado turned to Chief Warrant Officer Nunes, who sat at a workstation in the rear of the CIC.

"Grayson, Warrant. Find out who that is and where they live. Judging by the direction of the convoy, it's deep in the countryside, so a ranch or a farm."

"Yes, sir."

"I have no buddies to warn," Steiger said. "Come on, Sprax. Don't do this. I'm as loyal as the other four of your guards in this vehicle."

Delgado smiled. "She's telling us there are five deps with her."

"Sir," Nunes raised his hand. "The Grayson Ranch. It's a large spread. Thirty family members, seventy employees, and ten thousand square kilometers — not every part of it is arable or pasture. Look to the portside secondary display."

There, a map of the area shimmered to life, showing the Grayson Ranch, Tianjin, and the road between them, the same road taken by Sprax's convoy.

"Signals, get me Keres Niner and Erinye Niner. Make sure Moirae Niner can listen in."

"Aye, aye, sir." The petty officer opened a link with the lead shuttle, then said, "You're on."

"QD, Rolf, it's Delgado."

"Tell me you have good news, Skipper," Captain Vinn replied.

"The target is the Grayson Ranch. QD, get there as fast as possible. You have about an hour and a half to secure the place. Rolf is coming up behind the deps, so be the anvil to his hammer. Make sure the inhabitants are secure and out of the line of fire. You can keep the shuttles as gunships. Just park them out of sight until the main action starts. Rolf, block their vehicles with yours and take them from behind. The how of the operation is up to both of you. Just make sure everyone has their friend-or-foe blipper working so we don't get any blue-on-blue shots."

"Acknowledged," Both Vinn and Painter said.

"Now there's a wrinkle. Miko is in the lead van under guard by the deps. They suspect she's not one of them after all and plan on killing her during the attack to make it look like the Graysons got her. That obviously means you can't simply ambush the convoy before the deps have a chance to disembark, which would have been the ideal solution. Now I know she won't give up easily, so keep an eye out and get her away from the deps. That is your primary task ahead of trying to save the ranch's infrastructure from destruction or eliminating the bastards. But once you've secured her, you're free to terminate everyone else."

"Got it, Skipper. We'll do our damnest to extricate Miko," Vinn replied, echoed by Painter. "Anything else?"

"No. Delgado, out."

Ghost Squadron's commanding officer sat back and silently exhaled. QD Vinn and Rolf Painter were among the most experienced Special Forces officers in human space. Both were mustangs like him, command sergeants commissioned as captains after many years as special ops troop leaders, and what they didn't know about the business wasn't worth knowing. They'd adapt to the ground, the circumstances, and the unfolding events and win because they dared to do the unconventional, the risky, and that which allowed them to win. *Audeamus*, the motto of the Federation Marine Corps' Special Forces Regiments, meant just that — Let Us Dare.

His eyes went as if by instinct, to the CIC's primary display, now showing real-time images of the dep convoy, Erinye Company following one tactical bound behind them, and Keres Company's shuttles preparing to land near the Grayson Ranch. The only ones who didn't know what was going on were the deps and the Graysons. And the latter would find out within the next ten minutes that they were the insurgency's next intended victims.

"It's Bailo who put you up to this, right?" Miko Steiger's voice came over the CIC speakers again.

"What if she did?"

"Where are Bailo and her stooge anyway? Are they hiding somewhere?"

A rumble of male laughter.

"They're back at the pub, sleeping. Bailo and a few of her people used to come out with us but stopped once she saw we could handle ourselves. I figure she doesn't have the stomach to witness how we deal with colonists."

Delgado grinned. Steiger had just given him another target, and deliberately at that. He called Moirae Company's officer commanding, Lucius Farnes, who was sitting on the hangar deck with his troopers, armed and armored, ready to go.

"Luke, I need you to head for Tianjin and secure the pub serving as dep HQ. Don't worry about stealth. Just land half your company in the Old Quarter square, seize the building and arrest everyone inside. So that we don't trip over Keres and Erinye's part of the operation, loiter east of the town until they've engaged the enemy."

"What am I looking for?"

"A Siana Bailo, mercenary, and five of her acolytes. They should have the same clean appearance as the ones we have in the brig, so they won't be hard to identify. Try to take them alive, but if anyone resists, you're weapons-free."

"Roger, Skipper."

"Off you go, then."

Delgado sat back in his chair, exchanged an ironic glance with Chief Warrant Officer Nunes, and turned his attention back to the CIC's primary display, which showed his two companies and the dep convoy converging on the Grayson Ranch. Moirae Company's shuttles launched a few minutes later and spiraled toward Tianjin. And with that, he'd deployed his entire squadron.

— Twenty —

"Armed guards," the shuttle pilot said, nodding toward the side display.

Captain QD Vinn studied the two pairs slowly walking the perimeter of Grayson Ranch's main compound. The four shuttles carrying Keres Company were hovering five hundred meters above the ground, one kilometer north of the ranch. They couldn't see the dep convoy coming from the south, but Miko Steiger's beacon still registered, showing they were about an hour away.

"The trick will be to not get shot," the short, intense, dark-haired Vinn said.

"A direct approach will probably work. They're unlikely to carry anything that could hurt Old Bessie here," the pilot, one of *Iolanthe*'s petty officers, tapped the console in front of him. "We land her in the middle of the compound, flash our hidden Navy markings, and drop the aft ramp. You tell them we're friendlies come to help with the upcoming attack. Nothing to it."

"And what if they decide to take a potshot at me while I'm standing at the top of the ramp?"

The pilot grinned at Vinn.

"That's why you're paid the big creds, Captain."

Vinn clapped the man on the shoulder.

"I am indeed. Let's tell the other shuttles to stay aloft while we settle. Land us so our aft faces the big house."

He returned to the passenger compartment where the twenty-five special ops Marines of E Troop sat silently in their dark armor with helmet visors down, looking like malevolent, giant insects. Their heads turned toward him expectantly.

"We're about to land in the Grayson compound. Stay where you are while I tell the guards we're your friendly neighborhood Fleet operatives and not deps with delusions of grandeur." Vinn felt the shuttle descend and grabbed onto a strap dangling from the deckhead. "I don't expect any issues beyond them being surprised to hell and back."

The troop leader, sitting closest to the ramp, nodded once.

"Better you than me, sir."

Then, the pitch of the thrusters changed, and a few seconds later, the shuttle landed with a soft thump. The aft ramp dropped, revealing a well-lit set of two- and three-story buildings surrounding the center of the broad, open space, and Vinn walked over to the upper edge of the ramp.

"Hello, Grayson Ranch. I'm Captain QD Vinn of the Federation Marine Corps." Vinn's voice, augmented by his helmet, boomed across the compound. "In about an hour, approximately a hundred deportees aiming to kill everyone here will visit you. I'm looking to stop that from happening."

A male voice replied from behind a stack of crates, "Come out of that shuttle and let us look at you."

Vinn, hands held at chest height, armored palms facing outward, stepped onto the ramp and slowly raised his helmet visor, showing his face in the glare of the outdoor lights.

Another voice, deeper and sounding older, called out from the shadows of the sprawling family residence, "I'm coming out, Jonah. If he makes a wrong move, shoot him."

"Yes, Mister Grayson."

A tall, thin man with gray hair parted in the middle, and a drooping mustache emerged from the house and walked toward the shuttle, eyes taking in the Navy markings that had appeared on the normally blank identifier plates.

"Captain Vinn, I'm Redvers Grayson, the president and CEO of Grayson Enterprises. You said a hundred of the damned deps are on their way here?"

"Yes, sir. They're coming in a ten-vehicle road convoy, and they're about an hour away."

"How the hell do you know that? In fact, where did you even come from?"

"President Verrill requested assistance from the Fleet, and they dispatched my unit. We arrived a few days ago aboard a Navy transport and luckily caught the deps setting out from Tianjin toward your spread a while ago."

"Then why are you here and not ambushing the scum twenty kilometers away."

Vinn grimaced.

"They're holding one of ours in the lead vehicle, and we want to extract her before taking on the deps. And that means letting them approach this place and disembark under the belief no one's waiting."

"I see." Grayson rubbed his craggy chin with a long-fingered hand. "And what's your plan?"

"I've brought an entire company with me aboard four shuttles — this one and three others. I propose to bring the other three in, unload my troopers, and load you and your people. The shuttles will land in a clearing a few kilometers west of here and wait until everything is over. In the meantime, I will set up a defensive position that'll stop the bastards cold. Another company from my unit is following the deps in ground vehicles and will take them in a pincer. Ten, maybe fifteen minutes after they arrive, it'll be over. The deps will be prisoners or dead, and my shuttles will fly you back here."

"Well, I'm not sure I'm comfortable leaving my home with my people. I mean, I've only got your word that you're a Marine officer who's come to save us from rampaging deps."

Vinn thought for a few seconds.

"Okay. How about you and some of your people who are armed and know how to use their weapons stay? We'll evacuate the non-combatants. But those who stay will be subject to my orders and will take support positions. You won't be directly involved in the fighting. Deal?"

Grayson's eyes narrowed as he contemplated Vinn. Then he nodded.

"Deal."

"Okay, let me get the rest of my company while you gather the evacuees. We don't have all night."

Half an hour later, with the dep convoy less than thirty minutes away, the shuttles lifted off and headed for the clearing. At the same time, Redvers Grayson and twenty of his men took up firing positions inside the main residence, along with a corporal from E Troop to serve as control and radio link. QD Vinn spread out his company facing the main avenue of approach with sight lines to where he expected the deps would disembark. Within fifteen minutes, the Grayson Ranch fell deathly quiet. Anyone approaching would see nothing more than a target ripe for plucking.

Vinn, his first sergeant, and their wingers had taken up observation positions in a third-floor employee apartment from where they could see a broad swath of terrain, including the principal approaches. Then, they settled in to wait while watching the video of the road transmitted by a pair of nearly invisible drones hovering over it a kilometer away — an aerial tripwire, so to speak. The deps would probably make their final approach on foot, leaving the vehicles to turn around and be ready for departure.

The outside lights were still on, but Vinn had arranged for Grayson to switch them off on order, plunging the entire compound into darkness. Yet the Marines would still see their surroundings and the enemy bright as day thanks to the night vision function of their helmet visors, while the deps would be virtually blind.

***

They had driven on in silence once Sprax had relieved Steiger of her knife, and she hoped someone had heard her conversation with Sprax over the communicator in her jacket pocket. Otherwise, her situation would be dire the moment they arrived at the Grayson Ranch.

Soon, they saw the faint glow of the main compound's lights above the trees, and Steiger felt her heartbeat speed up. She'd have only one chance to escape Sprax and his men.

The faint glow grew, and Steiger figured they'd stop soon and make their final approach on foot, using the trees as cover. But Sprax didn't say a word. He just sat squarely, face impassive, eyes looking ahead as if focused on the upcoming attack and nothing else.

Then, the convoy slowed and Sprax nudged one of his men. "Muzzle, cuff, and leash her."

The enforcer, none too gently, manacled her wrists and put a collar around her neck, then slapped a piece of tape over her mouth.

They finally came to a halt and at Sprax's signal, they rolled down their balaclavas and disembarked silently, forming up by platoons.

Steiger was yanked out of the van and lost her footing, which earned her a kick in the ribs and another across the face as the man pulled her back up by the chain attached to the collar. Still, Steiger didn't so much as utter a grunt, which earned her a tiny bit of grudging respect.

Once the platoons reported ready, the column advanced toward the compound, hidden by the trees.

One tactical bound behind the deps, unseen and unheard, Erinye Company had also halted, climbed out of its vehicles and followed silently. And overhead, the drones put up by Keres Company watched them approach.

Vinn had spotted Steiger right away via the drones' video feed — she was the only one whose face remained visible, and he noted the degrading way in which she was dragged along. Extracting her from the mass of deps before they could kill her would be tricky.

He called his company snipers and briefly gave them the order to target the deps around Steiger on his signal, then advised the rest of the company of her situation and appearance. Hopefully she would see the men around her shot as a sign to drop to the ground while the rest of the company opened fire.

The deps soon spread out just inside the treeline and dropped to one knee, alert and carbines at the ready. For what reason, Vinn couldn't tell. Then, his helmet visor lit up with the signal that half a dozen tiny drones had been detected, coming from where the deps knelt and headed toward the compound.

His troopers were all hidden inside the various buildings and couldn't be detected visually. If those drones carried sensors, all they would pick up were life signs, but those would be expected by the attackers. Vinn briefly debated shooting them down, but then figured he'd better leave them be so the deps would come out from the trees and into the open when the drones had accomplished their mission.

And that happened moments later when they homed in on the compounds lights and zapped them with electromagnetic charges. Full darkness fell as the lights died, and Vinn saw the shadows of the deps rise to their feet and leave the treeline, headed for the buildings around the central square.

He also spotted the friend-or-foe transmitters of Erinye Company approximately fifty meters behind the deps, spread out in a wide arc — the hammer to Keres Company's anvil — and still undetected by the attackers.

When Vinn figured the deps were all out in the open, advancing cautiously, well spread out, looking for all the world like light infantry on a night raid, he homed in on Steiger.

"Snipers. Now!"

Twelve plasma rounds leap out into the night air and struck the dozen deps closest to Steiger. They collapsed almost in unison, leaving her to stand alone. Then, a fraction of a second later, she dropped to the ground, as Vinn had hoped.

"Keres, FIRE."

The darkness vanished as a hundred guns opened up, each round finding a target. A few of the deps, those with faster reflexes than most, also dropped and shot back, but with the Keres Company's troopers hidden behind windows and doors, the return fire was ineffective.

Erinye Company's carbines joined in, lighting up the treeline as they aimed at the last few deps still standing and those firing back, and then darkness reestablished itself. A darkness replete with moans of pain and the odd muffled scream. But of the hundred or so deps that had advanced on the Grayson compound, none remained effective.

Vinn emerged from the employee apartment block and stopped, looking at the grisly scene as Rolf Painter left the trees and headed for him. He was recognizable by his particular friend-or-foe transmitter which identified him as the officer commanding.

"That was short and sweet," Painter said once he was within earshot. "You got Miko out safely?"

"I hope so." As Vinn spoke, one of his troopers helped Steiger climbed to her feet and removed her shackles, muzzle and leash. He smiled behind his lowered visor. "I guess we did."

They watched Steiger approaching a large body lying on the ground near her.

"Hey, Arnis," she said, looking into the terrified eyes of a mortally wounded Sprax. "Seems like you've reached the end of the line."

"W-who are you?" His words came out in a hoarse whisper.

A cruel smile spread across Steiger's face.

"Let me introduce myself — I'm Chief Warrant Officer Miko Steiger, Federation Marine Corps, and the people who whacked you belong to Ghost Squadron of the Marine Corps' 1st Special Forces Regiment."

She leaned over and picked up Sprax's gun.

"Say your prayers, you depraved piece of filth. Where you're going, you'll need every bit of spiritual help you can get."

Steiger placed the tip of the carbine's barrel on Sprax's forehead and pulled the trigger.

— Twenty-One —

Leaving Sprax's body with a neat, charred hole in the forehead, Steiger walked over to where Vinn and Painter stood, watching her while Vinn made a brief report to Delgado via the secure surface-to-orbit radio network.

"Who was that you shot, Miko?" Painter asked.

"The leader of the Tianjin deps, a vile animal by the name Arnis Sprax. I'd promised myself I would take care of him personally. Are you going to put the rest of them out of their misery? Seeing as how none of them qualify as human beings, anyway."

Vinn and Painter glanced at each other, and the former nodded.

"I'll take care of it. I doubt any of them will last long enough to see the inside of a hospital. Ah, Mister Grayson."

The rancher was picking his way through the scattered bodies to where they stood, a stoic expression on his face.

"Nicely done, Captain Vinn. I suppose we owe you our lives."

"Just doing our duty, sir. Now, if you'll excuse me, I need to take care of those deps still drawing breath."

"You mean to kill them?"

"Yes, sir. Unless they get medical care quickly, which isn't going to happen, none of them will survive, so it'll be a kindness to put them out of their misery. Besides, considering what they've done to other innocent civilians, I figure they don't qualify for more humane treatment." With that, Vinn wandered off, unholstering his blaster. He made quick work of the dozen still twitching while the Keres and Erinye troopers secured the perimeter.

"What are you going to do with the bodies?" Grayson asked. "Can't leave 'em here."

Painter grimaced.

"The way I see it, we have two options. We can load them back aboard their vehicles, then drive those back to Tianjin and abandon them in the Old Quarter. Or we can use your farm machinery to dig a mass grave somewhere far from here and drop them in it."

Grayson shook his head.

"I don't want the bodies of a hundred black-hearted men and women blighting my land."

"Understood."

"What is?" Vinn asked, rejoining them. When Painter explained, Vinn nodded. "I can understand not wanting to risk the ghosts of evil spirits haunting the place. We'll load them aboard their vehicles. Can you provide drivers, Rolf?"

"Sure thing. Where do you think we should abandon them?"

"How about in front of the pub that serves as their HQ?" Steiger suggested. "It'll scare the living daylights out of the rest who'll lie low and thereby give the police a chance to regain control of Tianjin's Old Quarter."

"Good idea."

Ten minutes later, the Marines of both companies had stacked the bodies in the deps' vans, and the Erinyes climbed into theirs while Vinn called the shuttles back. By the time they arrived, the ground vehicles had vanished down the tree-lined road to Tianjin, and the only indications that remained of the brief, savage fight were bloodstains on the hard-packed earth and small charred holes in the walls of the buildings around the compound's center.

Another fifteen minutes saw Keres Company, along with Miko Steiger and the deps' weapons, lifting off, headed back to *Iolanthe*, their departure watched by a subdued crowd of Grayson family members and the ranch's employees.

"It was the damnest thing," Redvers Grayson said as the shuttles vanished into the low cloud cover. "One moment, the lights went out all by themselves. Then, fireworks started, and only a minute later, a hundred of the dep scum lay dead. Got to wonder who those Marines are. They're not the ordinary sort. Of that, I'm sure."

"Special Forces. Got to be," Lars Grayson, Redvers' son, who'd stayed behind with his father, said. "They weren't wearing normal armor, nor did any of them have rank badges or other insignia. But they sure as hell are deadly."

***

Once QD Vinn informed Delgado about the secure Grayson Ranch and the defeated enemy, Moirae Company descended from its circling position west of Tianjin. It made its way toward the plaza in front of the Old Quarter pub, which served as the late Arnis Sprax's headquarters.

Two of the shuttles landed and disgorged armored Marines while the other two circled overhead, ready to engage threats.

Their arrival in the middle of the night was so sudden that J Troop's lead operators broke through the front door unopposed. They dispersed throughout the ground floor while K Troop ran through the building to secure the back garden and keep anyone from escaping that way. With both troops having secured the points of egress, a section of J Troop quickly made their way up the stairs and began smashing down the doors leading to individual rooms. They seized those inside without regard to who they were or how much they protested, manacled them, and sent them out onto the plaza.

In the end, they had fifteen men and women lined up under the streetlights, guarded by Marines, and Captain Farnes walked along the row, examining each of their prisoners. All looked like deps — slovenly, sneering, and covered in tats.

"Where are Siana Bailo and her winger?" He asked.

"Who?" One of the deps replied, sniggering. He and most of the others were clearly under the influence of narcotics because they exhibited dull facial expressions and unfocused eyes.

Farnes walked over to the man and put his helmet visor against the man's nose.

"The mercenaries who help Sprax."

"Dunno." Another dep giggled. "One moment they were here, the next — poof, they were gone."

Curious faces appeared in the windows of surrounding buildings, but no one dared step outside. Not with fifty armed and armored troopers surrounding the plaza at oh-two-hundred hours, when honest folk are fast asleep in their beds.

Farnes stepped back.

"Can someone provide details on their whereabouts and departure time? Answer me that, and you'll be free to go."

A short, round female dep raised a tentative hand.

"I think they said they were heading to Iskellian, and I figure they left not long after Sprax."

"That wasn't so hard, now was it? How were they intending to travel?"

"Buggers had their own ground car, didn't they?" Another male dep said in a slurred voice. "An old, white Genova Tarlet. And it ain't here no more."

Farnes turned away from the bedraggled row of slack-jawed deps and flicked his radio to the orbital network.

"Niner, this is three-niner."

Within seconds, Delgado replied. "Niner."

"Apparently, Bailo flew the coop shortly after Sprax left. One of the pub's inhabitants said she thought they were bound for Iskellian, and another figured they took their ground car, a white Genova Tarlet."

"Acknowledged. You might as well come home. Leave the people be. They'll wake up to a brand-new horror once Rolf gets back to Tianjin."

Delgado described the plan for the attackers' bodies, and Farnes chuckled.

"That'll put the fear of the Almighty into the rest of them. Okay. Coming home."

"Niner, out."

Farnes switched to the company push.

"Climb aboard the shuttles, people. We're done here."

He glanced at the deps.

"Thank you for your cooperation. You're free to go."

***

Delgado turned to Chief Warrant Officer Nunes. "Go through the satellite recordings of Tianjin and look for a large white ground car near the dep HQ from about an hour before Miko's beacon came on. Once you've found it, trace its travel route."

"Already on it, sir." Nunes grinned at Delgado. He'd started the trace the moment Farnes reported. A few moments later, an overhead video began playing on the portside CIC display, showing two figures climbing aboard a car parked in front of the Old Quarter pub. "There we go."

Nunes sped up the video, and they watched as the car wound its way to the Iskellian Road and headed off in the capital's direction. The display turned blank as Nunes fast-forwarded the recording. After a few minutes, the video reappeared and showed the same car nearing the outskirts of Iskellian.

"That's now real-time, sir."

"And you're sure it's still them?"

Nunes gave Delgado a smug look.

"There's precious little traffic on the Iskellian-Tianjin Road at this time of night, unlike during the day when we can lose nondescript vans among the masses of other vehicles of the same sort. Besides, the satellite picked up no other white Genova Tarlet sedan."

Delgado raised both hands in surrender.

"Just checking."

They kept watching the car until it reached a building in one of the small industrial parks and disappeared inside a garage.

"Another safe house, I presume," Delgado said.

"Probably."

"Let's keep a close watch on it while I decide how we'll tackle this. It isn't the sort of thing I can simply throw a company at. That place is in the middle of a peaceful city."

***

The eastern horizon showed a pale pink band when Erinye Company lined up Sprax's ten vehicles in the plaza, and the drivers climbed out. As pre-arranged while they were on the road, four shuttles landed one beside the other a few moments later, and the one hundred troopers mounted up, abandoning their own vans to whoever wanted them.

Faces appeared in windows, including those of the pub, and once the small spacecraft had vanished into the still dark sky, a few of the less timid deps cautiously stepped out and ventured up to the vans. They found the four larger ones empty, but when a female dep opened the doors to one of Sprax's, she screamed.

— Twenty-Two —

"It looks like you departing Tianjin the moment Sprax left on his raid was prescient, Siana." Skyron Enneb looked up from his communicator as Bailo shuffled into the safe house's kitchen and headed for the coffeemaker.

"Why?"

"The newsnets are reporting mysterious overnight doings in Tianjin. Apparently, unidentified people wearing black armor with no markings parked a whole bunch of transport vehicles in the Old Quarter's central plaza. Bodies with distinct power weapon wounds filled ten of them. One hundred individuals in total, including the suspected deportee leader, Arnis Sprax."

If Bailo hadn't been awake before, she was now. She whirled around and leaned against the counter, her coffee forgotten, face white as a sheet of arctic ice.

"Say that again, Sky."

Enneb repeated the lines from the newsnets and watched her face crumble.

"They're all dead. The entire Tianjin assault force. Anything about the Grayson Ranch?"

He shook his head.

"Nothing. But it's pretty clear someone with plenty of firepower wiped Sprax and his people out."

"How is that possible? No one but Sprax knew about the target ahead of time. As usual, his people shouldn't have been told until they were there." Then her eyes widened. "Evana Kor. She has to be Fleet and must have betrayed Sprax by calling in the cavalry. But how?"

"Who?"

Bailo told her second in command about the woman who'd become one of Sprax's enforcers by playing on his desires.

"You mean Sprax got the hots for this Kor?"

"She's tall, muscular, and easy on the eyes — if you're a dep. Exactly the sort who'd appeal to a hooligan like Sprax." Bailo let out a sigh. "We might as well wrap things up around here. Tianjin was our best hope of destroying law and order in a major city. But with Sprax and his company gone in such a brutal fashion, the rest of the deps in Tianjin will lie low. The situation might even scare some into behaving like honest citizens. Tianjin is a lost cause now, and ramping up in Oshin and Holback will take longer than we have if there's a Fleet Special Forces unit on the ground."

"So, we just pack up and go home? Upari won't be happy about that. He was furious when I told him about the entire M-147 shipment and the training team vanishing."

"Then I'll make it clear to Upari that it's over. We've completely lost the gains we made over the last few months. The police will retake control of central Tianjin in a heartbeat, and I have no doubt they'll not be tender with the deps this time around. And once the Garonne government cuts off all the benefits that have kept them idle and free to scheme, they'll either work and have no more time nor energy for mischief or starve. We can't fight the Federation Fleet, and at this point, I'm convinced there's a Navy ship in orbit and a Special Forces squadron, if not on the ground, then aboard the ship, ready to pounce again at the drop of a hat."

"You go explain that to him, Siana. I'll be hiding in the cellar. In the meantime, pour yourself a coffee and grab some breakfast. Upari can wait. Maybe once he hears the report from the newsnets, he'll understand the situation before you even explain it to him."

***

Chief Superintendent Kyra Bain listened to Delgado's proposal, and when he fell silent, she nodded thoughtfully.

"You're entirely correct. It would probably be better if the arrest were a police action rather than a military one."

"So long as we can interrogate Bailo and her minions, I'm happy."

"And once you've done so, what do you propose we do with them? I suppose the Garonne government can charge the lot with subversion, being accessories to mass murder and abetting an insurrection, among other grave offenses."

"It could. Or you can hand them over to us. We'll try them under the code of service discipline, seeing as they're a hostile military force — albeit private — operating on Federation territory. If found guilty, the court will send them to a penal colony on Parth, possibly for the rest of their lives."

Bain cocked an eyebrow at Delgado.

"I'm pretty sure President Verrill wouldn't mind giving you jurisdiction. He has enough on his plate right now. So long as he can declare the emergency over and give the public a full accounting of what happened, he'll be content."

"Okay. We'll play it that way. Did you want any of my people to accompany you?"

"As observers, sure. Perhaps a dozen to give my team an impression of greater heft."

"A section of troopers, along with my Constabulary liaison and intelligence officer, then."

Miko Steiger, now wearing the same sort of uniform as the rest of Ghost Squadron, with the tattoos and piercings gone and her now-blond hair in a conservative, albeit short style, entered the CIC at that moment and joined Delgado at his workstation. Her face still bore the bruising from the kicks she'd received but the cuts had been seen to by *Iolanthe*'s sickbay.

"I understand you've run the mercenary bastards down."

"We have. Chief Superintendent Bain, meet Chief Warrant Officer Miko Steiger of Naval Intelligence. It's thanks to her the Graysons are alive, and Sprax and his scum are dead."

Bain nodded politely.

"A pleasure, Chief Warrant Officer. I can't imagine what you must have gone through."

"Likewise, and you really don't want to imagine what I've seen."

Delgado glanced up at Steiger.

"I've just been discussing the arrest of Bailo and her mercs with the chief superintendent and will send a section from D Troop as well as Aleksa and Jake to back up the Constabulary team that'll take them in."

"I want in on it, Curtis. If only to see Bailo's face when I appear as if by magic, looking nice and clean."

"You good with that, Chief Superintendent?"

"Sure. Chief Warrant Officer Steiger deserves a bit of satisfaction after what she did."

"Right then. I'll have them at the spaceport in one hour. That should give you enough time to organize the arrest team."

"In that case, I'd better get going. Thanks for letting us have this one and for the intel on the site."

Delgado waved her words away.

"De nada. We're on the same team, and I figured we'd better do this one in accordance with the legal niceties. You won't need a warrant?"

"No. This comes under operational exigency since you provided us with the data necessary to effect an entry and arrest."

"In that case, talk to you later."

"Bain, out."

Her image faded from the workstation display, and Delgado climbed to his feet.

"I hope you'll behave down there, Miko. Siana Bailo and her people are to be afforded all the rights of a military prisoner."

"No worries. I meant it when I said I only wanted to see Bailo's reaction when she realizes her worst fears were true. Besides, my ribs are still a tad tender from the shit kicking I received, so I won't be getting frisky."

***

A boxy, gray armored personnel carrier with eight oversized wheels and Constabulary markings was waiting at the end of the Iskellian spaceport runway when the shuttle carrying Staff Sergeant Osmin Sberna's section along with Nunes, Kine, and Steiger landed. All carried plasma carbines and wore black armor but with the helmet visors raised so their faces were visible.

A Constabulary corporal climbed out of the APC as the shuttle's aft ramp dropped, and the Marines filed out. He studied them, looking for rank insignia or unit badges, but found nothing.

"You must be the folks my chief super told me to pick up," he finally said.

Sberna nodded, smiling.

"We are, and we're Federation Marines. I'm Staff Sergeant Sberna, in charge of this little group."

"Well, climb aboard. My orders are to take you to the incident van the chief super is setting up for this operation."

As soon as the side door slammed shut, the corporal put his heavy vehicle in gear and sped off the tarmac, along the spaceport ring road, and through the security gate without slowing. In a surprisingly short time, the APC came to a stop, and the door opened again, revealing a large cube van, also gray and with Constabulary markings, sitting in the yard of a small industrial park behind a tall wall. Several platoons of armed and armored constables stood in three rows, waiting patiently.

Sberna climbed out and looked around for the highest-ranking officer. He spotted Chief Superintendent Bain and, with Steiger, Nunes, and Kine at his heels, walked over to where she was talking with an inspector wearing police armor and carrying a holstered needler.

When Bain acknowledged them, they stopped, came to attention, and saluted.

"Staff Sergeant Sberna, Chief Warrant Officers Steiger, Nunes, and Kine, and seven troopers reporting."

Bain returned the salute and smiled. "Glad to have you with us. I'm just about to go through the latest on the target with Inspector Zendu, who'll be the arresting officer. Please go ahead, Keith."

"Yes, sir." The inspector was an imposing man with a dark complexion and a deep voice. "Sensors identified twenty-two separate human life forms in the target building, a disused small business with large rooms on the ground floor and offices on the second floor. It shouldn't contain any people at all, let alone that many. Ten of those life forms are prone in upstairs rooms, indicating that they're sleeping. The municipal records show the building doesn't have a basement, which means the only escape routes are via the front and back doors, the garage, and the windows. It'll be a straightforward entry via both doors simultaneously. We'll break them down, toss in a pair of screamers, and arrest everyone while they're dealing with them."

"What if there's any resistance?" Steiger asked.

Zendu grinned at her, revealing straight white teeth.

"Not after the screamers. They have a habit of giving everyone within a dozen meters a bad case of involuntary spasms, which is why I recommend you shut your visors when we go in."

"So noted."

"I understand you're Fleet observers. Please stay well behind my people until we secure the premises."

"Of course, sir."

Zendu stiffened as he faced Bain.

"With your permission, I will carry out the operation, sir."

"Go, Inspector."

Zendu turned on his heels and pointed at the platoon to his left. "You go with them, Sergeant. Do not enter the building until I call the all clear."

"Yes, sir."

— Twenty-Three —

The Marines jogged behind the twenty-strong Constabulary platoon tasked with entering via the front door as it left the industrial park and headed along a side road to where the building used by the mercs as a safe house stood. They stopped just around the corner from it and waited for the other platoon to get into position.

A few minutes later, the master sergeant in charge of the platoon made a hand signal, and two of his constables rushed forward, one of them carrying a breaching device and the other a screamer. The rest of the platoon followed.

The bored mercenary sitting in front of video displays showing the front and rear pathways leading to the doors suddenly caught movement. But before he could alert anyone, the first constable attached the breaching devices to the door panels and blew them inward. Immediately after that, the second constable threw in a screamer that emitted a piercing, high-pitched sound, causing a reaction similar to an epileptic fit in anyone nearby.

While the screamers howled, the constables entered, needlers in hand, and cleared each room, cuffing the mercenaries spasming on the floor. Once those on the upper floor had been manacled, the screamers died away, and the mercs regained control of their bodies.

Sberna, the three chief warrant officers, and his troopers entered the building and found themselves in a small lobby with open doors on either side and stairs heading up at the back. The place gave no indication of its past purpose, but it looked well-maintained and showed minimal signs of use.

Steiger quickly went from room to room while the other Marines spread out until she found who she was looking for, lying prone with her hands tied behind her back. She knelt and turned Bailo around so the latter could see her, then removed her helmet and stood again.

"Hello, Siana. Remember me?"

"W-what happened." Bailo was clearly still shaking off the screamers' effects, and Steiger smiled.

"The Constabulary subjected you to a crowd control device that emits sounds at a frequency causing spasms in human beings."

Bailo frowned as she studied Steiger.

"Do I know you?"

"Sure, you do, Siana. I used to go under the name Evana Kor when I infiltrated the late Arnis Sprax's gang of vile psychopaths."

Bailo's eyes widened.

"I knew it. I was sure you were up to no good. Was it you who alerted the cavalry?"

Steiger bowed her head.

"Guilty as charged. I'm also the one who killed Sprax with his own weapon. You could say my mission was a complete success."

"Who the hell are you?"

"My name isn't important, but I'm a Federation Marine Corps chief warrant officer with more undercover experience than most of my sort. You have to admit I was pretty convincing, seeing as how I had Sprax take me on and trust me, at least until you showed up."

Chief Warrant Officer Nunes entered the room and asked, "Who do we have here?"

"Siana Bailo, the mercs' leader."

"Ah, Major Bailo. Glad we caught up with you."

Steiger gave Nunes a curious glance.

"Major?"

"We suspect she's still serving in the Celestan National Guard. Our database of Commonwealth military personnel shows her as a member of the Guard's Special Forces branch. Admittedly, it's two years old, but Special Forces officers don't suddenly decide to go mercenary if they still have a few years left in uniform, and she's still plenty young. What do you say, Major?"

Bailo gave him a baleful stare but didn't reply. Instead, she asked, "How did you find this place?"

Nunes grinned at her as he pointed upward.

"Our eyes in the sky tracked your car from Tianjin to here. It was actually quite easy once some helpful deps told us what vehicle you were riding and when you left Tianjin."

"Damn deps. Useless, the whole lot." Bailo spat out the words.

"And yet you used them as your shock troops to — do what, exactly?"

"You figure it out."

"Oh, we will. Have no fear."

A pair of constables appeared, and one of them said, "If you'll excuse us, we need to assemble the prisoners for transportation and processing."

Steiger and Nunes stepped aside, and the latter gestured at Bailo.

"Be our guest. We'll have plenty of time to chat with Major Bailo once she's safely in a cell."

In the lobby, twenty-two mercenaries waited silently, hands tied behind their backs, as Chief Superintendent Bain entered the building. She stopped in front of the cluster of mercs and examined them. They, in turn, studied her with emotionless eyes.

"You are under arrest for subversion, being accessories to mass murder, abetting an insurrection, and operating a private military corporation without Adjudicating Authority oversight. More charges are likely in the coming days as we unravel your activities because I understand we've seized several computers, and forensic analysis will provide us with more evidence." She paused for a few moments.

"Now, I have no doubt you're Commonwealth citizens, seeing as your leader is a Celestan. Therefore, a military court will try you instead of civilian authorities because, according to Federation law, foreign mercenaries operating against a Federation government are considered hostile military personnel. This means that each of the charges I've listed is sufficient for a lengthy stay on Parth. If you are found guilty of all of them, there is a distinct possibility of receiving the death penalty. As a result, you'll be handed over to the Federation Armed Forces for interrogation, formal charges, and the inevitable trial. Of course, full cooperation will help mitigate your sentences." Bain let that sink in before continuing.

"With that, we've made a change in plans. We will now take you to the spaceport, where you will board a shuttle and be transferred to a Navy ship in orbit instead of our own cells. Sergeant Sberna?"

He snapped to attention.

"Chief Superintendent."

"Your colonel figured it would be better if we hand the prisoners over to you as soon as possible. A bus is waiting outside. If you think your troopers will suffice to guard the prisoners, then we'll leave you to it."

"No problems," Sberna replied. "Any of those buggers gives us grief, we'll just shoot 'em."

Bain fought to restrain a smile at Sberna's casual drawl and said, "Try keeping them alive, at least until they've told you everything they know."

"No promises."

Sberna turned to his troopers and issued brief orders while Steiger and Kine headed outside to ensure the bus wouldn't pose a problem. A few minutes later, Sberna's Marines shepherded the silent mercenaries aboard, and the bus left for the spaceport. All the while, Bailo never stopped glaring at Steiger as if blaming her for the reversal of fortunes she'd suffered, which wasn't far from the truth.

As Sberna had expected, their easy capture totally demoralized the mercenaries, and they were in no mood to balk at his orders. Of course, having eleven armored and armed guards helped keep them quiet.

***

"Any problems?" Delgado asked when Sberna walked up to him on *Iolanthe*'s hangar deck and saluted.

"None whatsoever, sir."

"Good. I had hoped the change in plans to have you bring them up directly wouldn't be an issue."

"They're just a bunch of sad sacks who know they've been beaten by pros." Sberna turned to watch the mercs shuffle off the shuttle and into the arms of a half dozen armed bosun's mates. "But their boss, this Siana Bailo, she's been looking like she wants to kill us ever since she shrugged off the screamer's effects."

"No doubt, seeing as how she's probably still Celeste National Guard and has been caught operating on a planet belonging to another star nation." Delgado jerked his chin at one of the female mercs giving him a baleful stare as she walked by. "Would that be her?"

"Yep."

Steiger, Nunes, and Kine joined them, and Kine asked, "Did the crew organize enough secure compartments for all of them, sir?"

"Yeah. They had to strip vacant cabins and install surveillance sensors, though. But at four per with the doors locked from the outside, they'll live in reasonable comfort until we get rid of them."

"When do you want us to begin interrogations?"

"As soon as possible. We need to find out if there are more of them on Garonne, whether they've armed other dep groups, and, most importantly, who sent them here and why."

Nunes and Kine glanced at each other and the latter said, "We start with Bailo?"

"Sure. If Miko can get the names, ranks, and serial numbers of the rest, that would be helpful."

Steiger nodded.

"Will do. And as soon as they get locked away before they have a chance to think about their predicament. I'll need two escorts, though. Just in case."

"I'll see that Rolf assigns a pair," Delgado said.

— Twenty-Four —

Kine and Nunes observed Siana Bailo sitting in the interrogation room via video feed for a while, noting her demeanor, nervousness, or rather lack thereof, and the rage still burning in her eyes. Her hands were tied in the back, which made for awkward seating on the metal chair facing the bare table.

"Seems like a real sweetheart," Nunes remarked. "Do we free her or leave her like this?"

"Let's leave the restraints on for a while. It'll put her at a psychological disadvantage."

"Shall we?"

They entered the room and took seats opposite Bailo.

"I'm Chief Warrant Officer Aleksa Kine, and my colleague is Chief Warrant Officer Jake Nunes. We'd like to ask you a few questions. As Chief Superintendent Bain said earlier, cooperation will go far in mitigating any sentence you'll get from the military tribunal you'll face for your crimes. It might even save your life."

Bailo merely glared at Kine without acknowledging her words.

"First, let's begin with something easy. You're Major Siana Bailo, Celeste National Guard, correct?"

No reply, though Bailo's eyes slipped over Kine's left shoulder and fixated on the bare metal bulkhead.

"You do realize we're authorized to use invasive interrogation methods should you not cooperate, right?"

Bailo finally spoke, though she kept staring over Kine's shoulder. "I've been conditioned against interrogation, so go ahead and kill me."

"I'd rather avoid that, Major. Let's assume your cooperation would mean not appearing before a military tribunal but getting released to go home?"

A bark of humorless laughter escaped Bailo's throat, and her eyes met Kine's again.

"Yeah, considering what would await me back on Celeste if I told you everything, and it got out — which it would — I'd rather take my chances with the tribunal."

Kine smiled at her.

"Just checking. So, you're still a serving officer. Otherwise, you'd not be worried about going home after talking to us."

Bailo shrugged irritably, confirming Kine's words.

"And you're still assigned to the Celeste National Guard's Special Operations Division?"

"Bailo, Siana, Major, RT9347853," Bailo replied in a tired tone.

Nunes cocked a weary eyebrow at her.

"Cute. Name, rank, and serial number, just like in the old war stories."

He leaned forward, eyes meeting Bailo's defiant gaze.

"On further reflection, Aleksa, I think we should inject her with interrogation drugs just to see if she really is conditioned. We can always move on to her second in command, who should know everything she does. And if he's a real merc and not a regular officer posing as one, he won't be conditioned."

"Somehow, she doesn't strike me as the suicidal type. Are you, Siana?" When Bailo didn't answer, Kine said, "Why don't we let the major reflect on her upcoming life decisions and move on to the next one in line?"

"Sure."

Kine and Nunes stood and left the room while a pair of bosun's mates took her back to the brig, where she enjoyed the last available cell in solitary splendor. They undid her restraints before gently shoving her through the door.

The two chief warrant officers met Miko Steiger in the wardroom, where she was taking a quick cup of coffee.

"You finished with the rest of the prisoners?" Nunes asked as he sat across from her, steaming mug in hand.

Steiger nodded.

"Yes. They appear to be genuine private military corporation employees and not regulars. The second in command, who identified himself as such, is a Skyron Enneb, a citizen of Celeste and a long-time employee of the Mahkteere PMC, which is headquartered on Celeste. I checked our database, and it's been in existence for the last twenty years. Interestingly enough, he volunteered that he did two hitches in the Corps before leaving as a buck sergeant."

"Nicely done, Miko." Kine clapped on Steiger's shoulder before taking a seat beside her. When Miko winced because of her bruised ribs, she added, "Sorry."

"No harm done."

"And he gave that up just on your initial questioning?"

"Yes." Steiger nodded. "Enneb seems keen to redeem himself with the Federation Fleet. I guess he took Chief Superintendent Bain's words to heart."

Nunes snorted.

"He's obviously a PMC amateur who figures soaping up the pros will get him a bye."

"Don't knock it, Jake. That's how we'll get most of our intel," Kine replied. "It sure as heck won't be from the Siana Bailos of the galaxy."

Nunes raised both hands, palms facing outward.

"I agree. Shall we interview Mister Enneb?"

"Let's."

Kine had the bosun's mates guarding the prisoners bring Enneb to the interrogation room, and, as with Bailo, she and Nunes observed the man remotely via the video pickups. He also had his hands bound behind his back and sat uncomfortably. But contrary to Bailo, Enneb looked around, his head jerking in all directions while he licked his lips almost obsessively and blinked at an unnaturally rapid rate.

"Clearly nervous. I think he'll tell us everything he knows."

Kine nodded in agreement.

"You're probably right. Time to have a conversation with our guest."

They entered the interrogation room and took chairs across the table from Enneb, who stared at them with visible anxiety.

"Skyron Enneb, I'm Chief Warrant Officer Aleksa Kine, and this is Chief Warrant Officer Jake Nunes. We'd like to ask you some questions."

Enneb nodded.

"I'll do my best to answer them."

"You're a former Marine, I understand?"

"Yes, Warrant. Two enlistments. I left as a sergeant."

"What was your MOS?"

"Infantry. I served in the 2nd Regiment."

"Why did you leave the Corps?"

Enneb gave Kine a shrug.

"Got tired of being a garrison trooper, and the CO wouldn't approve my transfer to an OutWorld-based regiment."

"Why not?"

"Dunno. He didn't authorize any transfers out of the 2nd."

"And once you left?"

"I returned home to Celeste, bummed around for a while, then found out the Mahkteere PMC was hiring. That was ten years ago. I've been running independent jobs for the last five, but this one, they put me under Siana Bailo. You're aware she's a Celeste National Guard regular, right?"

"We do. Is she the only regular on this job?"

He nodded.

"Yep."

"Do you know why she's masquerading as a PMC employee?"

"Search me. When the company got the contract six months ago, she just showed up, and they put her in charge because she was supposedly a retired major. I only found out she was still a regular because of something she said in the early days. None of the others know."

Enneb's nervousness was fading away, replaced by a need to unburden himself.

"Speaking of others, are there more than just the twenty-two of you down on Garonne?"

"Yes. There are six in Holback and six in Oshin working with the deps there."

"What sort of progress have they made so far?"

Enneb grimaced.

"Not much. There are fewer deps in those places and many of them have jobs. Tianjin was always the main effort simply because of the numbers and the length of time since they've been dumped there."

"Can you tell us how to find them?"

"Sure. There's a safe house in each location." Enneb rattled off a pair of addresses. "If you send the

Constabulary, they'll come nicely. No need for those howling thingamafucks you used on us."

"Do you know who hired your company to train and equip the Garonne deportees?"

"No. But we're rarely told who engaged our services. Mahkteere prides itself on confidentiality."

"Then how do you get your orders? Celeste is a fair way off, and you don't have independent access to the subspace network."

"Through Bulsar Upari. He's our controller for this job. Upari's in Iskellian." Enneb gave another address.

"Is he from Mahkteere as well?"

"Nope. Never knew the man before we arrived here. I figure he works for the people who hired us. Leastwise, he gives us our instructions and we have to report everything back to him." Enneb let out a brief, albeit humorless, chuckle. "Like when I announced someone had taken our freshly delivered stocks of M-147s and the training team the other day. I guess you did that. But boy, was he ever mad. You see, Upari arranges the weapon deliveries, which, I suppose, his employer pays for."

Kine and Nunes looked at each other, and the latter said, "I think we must invite Mister Upari for a little chat."

***

"Another twelve mercs and a controller? It's a good thing *Iolanthe* has plenty of spare room. Well done, both of you." Delgado grinned at Kine and Nunes when they finished debriefing him on Enneb's interrogation. "I'll ask Chief Superintendent Bain to pick them up and deliver them to the various spaceports. Let's hope they'll be as docile as your man says."

"I'd rather we pick up the controller, Bulsar Upari, ourselves," Kine said. "And quickly. He surely watches the newsnets and knows the Tianjin deps failed in their attack on the Grayson Ranch by now. It wouldn't surprise me if he's frantically trying to contact Bailo or Enneb to find out what happened. If we wait too long, he might decide discretion is the better part of valor and vanish. Since I'm a Constabulary officer, I have the necessary powers of arrest should we wish to keep things strictly legal. At least on the ground."

"Very well. I assume you'll be wearing civvies?"

"Oh, yes. No point in advertising."

"I'll get a shuttle warmed up for you and call Bain so she can arrange transport as well as pick up the mercs in Holback and Oshin."

An hour later, Kine and Nunes, clad in casual business clothes, the sort detectives would wear, complete with needlers in hip holsters hidden beneath jackets, climbed aboard an unmarked Constabulary staff car. Kine gave the driver, who wasn't wearing his uniform either, the address and settled back. Once they were on their way, the driver reached back and handed her an envelope.

"The warrant I asked for?"

"Yes, sir."

"Mighty quick."

The driver grinned at her over his shoulder.

"The Chief Super doesn't mess around."

Soon, they turned onto a quiet, respectable street with storefronts and professional offices on the ground floors and lodgings above. The driver stopped in front of the one bearing a brass plate beside the door that said *Bulsar Upari - Factor and Forwarder*.

"Here we are."

"Thanks. This shouldn't take long."

"No worries, sir. I'm yours for as long as you need me."

Kine and Nunes climbed out of the car and went up the steps to the door, which didn't open at their approach, nor did they see any handle or knob. Instead, the door's stone surround had a discrete com panel embedded in it, and Kine touched the surface.

A few heartbeats later, a man's harsh voice asked, "What do you want?"

"We'd like to speak with Mister Bulsar Upari."

"Why?"

"I'm a Constabulary detective named Aleksa Kine, and he's Jake Nunes." Kine pulled her credentials from an inner jacket pocket and held them up to the com panel, which presumably hid a video pickup. "And we believe you might have information that can help us in our investigation of a commercial fraud case. May we come in?"

Upari didn't immediately reply, evidently wondering whether it was a trap. He finally said, "Do you have a warrant?"

"Of course." Kine pulled out the envelope and extracted a plastified sheet, which she held up to the panel. It was signed by a federal judge and laid out precisely the same thing Kine had told Upari.

"All right, then."

The door slid open, and they stepped into a small, neat foyer with chairs along white walls and a door leading deeper into the building. That door opened to reveal a stocky man with thick black hair, a drooping mustache, and small, suspicious eyes beneath beetling brows. He wore an expensive business suit, small gold hoop earrings, and a brooch depicting a mythical beast on his left breast.

"Thank you for agreeing to see us, Mister Upari." Kine nodded politely at him.

"As if I had a choice." He turned on his heels and waved at them to follow.

— Twenty-Five —

Upari led them into a spacious, well-appointed office that reeked of understated wealth and gestured at a pair of chairs in front of his desk as he sat behind it. Kine and Nunes, however, remained standing, with the latter strolling around the room, studying the artwork on display.

"Let's get this over with. Time is money, and every minute I spend with you costs me. You said I could help in a case of commercial fraud. Explain yourselves."

"Are the names Siana Bailo and Skyron Enneb familiar to you?"

Upari frowned, and Kine could read both surprise and apprehension in his eyes, dispelling any last doubts about his involvement.

"No. Should they be?"

"I believe you're acting as their controller for interests on Celeste."

He laughed, but it sounded false to Kine's ears.

"Whoever told you that is seriously mistaken. Now, if that's the information you're acting on, this conversation is over." Upari stood. "Please leave."

"Not without you, old chum," Nunes said, producing his needler and aiming it at Upari's face.

"You can't threaten me in my own home. I have rights." Now, the fear was evident in his expression.

"Sure, I can. I'm not a cop, but a Marine. She's the cop. You can complain to her about my not respecting your rights, but for now…"

"Bulsar Upari," Kine said, "you are under arrest on suspicion of fomenting insurrection, smuggling weapons, and organizing illegal mercenary activities on a Federation world on behalf of another star nation. You may be charged with further crimes as our investigation continues."

"Bullshit." The man bristled. "I'm a factor, not an insurrectionist, let alone a mercenary enabler."

"I have witnesses that say otherwise." Kine produced restraints and dangled them in front of her. "Please put your hands behind your back."

"I most certainly will not."

Kine glanced at Nunes.

"You want to take him, Jake?"

"Sure."

In a matter of seconds, Nunes forced Upari down on his knees by twisting one arm behind him. Kine slapped the restraints on that arm's wrist and forced the other to join it.

"Shall I drain his computer?" Nunes asked.

"The warrant allows it."

"Hey, you can't—" The needler thrust into Upari's face silenced him, although he gave Nunes a murderous glare.

"Don't move. Don't speak. Just stay where you are until we're done, Sunshine."

Nunes sat behind Upari's desk, called up the virtual workstation, and grimaced.

"You didn't lock it before letting us in? Shame on you, Bulsar."

He fished a data wafer from his jacket pocket and placed it on the reader, then he ordered the workstation to download all the information it held. A few seconds later, he retrieved the wafer and stood.

"Done. I'll analyze it once we're back aboard. Can you stand on your own, Bulsar, or should we pick you up?"

When the man didn't answer, Nunes and Kine went over to where he knelt and lifted him to his feet with the greatest of ease.

"You can come along quietly, or I can sedate you."

Upari sneered.

"I'll come quietly."

"Any items of sentimental value you'd like to bring along? Because you're not returning here ever again." When Upari didn't answer, Nunes shrugged. "I guess not. You're probably the sort of agent who travels light and doesn't stay put in any given place once a job is done. Am I right?"

Without waiting for an answer, Nunes wrapped his hand around Upari's upper arm and guided him to the door.

"Tell me, my friend," Nunes said once they sat in the back of the car. "Are you conditioned?"

Upari stared at him and said, "Conditioned against or for what?"

"That answers my question nicely." Nunes smiled at Upari. "I think we'll have this one singing very quickly, Aleksa."

Back aboard *Iolanthe*, they immediately sat Upari in the interrogation room and left him to stew while they observed via video feed.

"You want to inject him right off the bat, Jake?"

"Yeah. I get the feeling he's not going to be anywhere near as helpful as Enneb, and he's the link with the mercs' employer back on Celeste. If he doesn't even know what conditioning is, then we might as well not waste time cajoling him."

"Okay. Your call. But we'll no longer be within the bounds of legality when dealing with a civilian."

"He's as guilty as the mercs and will be tried by a military court alongside them. I'll go get my interrogation kit."

Nunes returned with a small metallic case, and they entered the interrogation room.

Upari scowled at them, but Kine could sense his nervousness. He'd obviously never been in this kind of situation before and knew they had him dead to rights.

"I'm Chief Warrant Officer Aleksa Kine of the Federation Constabulary and this is Chief Warrant Officer Jake Nunes of the Federation Marine Corps, and we're here to interview you. Will you answer our questions truthfully?"

"Get bent," Upari growled.

"That's a no, then."

An evil smile briefly lit up Upari's face.

"Correct."

"Then let me tell you what's going to happen. Chief Warrant Officer Nunes is a real wizard with interrogation chemicals that'll loosen your tongue. But there's a risk involved, and that risk is you'll suffer heart failure at some point and face premature death. It may affect one in five hundred individuals."

The odds of suffering cardiac arrest were much smaller, perhaps one in ten thousand, and good interrogators were always prepared to revive interviewees. But Upari didn't know that, and a look of alarm entered his piggish eyes. Yet he remained defiant.

Kine glanced at Nunes.

"You might as well go ahead and drug him. I'll stand by to call the sickbay if he goes into convulsions."

Nunes opened the little case and took out an injector. He confirmed its contents, then stood up and moved around the table to position himself behind Upari.

"Last chance, little buddy," he drawled. When Upari didn't react, Nunes pressed the tip of the injector against the side of Upari's neck, and with a little hiss, the drug entered his bloodstream.

Nunes sat again and kept his gaze on Upari's face, looking for the telltale signs the chemical cocktail was taking effect. When the man's eyes began losing focus, and his facial muscles slackened, Nunes smiled.

"What's your name?"

"Berlocq Morley." He was slurring his words, another sign the drug had spread through his system.

Nunes and Kine exchanged a quick glance. That he'd been working under an assumed name wasn't exactly a surprise to either of them.

"Pleased to meet you, Berlocq."

"I can't say the pleasure is mine." Morley giggled. "But I sure feel funny."

"Berlocq, how long have you been on Garonne?"

"A year or so."

"And do you actually run a factoring and forwarding business?"

"Sure. It just isn't particularly profitable. But then, it doesn't have to be since I'm well paid to control the private military corporation consultants." He giggled again.

"Who pays you?"

"A Celeste consortium interested in causing chaos on their former colony."

"Can you tell me who belongs to this consortium?"

A guffaw. "I can."

He tried to put on a sly expression, but his slack facial muscles didn't allow it to fully form.

"Who are they?"

"Zan Tillman, Jorus Pritchett, and Commonwealth Senator Aleane Quizar."

The names meant nothing to either Kine or Nunes.

"Why are those three interested in causing chaos on Garonne?"

Morley gave them a silly grin.

"Because they all suffered significant losses when Garonne aligned with the Federation and seek retribution."

"And how did they hire you?"

"I am a freelance consultant who specializes in disrupting businesses and governments, big or small, and I'm damned good at it. They reached out to me. Or rather, Tillman did. He's the leader of the consortium and offered me an enormous sum to take on this job. All three of them are wealthy enough that they can indulge their fancies."

"You hired the Mahkteere PMC to put boots on the ground?"

"Yes. They're small but effective. This wasn't the first time I used them."

"Did you know Siana Bailo is a serving Celeste National Guard officer masquerading as a mercenary?"

"Of course. Senator Quizar arranged to have her participate in this project so that the PMC employees could get professional leadership and planning. It was I who suggested they find a regular to head the mission." Morley seemed quite proud of himself. "She's also something of an insurance policy. If the job derailed, she would be accountable for removing the mercenaries to ensure there are no loose ends."

Morley let out a bark of laughter.

"And it has gone off the rails. Did she terminate them?"

"No. We have every last one in custody, Bailo included."

"Oh! That means it's failure all around." He sounded incredibly sad, and tears appeared in the corners of his eyes. "And the first time I got cut down in mid-stride."

Then, suddenly, his head fell against his chest, and his body slumped forward.

"Is he dead?" Kine asked, alarmed.

"No." Nunes grinned at her. "Listen."

The sound of soft snores reached her ears, and she laughed. "He fell asleep."

"Most of them do. But we got the essential elements of information."

— Twenty-Six —

"Curtis has been heard from." Brigadier General Zachary Thomas Decker dropped into a chair facing the desk of his wife, Rear Admiral Hera Talyn. "He's solved most of the problem on Garonne in record time."

Decker summarized the report Delgado sent to SOCOM, adding, "Ghost Squadron is still collecting weapons and neutralizing violent deportees based on the interrogation info they're getting from the mercenaries, but essentially, it's over. Or at least back to the situation before those mercenaries set up shop and began training the deps as guerrillas."

"Excellent. I knew young Curtis would do well. So, this Zan Tillman is behind it. Let me see what we have on him." The head of Naval Intelligence's Special Operations Division turned to her virtual workstation and entered the name. She read for a bit and then nodded. "I thought the name was faintly familiar. He's reputedly the richest man in the Celeste system, although no one has any idea of his net worth since he's an extremely private individual.

However, he's a rabid centralist, which is the main reason I remember him. And he had extensive holdings on both of Celeste's colonies, Garonne and Marengo, which he lost when they joined the OutWorlds in seceding, which means revenge is a plausible motive. But I think it's more than that."

Decker cocked a questioning eyebrow at her.

"We're picking up signs of Commonwealth activity designed to destabilize governments throughout the Federation. As a centralist, Tillman would naturally cooperate with the Sécurité Spéciale in sowing discord on Garonne to undermine Verrill's administration. He and Verrill will surely have become enemies ever since you and I forced the issue of granting Garonne greater autonomy years ago."

"And what better way to screw with Garonne than a private venture, which gives the Commonwealth government plausible deniability."

Talyn nodded.

"That's what I think. We're definitely in a cold war with the Commonwealth, though we haven't acknowledged it yet."

"Is Marengo experiencing any issues? I haven't heard anything coming from that star system in a long time."

"No more than others in the Rim Sector."

"Perhaps the *Sécurité Spéciale*, via Tillman, is using Garonne as a test run. But then, I do recall Marengo getting a lot fewer deportees in the past."

"It is less hospitable, both in terms of physical environment and societal attitudes for involuntary colonists. Marengo has more successfully resisted large-scale dumping than Garonne. Still, I'll send a pair of undercover agents to that star system in case something like Garonne is brewing beneath the surface."

"You got anything on Jorus Pritchett and Senator Quizar in your secret database?" Decker asked.

"Let me check." Talyn called up both names and spent some time reading the results. "We have little on Pritchett other than he's a close associate of Tillman and is enormously rich in his own right, but it appears he inherited much of his wealth rather than earned it like Tillman. Aleane Quizar is the junior Commonwealth senator for Celeste and also a centralist. She sits on the shadowy Senate Interstellar Security Committee, formed after the Federation seceded. We suspect that committee oversees the Commonwealth's efforts to destabilize Federation star system governments, which means she'll be dealing directly with the *Sécurité Spéciale*."

"And she could well have been the one who came up with the plan of using mercs hired by Tillman and Pritchett to arm and train deps on Garonne as a guerrilla force."

"Quite possibly." Talyn gave her husband a small smile. "And if so, it means the Commonwealth government has been orchestrating events on Garonne at a remove, events that caused hundreds of violent deaths."

"The cold war heating up?"

"Probably." Talyn tapped her chin with an extended index finger, lost in thought. "It seems to me we shouldn't just let it slide. This might be the perfect occasion to let the Commonwealth know that their actions, covert as they might be, have consequences."

"What's cooking in that fertile brain of yours?"

"It might give the Commonwealth pause if we terminated Tillman, Pritchett, and Quizar as examples. The lives of three entitled, arrogant sociopaths against the lives of many future victims of Commonwealth interference."

"And you can authorize that?"

"Hell, no." Talyn grinned at Decker. "My permission to take independent action stops at the point where the Commonwealth and Federation spheres intersect. This is something I need to run by the Grand Admiral. And even he doesn't have the full authority to operate within the Commonwealth. Although I think a small, surgical strike against the three named individuals will fall within his remit if it's done on a plausible deniability basis."

"So you're planning on a pair of assassins?"

"No. That would be too subtle and cause the powers that be over there to miss the point. It must be something the authorities can't just sweep under the rug, something that will generate a certain amount of public controversy."

"Full-scale raids on the three while they're sleeping?"

Talyn snapped her fingers and pointed at Decker.

"Give the brigadier general an extra kiss when he gets home. That's precisely what I mean. They tried to start a war. We've ended it with a victory, which means the losers' leaders get to pay with their lives, so no one else tries."

"I like the way you think. You want me to send Ghost Squadron on a blacker-than-black operation behind enemy lines?"

"If the Grand Admiral authorizes it."

"And what about the thirty-six prisoners currently in *Iolanthe*? You want to make an example of them too?"

"Hmm." Talyn pursed her lips. "On the one hand, they deserve to be tried by a military court for what they did and would serve long sentences in a penal colony on Parth. On the other hand, sending them home would clearly signal the failure of their mission, and they'd likely be unemployable after this. Major Bailo could even suffer dire consequences from her own superiors. The Celestan National Guard, as you might recall, doesn't handle disappointments well.

"So, take full biometric scans of everyone, load them aboard the free trader *Iolanthe* captured, tell them if they're ever seen in the Federation again, it's off to prison, and send them home."

"I am leaning toward that solution. There's nothing worse than slinking home after losing so decisively. Besides, we'll save the Federation a lot of money by forgoing trials, let alone incarceration."

"Can you authorize that?"

Talyn nodded.

"Yes. They're prisoners taken by *my* black ops squadron."

"And what about the Grand Admiral?"

"Let me see when he's available for a quick chat." Talyn turned to her workstation again and touched the controls. "His calendar is open right now."

She activated her office communicator, and a cheerful male voice said, "Admiral Talyn. I'm guessing you want a few minutes of the Grand Admiral's time."

"If that's convenient, Zane. And I'd like to bring General Decker."

"I'll ask. Wait one." Thirty seconds later, Navy Captain Zane Dubreas, Grand Admiral Antar Kessler's senior aide, came back on the link. "You and the general can have ten minutes right now."

"On our way. Talyn, out." She climbed to her feet. "Come on."

They walked across the sprawling HQ structure and up to the top floor where the Grand Admiral's spacious office overlooked Joint Base Sanctum's spaceport. When they entered the antechamber, Captain Dubreas stood.

"You can go straight through, Admiral." He gestured at the open inner door behind him.

Talyn smiled at him.

"Much appreciated, Zane."

With Decker on her heels, Talyn marched through and halted the regulation three paces in front of the Grand Admiral's desk.

"Thank you for seeing us, sir."

Antar Kessler, a large, dark-complexioned man with short iron-gray hair and a seamed face, stood and gestured at the settee group to one side of the office.

"When you ask for a few minutes of my time, Hera, they're never wasted. Let's take our ease." When they were seated, Kessler said, "If you've brought Zack with you, can I infer that it's related to the Garonne operation?"

"It is, sir. Zack will give you the background."

Decker summarized Delgado's report, and Talyn presented her idea of launching a punitive black op on Celeste. When she finished, Kessler sat back, elbows on the chair's arms, fingers steepled below his chin.

"You realize that striking against those three with a Special Forces squadron on Commonwealth soil could be construed as an act of war."

"Definitely, sir. Except, as always, Ghost Squadron will have plausible deniability. And because no one expects an attack, the chances of success are excellent. Besides," Talyn allowed herself a cruel smile, "the Commonwealth is in no condition to declare formal hostilities on the Federation. They know we'd crush them. Therefore, the worst that could happen is a protest by their ambassador and possibly a few sanctions, not that they can materially affect us in any case. I figure they'll take their lumps and be more circumspect in the future."

Kessler frowned as he mulled over the idea. Then, he said, "Do it. Making examples out of the targets might cause the Commonwealth to reconsider its activities in other star systems."

"Yes, sir."

"Was there anything else?"

"I plan on releasing the Celestan mercenaries Ghost Squadron took prisoner and have them shipped home to rub the Commonwealth's nose into their failure rather than hold and try them in our courts."

Kessler shrugged.

"If you think that's best, then so be it."

"That was it, sir."

"Then you're dismissed." Kessler made a vague gesture toward the door but didn't rise himself.

He watched them leave with an ambivalent feeling. There was no doubt that both ranked among the most effective flag officers in the entire Federation Armed Forces, but occasionally, they seemed just a bit too bloodthirsty.

Still, they were trying to keep matters to a low simmer, using intimidation and targeted strikes rather than massive violence wherever possible and he should be thankful for that. It still sent the right message without killing a lot of innocent people alongside the amoral, greedy bastards behind the troubles.

— Twenty-Seven —

"Chief Superintendent Bain tells me you've solved our problems, Colonel," a beaming President Verrill said when his face appeared on one of the CIC's secondary displays.

"Not every last one of them, Mister President, but we've captured the mercenaries who were behind the deportee uprising, as well as their controller and the weapons they brought with them. We also killed the deportees who carried out the attacks, a hundred of them. I don't know whether more lurk in the shadows, but I doubt it. Hopefully, our actions will have quashed any desire by the deps to try again. But you will need to deal with their reaction when you cut off the benefits they've enjoyed since time immemorial. Still, at least Tianjin can come back under government control now that we've eliminated the core group of deps holding it hostage."

"Absent the hard core of fighters which you eliminated, our police and the Constabulary should suffice to keep them quiescent. But I still wouldn't mind a Marine battalion stationed here permanently."

"I'll pass along your request to Fleet HQ, sir. Rotating a battalion through every six or nine months may be possible for a few years. But you'll be responsible for building a base to house them. Yet you really should consider forming your own National Guard."

Verrill let out a humorless burst of laughter.

"For now, we simply lack the funds to do so. Maybe in ten years, we can reconsider the idea. How much would building a base for a battalion cost?"

Delgado grinned.

"A lot less than forming a Guard."

Very well. You can informally pass along my request to the Fleet, and I'll make it formal to the SecDef on Wyvern. In any case, you have my thanks and those of the planet's citizens for neutralizing the threat so quickly. What'll happen to your prisoners?"

"I don't know. I've submitted my report to SOCOM and am waiting for orders. With General Decker and Admiral Talyn involved in the decision-making process for my squadron's missions, I'm always expecting the unexpected."

Verrill frowned.

"Zack Decker and Hera Talyn?"

"Yes."

"I'm glad to hear they've prospered. They were a great help to the Garonne Independence Movement many years ago. I believe Hera was a commander and Zack a chief warrant officer at the time."

"And she's now a rear admiral, and he's a brigadier general. And both are involved in some extremely high-level stuff."

Verrill chuckled.

"Zack really went up in the world."

"He's a superb leader and the perfect example of a highly competent Special Forces officer. I don't think anyone has surpassed him in living memory."

"Well, Zack certainly was effective in helping the Movement achieve victory. If only the Senate and the Supreme Court had granted us full independence at the time, the recent unpleasantness might have been avoided."

"Agreed, sir."

"Will you be staying for a while?"

"No idea. My unit is in high demand, and SOCOM might send us on another mission right away without returning to Caledonia first."

"I suppose it makes for an exciting lifestyle."

"We wouldn't be in Special Forces if we didn't enjoy it, and most of us will do nothing else for the rest of our careers, which should tell you something."

Verrill chuckled.

"Understood. Still, I'd like to host you for a small, private dinner if your time permits. Just you, me, and Chief Superintendent Bain."

"I appreciate the invitation, but I'll need to stay aboard the ship in case orders arrive requiring an immediate departure."

"Alright, then. Once again, thank you. Verrill, out."

And Delgado's orders came through moments later, proving once again that the universe still had a sense of humor.

"Sir, an encrypted message from SOCOM for you. I've sent it to your workstation."

"That was a fast turnaround. Thanks, PO."

Delgado decrypted and read it, then sat back in his chair, eyes staring at the display while he processed his orders. Calling them unusual didn't do the contents justice. He set up a meeting involving his command team, Miko Steiger, and *Iolanthe*'s captain and withdrew to his quarters so he could carry out some preliminary thinking in peace and quiet.

Two hours later, he walked into *Iolanthe*'s main conference room and saw everyone was already sitting around the oval table.

"Folks, we've received fresh orders, and you'll find them interesting, to say the least," Delgado said, taking his seat at the head of the table. "First of all, we're releasing the prisoners and sending them back to Celeste aboard *Zenobia*."

The reaction around the table was immediate and primarily negative.

"Why?" Major Tesser asked.

"So they can spread the word of their utter defeat. I have no doubt they'll find themselves unemployable as private military contractors after this. And Major Bailo will have sharp questions to answer from a chain of command that doesn't forgive or forget."

"*Zenobia* isn't equipped to handle thirty-six people, especially for such a long run," Commander Ardross said. "She has cabins for half a dozen at most."

"Tough. They'll have to sleep in cargo holds and line up for the heads. We'll give them enough ratbars to keep them fed for the run back to Celeste, but that's it. Consider it part of their punishment."

Ardross nodded.

"Fair enough. The environmental systems will be strained, but not to the point of rupture."

"We'll ship them over to *Zenobia* the moment we're done here and tell Captain Hextar to leave as soon as possible. Until they're gone, *Iolanthe* must remain in Navy cruiser mode so they don't recognize her because we're going to Celeste as well, but in freighter mode. Keever, I hope you have a beacon identifying us as a Commonwealth ship."

"Yep. We registered *Iolanthe* as the transport *Gitane* on Meiji a few years ago, before the Federation seceded. Meiji is the prime Commonwealth star system for flags of convenience, so one more wearing the lotus banner in Celeste orbit won't attract attention."

"What will we do on Celeste?" Major Tesser asked.

A lazy grin spread across Delgado's face. "We're terminating the three clowns behind the Garonne mess — Zan Tillman, Jorus Pritchett, and Aleane Quizar — to give the Commonwealth an object lesson in why messing with the Federation is a terrible idea. And we'll do so in a manner that leaves no doubt in the minds of the

Commonwealth government who carried out the terminations and why."

"Ah. I'll bet that idea came from General Decker or Admiral Talyn. Probably both."

"Of course it did," Captain Painter said, chuckling.

"We won't know what we face until we're there," Delgado said. "So there's no point planning anything. Miko, apparently, there are two of your colleagues on Celeste. They'll receive a warning about our arrival and scout the targets for us while we are in transit. You're to contact them when we arrive, using a special encryption. I'll give you the code when we're done here."

Steiger nodded silently.

"That's everything I have for now, folks. Let's get the mercs on their way. Once they go FTL at Garonne's hyperlimit, we'll transform into *Gitane* and leave ourselves. With any luck, we should get to Celeste a day or two ahead of *Zenobia*."

"Possibly even three," Ardross said. "We're built for speed. She's not."

An hour later, the prisoners found themselves in three ranks on the hangar deck, wondering what was about to happen. They weren't wearing handcuffs, but armed bosun's mates surrounded them.

Delgado passed through the hangar's inner airlock and stopped in front of the formation.

"We are releasing you on your own recognizance and sending you away aboard *Zenobia*. You're free to go wherever you wish so long as it's out of the Federation's sphere because you're no longer welcome on any of our worlds."

"Let me guess," Siana Bailo said with a sneer. "You've rigged *Zenobia* to blow the moment she switches on her hyperdrives. That way, you won't have to worry about us anymore."

Delgado scoffed.

"If we wanted you dead, we'd have had no hesitations in tossing you out the airlock one by one. Our controllers have decided to let you go home as a way of giving your employers notice of your failure. Whatever happens to you once you're aboard *Zenobia* will no longer be our concern. By all means, tear her apart on your way to the hyperlimit so you can assure yourselves we didn't sabotage her. But you will leave shortly after we drop you off. Now, if it were up to me, I'd send you to Parth so you can stand before a military tribunal and then spend a few quality years in a penal colony, but I have my orders. We've put a case of ration bars in the shuttle that'll take you over. Enough to feed the lot of you until you reach Celeste. I hope Captain Hextar keeps his environmental filters pristine. Otherwise, you'll be drinking funky-tasting water after a few days. But that's none of my concern."

He turned to *Iolanthe*'s bosun and gestured at the mercenaries.

"Load 'em up and get 'em out of here. They're stinking up this ship."

"Aye, aye, sir."

Zenobia broke out of orbit an hour later and headed for Garonne's hyperlimit. She vanished into hyperspace soon afterward and the Federation Navy cruiser *Iolanthe*, second of her name, turned into the civilian transport *Gitane* and accelerated on the same heading as *Zenobia*.

— Twenty-Eight —

"Come in and sit," Secretary General of the Commonwealth Brodrick Brüggemann turned away from the office window overlooking Lake Geneva and took the chair behind his enormous, ornate, yet curiously bare desk.

"Sir." Andreas Bauchan, Director General of the *Sécurité Spéciale,* the SecGen's own secret police and intelligence agency, did as he was bid and crossed one leg over the other at the knee.

"If you asked to see me now and not wait until our regular Friday morning update, the news can't be good." Brüggemann sounded testy, as if in a bad mood.

Bauchan gave him a languid shrug.

"Nowadays, it rarely is, sir. And what I have to report won't improve your disposition."

The SecGen sighed and made a come-on gesture with his right hand.

"Tell me."

"The operation to destabilize the Garonne government has utterly failed. Our operatives on Garonne report that the deportee strike force, which carried out the attacks, was completely wiped out. Additionally, all of the mercenaries who trained and equipped them were taken into custody and removed from the planet's surface. No one knows what happened to them. The weapons provided to the deportees have also vanished. Those responsible have not been spotted — the arrests of the mercenaries were made by the Constabulary. But my people suspect the Federation Fleet sent a Special Forces unit to Garonne when President Verrill asked for aid. And not just any Special Forces unit but the one they call Ghost Squadron. Its members are the Federation's foremost black ops specialists."

Brüggemann frowned. "That is rather annoying."

"And since Garonne was one of our test beds to develop the best kinetic techniques for disrupting Federation planetary governments, I'd say we must take a few steps back and reassess what we're doing. No one expected such a rapid deployment of Federation Fleet assets, let alone that those assets would be the best and most ruthless Special Forces unit in the known galaxy. I recommend we slow-walk the operations on Marengo and New Oberon, the other two test beds, until my people can analyze what happened on Garonne. It would be best if we didn't so comprehensively lose our resources in those two star systems as well."

"I'd rather you kept the momentum going, Andreas. Creating havoc on Federation worlds is your priority."

Bauchan inclined his head.

"Of course, sir."

"Poor Zan Tillman, though. Losing a hefty investment like that."

"We'll ensure he doesn't lose the one he made on Marengo as well. But he knew the risks going in."

Brüggemann cocked a skeptical eyebrow at Bauchan.

"Did he, though?"

"Maybe not completely. But then, none of the people we're using to hide the government's involvement in subverting Federation worlds do."

"Useful idiots?"

Bauchan let out a bark of laughter.

"I wouldn't go quite so far, sir. Useful, sure. But idiots, no. They're well aware of the role they play and are participating with gusto, mainly because they all lost a lot when the OutWorlds seceded and want revenge, the risks be damned. This desire for vengeance, no matter the cost, appears to be a quirk of the ultra-wealthy. And I will take advantage of it to the utmost."

"I'm happy as long as we ensure that the damned Federation is occupied with internal problems and unable to bother us."

"Are you sure you're not into a bit of revenge yourself, sir?" Bauchan asked in a disingenuous tone.

A smile spread across Brodrick Brüggemann's face.

"I'd be lying if I didn't admit it being one of my motivators. The bastards broke up the Commonwealth and left us with a much smaller sphere, surrounded by the Federation."

"But we still outstrip them in population, shipyards, industrial capacity, and many more indicators of advanced civilization and will for a long time yet."

"Until we don't. They did take two-thirds of the Commonwealth's military strength with them. Surely, you've figured out their long-range plan is to absorb us and remove all power from Earth."

"Let them try. They will not succeed, mainly because their military strength is occupied with securing their outer frontiers and unavailable for action against us.

"I wish I could be as sanguine about it as you are, Andreas. But my instinct, which has never led me astray, says we've got maybe ten or twenty years of peace before the Federation makes a bid to take down the Commonwealth for good."

Bauchan gave him a languid shrug. "You're perhaps a bit too pessimistic, sir. The Federation might control a vaster expanse of space than we do, but that's to our advantage. We are more compact, easier to defend, and our Armed Forces are growing rapidly."

"Still…" Brüggemann swiveled his chair around to look out the windows again.

"And we'll eventually find the right formula for destabilizing Federation star systems long term, keeping them busy looking inward rather than casting covetous eyes on us. I think we'll be safe from attack for more decades than you might expect, sir."

"From your lips to the Almighty's ear, Andreas."

Bauchan merely smiled at the old fraud's use of the Almighty's name. If anyone in government was the furthest thing from a believer, it would be Brüggemann. But he'd learned to mouth pieties with a straight face long ago.

— Twenty-Nine —

By the time *Iolanthe* emerged at Celeste's hyperlimit, she was emitting a beacon identifying her as *Gitane*, a transport registered on Meiji, and her crew — Marines included — wore civilian clothes rather than merchant uniforms. It further served to mark the Q ship as belonging to an owner-operator rather than a shipping line, therefore looking for any cargo that would cover expenses and giving her an excuse for loitering in orbit and sending down shuttles.

Humanity colonized Celeste during its first outward migration, making it one of the oldest extra-solar worlds. And although the big cities on Celeste faced increasing social problems, its infrastructure remained highly advanced.

An automated traffic control system that read *Gitane*'s beacon directed her into orbit, compared the information contained in the signal with a Commonwealth database of known starships, and matched her visually with the images it had. Since *Gitane* had been entered into the database shortly after her launch five years earlier, three years before the OutWorlds seceded, the ATCS was satisfied about her identity and didn't refer her arrival to a human overseer.

"We're here," Captain Ardross said over his shoulder to Delgado. "The control of the mission reverts to you, Curtis. What's your next step?"

"Miko contacts her colleagues on the ground. They should have information about the targets for us. I'll take it from there."

"Will she use the ship's radios?"

"I believe so. But she'll use Naval Intelligence-grade encryption, so it'll be gobbledygook to any Celestan eavesdropping. Besides, wouldn't a trader communicate with his comprador in code?"

Ardross nodded.

"Always."

"Which means we're at the mercy of our resident spook. Who I'll be talking to in a moment." Delgado grinned at Ardross and then stood, stretched, and left the bridge, looking for Steiger.

He found her in the wardroom, chatting with Rolf Painter and Lucius Farnes.

"Miko. Time to call your buddies and see what they have for us."

"Right." She climbed to her feet. "CIC?"

"Yeah. The bridge is a bit busy right now."

Steiger entered the CIC and headed for the signals alcove. She smiled at the petty officer on duty.

"PO, I need to send a quick message to an untraceable node. Mind if I take your seat for a few minutes?"

He smiled back at her and stood.

"Be my guest, Warrant."

Steiger sat at the workstation, established a connection with an anonymous, numbered node, and sent a message consisting of a single encrypted word — *¿Qué?* Then she disconnected, erased every trace of the link, and rose.

"Thanks, PO. I'll be back every hour to query the same node."

"If you like, I can monitor it."

"As convenient as that might be, it's best if I was the only one who knows how to connect."

"Your call, Warrant. I'll tell my replacement at watch change."

"Excellent." Steiger sketched a salute and left the CIC.

On her fourth check, she finally found a lengthy encrypted message on the node and downloaded it. Then, she erased the message, leaving the node pristine.

"You want the bad news first?" Steiger asked as she entered Delgado's cabin once she'd decrypted the missive.

"Sure."

"Senator Quizar is on Earth, so you can scratch her off the target list."

"Darn. Eliminating her would have reverberated far more across the Commonwealth's political structure than the other two. But I suppose even if SOCOM allowed a raid on Earth, it'd be damn near impossible to get at a senator in Geneva."

Steiger, who'd spent a lot of time in the Commonwealth's capital, shrugged.

"An assassination is still possible. If I recall correctly, someone terminated Secretary General Sara Lauzier in a Geneva restaurant at the end of the last century.

"I don't think our bosses would go for it. Too much risk of getting caught. I hope that was the bad news."

"Yes. Tillman and Pritchett are on Celeste. I've obtained the coordinates of their mansions in the hills above Angelique. Both live in quasi-fortresses and work from home. They're not precisely recluses, but they don't go out much. Apparently, they have everything a wealthy human could need, including, in Tillman's case, an eighteen-hole private golf course, among other things.

"The biggest issue is that my colleagues cannot even reach a point where they might see the mansions. They're more secure than the Palace of the Stars or Joint Base Sanctum. And trying to obtain jobs there, don't even think about it. Both mansions have considerable staffs, including their own private armies, and they vet everyone meticulously. It seems they turned their properties into impregnable citadels shortly after a raid by unknown parties on Arcadia, which resulted in the gruesome deaths of Elize and Allard Hogue, once the most powerful persons in the Arcadia system." Steiger cocked an ironic eyebrow at Delgado. "You wouldn't happen to know anything about that, would you?"

"No comment," he growled.

"All that to say, my colleagues apologize, but they cannot get close to either Tillman or Pritchett nor can they scout their lairs. We're pretty much stuck doing recon from orbit and perhaps a few overflights at lower altitudes. Anyway, everything is on there." She handed him a data wafer.

"Of course, we don't dare put up surveillance satellites. It wouldn't take long for Celeste's traffic control to notice unauthorized orbiters. Why the hell did I think this would be an easy in-and-out?"

Steiger smirked at Delgado.

"Because you're an incurable optimist."

"A character trait I'd better lose if I want to become commanding officer of the 1st Special Forces Regiment."

"Oh? Why?"

"Because the CO needs to be a realist, not an optimist nor a pessimist."

An exaggerated wink. "Better work on it then."

"I'll work on hammering the target areas with scans right now." Delgado swung to his feet and exited his cabin, headed for the CIC.

"Well, leave a girl then," Steiger murmured, smiling. She headed to her own quarters and a lie-down until someone found a mission for her.

"Chief," Delgado made his way to the sensor workstation, data wafer in hand. "I have two targets on the planet that need coverage down to the millimeter and from every possible angle."

"Sure, sir. Just give me the coordinates."

Delgado handed him the wafer. "They're on this."

"It'll take a bit longer than usual since we can't deploy any satellites to achieve constant coverage and, therefore, only have periodic visibility of the target area."

"Understood and expected, Chief."

"I'll get right to it, beginning the next orbital pass, sir."

Over the following hours, Delgado and Chief Warrant Officers Testo and Nunes studied the scans of both properties as the data came in during each pass. The first run was visible spectrum, the second infrared, the third, ground-penetrating radar, and the fourth, life signs, and they began building a detailed, dynamic image of both properties.

As Steiger had said, they were immense, covering hundreds of hectares, most of it forest, except Tillman's private golf course. And even though the properties were sizable, tall fences surrounded both, no doubt wired into a comprehensive sensor system.

At the heart of each stood a central mansion surrounded by a dozen outbuildings, some of them quite large. The life sign readings at Tillman's showed more than three hundred humans, a hundred of whom were concentrated in a two-story structure that looked like barracks with a fancy façade. Pritchett's held well over two hundred and fifty, with almost half in a building very much like the one on Tillman's spread.

"What do we think?" Delgado asked, staring at the video of a pair of men wearing tactical clothes and carrying carbines patrolling a main house perimeter. "A hundred and fifty to two hundred armed guards securing Tillman's. A little less for Pritchett's?"

Nunes nodded. "Sounds about right, sir."

Delgado rubbed his chin.

"You know, I'm beginning to think we'll only be able to strike one place. We'll need the entire squadron for a single target, and once we've hit it, we need to get the hell out of this star system."

"Tillman?" Testo asked.

"Yep. At least we know for sure he's home. Pritchett, not so much."

They'd spotted Tillman walking around his property and playing golf. He was obvious even from orbit — tall, muscular, with thick gray hair and a generous gray beard.

"And what are those small mounds on what looks like artificial hillocks?" Delgado pointed at a secondary display showing a square kilometer of Tillman's property with the mansion at its center. The two promontories in question were bare, as was the terrain immediately around them. "The IR reading makes them different from the surroundings."

"Aerospace defense domes? Tillman probably possesses the kind of influence to have some installed even though the Commonwealth doesn't permit them in civilian hands. That'll have the potential for complicating matters."

"Rods from God, Jake, my friend," Testo said, smiling. "Have *Iolanthe* launch kinetic penetrators so they arrive a minute before our shuttles and voilà. Done."

"It'll hardly be a quiet insertion in that case."

"If the domes are live, we'd trigger the alarm anyway, so we might as well dispose of them."

Delgado rose and wandered over to the CIC's sensor station.

"You can stop monitoring Target Beta and concentrate your resources on Target Alpha."

"Aye, aye, sir." A momentary pause as his eyes shifted to a secondary readout, then, "Sir, *Zenobia* just entered orbit. Or at least a ship with her beacon did."

"I guess they decided to come home."

"And they'll tell Tillman about what happened on Garonne," Nunes said. "I wonder whether he'll increase his personal security from massively impressive to ridiculously tight."

"Good point." Delgado nodded. "But considering his setup and the fact he probably considers himself immune from any sort of retaliation — his sort of wealthy always do — especially from Federation authorities, I doubt he'll so much as add another rent-a-cop."

He stretched, joining his hands above his head, and cracked his knuckles.

"I think that will do for now. PO, call me if anything unusual happens at Target Alpha."

"Sir."

"Come on, guys. Let's grab a cup of coffee and a sandwich."

— Thirty —

The communicator's buzz pulled Curtis Delgado from a deep sleep, and he reached clumsily for it.

"Delgado."

"Chief Rasmussen, CIC sensors, sir. You asked to be called whenever something unusual happened at Target Alpha."

The last wisps of Morpheus' embrace dissipated almost instantly, and Delgado swung his legs over the cot's edge.

"What's up?"

"A shuttle landed on the pad in front of the mansion a few minutes ago, and we saw Zan Tillman and an unknown woman climb aboard. It's taking off as we speak."

Delgado bit back a choice curse.

"Track it. We'll lose him if he's headed to a ship in orbit."

"Not necessarily, sir. If we can find the ship he's boarding and it stays in orbit long enough, we can send a probe that'll attach a subspace tracker with enough power reserves to stay active for at least thirty days."

"Could you have one prepared right away?"

"I'll need to clear it with Commander Ardross first, but yes, we can have it ready by the time the shuttle reaches orbit."

"Then please do so."

"Aye, aye, sir."

"I'll be in the CIC in a few minutes. Delgado, out."

He finished getting dressed and quickly swung by the wardroom for a cup of coffee, which he carried into the CIC. As he took his accustomed workstation, Chief Rasmussen turned around.

"I've cleared the tracker probe with the captain, and we'll deploy it when we know where he's going."

"Will there be any problem spotting the ship if we're on the other side of Celeste when he boards?"

"Considering the captain ordered an increase in our orbital speed, we should know which it is well before then. There aren't that many FTL-capable vessels in orbit, and they're well-dispersed thanks to traffic control. We've been tracking them as a matter of course since arriving, so the moment the shuttle aims for a particular one, we'll launch our probe."

Delgado grinned at the chief. He enjoyed working with an efficient crew, and *Iolanthe*'s was proving to be the best of the best.

They lost sight of the shuttle when Celeste masked it from the Q ship. But once they caught it again, the tiny spacecraft was clearly headed for an FTL-capable megayacht whose beacon identified it as the *Manticore*, owned by Liparus Enterprises.

A quick search showed Liparus being a subsidiary of a numbered shell company whose ownership was undisclosed, at least to the public sources Chief Warrant Officer Nunes consulted.

"How much do you want to bet Tillman owns Liparus through enough twisted corporate layers that even the Celeste Commercial Regulatory Agency can't untangle them and definitively determine that *Manticore* is his?" He asked.

Delgado grinned at him.

"No bet, Jake."

"The probe is on its way, sir," Chief Rasmussen announced just as Commander Ardross entered the CIC and took the command chair.

"Excellent, Chief," Ardross said before Delgado could express his thanks. "Put its video feed on the primary display."

"What are the chances of them detecting it?" Delgado asked instead.

"Almost nil, unless they're specifically pinging aft instead of keeping watch forward for stray satellites or other objects in orbit, and even then, the probe will show up as debris."

They watched *Manticore* grow on the screen as the probe neared it. The yacht, almost as big as a frigate, had a rounded, sweptback wedge shape with large hyperdrive nacelles hanging from short struts on either side and low blisters on both sides, indicating retracted defensive weapons. She was a blinding white and had her name and registration number picked out in square black characters on the nacelles and the back, between the sublight drive nozzles and the hangar deck doors that were closing after Tillman's shuttle had landed.

A small disk appeared in the viewer, headed for a point above the drive nozzles, and Chief Rasmussen said, "The probe has released the tracker."

The disk lightly touched *Manticore*'s hull and activated its magnetic grapples, affixing itself securely.

"I'm getting a signal, sir." The yacht's sublight drives lit up. "And not a moment too soon, either."

"Let's see which direction she's headed before we decide on any move," Ardross said. "If she's off toward Earth or any other Commonwealth system, we'll wave a fond farewell and decide whether you hit Pritchett — without knowing whether he's actually at home — or head back to Federation space, Curtis. Fair enough?"

"Sure." Delgado nodded.

The video feed from the probe died away as it shut down, its mission completed, and the CIC's primary display reverted to a straight-ahead view of Celeste's shimmering arc and her low orbitals. But it, too, shifted to focus on *Manticore*, now accelerating toward the planet's hyperlimit. After a while, Ardross rubbed his chin, eyes narrowed in thought.

"Nav?"

A few seconds later, the holographic image of *Iolanthe*'s navigator — who was at his station on the bridge — popped up beside Ardross' command chair.

"Yes, sir?"

"Tell me the ship we're tracking is on a course toward the Federation."

"Wait one." Then, "It sure looks like it, sir."

"In that case, we need to get on a parallel bearing and arrive at the system's heliopause before she does so we can determine her heading when she goes FTL in interstellar space."

"On it. Did you wish to leave before she jumps on her first leg out?"

"We might as well. She looks like a fast ship. Let's go in five minutes."

"Aye, aye, sir. Breaking out of orbit in five minutes on a parallel course."

A klaxon sounded, followed by a male voice announcing *Iolanthe* would be on her way in five.

Delgado, who'd been tapping his chin with an extended index finger, said, "You know what? I think *Manticore* might be en route to Marengo. Maybe Tillman hired mercenaries to disrupt the pair of former Celeste colonies because he lost a lot of money on both. With the uprising on Garonne having failed, he could be aiming for Marengo to help ensure the insurgency there is a success."

"We'll know when *Manticore* goes FTL interstellar at the heliopause."

"I'd better prepare a message for SOCOM on this development. Do you think the Commonwealth subspace network is still speaking to the Federation's?"

"Of course. Communications are vital to commercial enterprises, and the volume of trade between the OutWorlds and the old Commonwealth is as healthy as ever. We just don't have access to the classified military bands out here, so you'll have to address it to a civilian node and ensure it's encrypted with the newest algorithms. Anything older than two years, the Commonwealth counterintelligence spooks can read."

Delgado smirked at Ardross.

"Thanks, Captain Obvious. No one uses two-year-old algorithms nowadays, and if you didn't know it, our signals boffins have created a series of codes that are radically different from the previous ones. The Commonwealth doesn't have a hope in hell of decrypting them."

Ardross winked at Delgado.

"Just making sure you radioactive glass eaters are aware of the most recent developments in encryption technology."

Delgado burst into laughter and gave Ardross the rigid digit salute at using the latest lame insult the Navy had come up with for Marines.

"We are aware, Captain, sir. And probably more so than most squids. Now, if you'll excuse me, I have a message to encrypt and send to SOCOM's covert subspace node."

Manticore didn't change her heading and jumped on the first leg to the heliopause, heading in Marengo's general direction. *Iolanthe* went FTL shortly after that. Ardross had her push the upper in-system hyperspace bands so she could get to the heliopause ahead of *Manticore* and confirm her interstellar course, betting the civilian yacht would travel at a more sedate pace to avoid overstraining her hull and drives. Naval vessels were built to take greater punishment.

In the end, *Iolanthe* waited almost ninety minutes before picking up the subspace tracker as *Manticore* dropped out of hyperspace to confirm her course and jump into the interstellar bands, which were exponentially higher than the in-system ones.

"She's on a direct course for Marengo, sir," the navigator said after calculating *Manticore*'s heading when she went FTL again.

"You were right, Curtis," Ardross said over his shoulder.

"It just made sense, Tillman leaving shortly after *Zenobia* arrived, carrying his mercs from Garonne. Guys like him, they're the take-charge type. If something isn't going the way he wants, he'll step in and take over himself. I just wonder how that'll affect any plans the *Sécurité Spéciale* might have for Marengo. Because, sure as the Almighty made little apples, they're behind all of this since the SecGen ordered them to cause havoc on the OutWorlds just after we seceded. In any case, I'll also send a quick confirmatory message to SOCOM before we go FTL."

— Thirty-One —

To say Zan Tillman was an angry man would have been an understatement. But he suppressed his ire through a determination to see the Marengo operation succeed where Garonne had failed. True, it was a different sort of undertaking, a slower and costlier one. But he was bringing something with him to speed up the undertaking.

As he paced the saloon, lost in thought, his principal adviser, who might have been called consigliere in a different age and on a different world, watched him while sipping a Celestan white wine that fetched hundreds of creds a bottle. A slender, narrow-faced woman of indeterminate age with a shock of short, graying hair above an aquiline nose and deep-set blue eyes, she wore an expensive business suit of the sort few could afford on Celeste.

"You might save a lot of energy if you stopped that, Zan."

Tillman gave her an irritated look.

"Stopped what?"

"Pacing like a caged predator, looking for some way to make the Marengo operation succeed where Garonne failed. Federation Special Forces called in at President Verrill's request ended the Garonne insurrection, or at least that's what Siana Bailo maintains. But they don't know about Marengo because it hasn't spun up yet. So relax and enjoy the trip."

Tillman dropped into a plush chair across from her, ran his hands through his thick hair, and said, "Okay. I'm relaxing, but pacing helps me think. You know that."

She smiled at him.

"Yet I still think the entire enterprise is ill-advised, Zan. Let it go. You experienced defeat on Garonne. Take the loss and move on."

He glowered at her, but Artemis Ferran's serene smile never wavered. She'd been his confidential adviser and sometime lover for over twenty years, and she knew Tillman better than he did himself. He was a driven man who, once he sunk his teeth into a problem, didn't let go until he was satisfied, and to hell with anyone or anything that got in his way. Tillman became extremely wealthy because of his ability to zero in on the essential things and exploit them to the utmost.

Yet this desire to create havoc on Celeste's former colonies to avenge his financial losses was out of character. She wondered again, as she had so often in the last year, what the high-ranking federal official who'd visited him discussed behind closed doors. Tillman steadfastly refused to talk about it. But his obsession with Garonne and

Marengo had started shortly afterward. And nothing Ferran said could change his mind.

"Defeated?" Tillman shrugged irritably. "It's merely a setback. We didn't bargain on a Special Forces unit showing up so early in the game and ruthlessly eliminating our players. It won't happen again. I fully intend on a second try at Garonne, a successful one this time. But first, I must ensure the Marengo operation goes off without a hitch."

"Why, Zan?"

"Why what? Making sure Marengo works or trying Garonne again?"

"Both."

"We've already had this conversation, Artemis. I don't intend to rehash the subject." Tillman looked away, jaw muscles working.

"And I still think you're tempting fate by pursuing your obsession with vengeance."

He held up his hand.

"Enough."

***

"Sir?"

Andreas Bauchan, Director General of the *Sécurité Spéciale,* looked up from the workstation's virtual display at his chief of staff, Edouard Metivier, who stood in the doorway to his office at the agency's headquarters, north of Geneva, near Cessy.

"Yes?"

"We just received an operational immediate from our agent embedded in Zan Tillman's staff. The mercenaries Tillman hired to cause trouble on Garonne arrived back on Celeste and reported their defeat. A few hours later, he decided to head for Marengo aboard his yacht *Manticore*."

Bauchan sat back in his chair, eyes on Metivier.

"What does Tillman think he's playing at?"

"I suspect after the failure on Garonne, he decided to get involved personally so he can ensure success on Marengo. It would be his style, based on his personality profile."

"I suppose we always knew about the risk of our intermediaries taking too personal an interest in the activities they were sponsoring."

"There's certainly nothing we can do about it, sir. Tillman's field executive, a former Marine by the name of Avram Meltes, controls the assets on Marengo. Since we have no influence on him, we'll have to let it play out and see what happens."

"Still, if the Federation apprehends Tillman, that will suggest Commonwealth involvement, even if it is through private means, and could increase tensions. Yet, as you said, we can't do anything to stop him. Let's hope he sees sense and backs off. Or if he doesn't, we can always pray his intervention lights up a conflagration on Marengo that'll destabilize the entire sector."

***

"Curtis is pursuing Tillman to Marengo?" Talyn frowned. "That means, of course, Tillman's got something going there we don't know about yet. And that my agents are still trying to figure out."

"I reckoned Marengo was too quiet lately. The guerrillas didn't disappear after all — they've simply been lying low in recent years and building their strength. And to think the Corps sent the last battalion of the 14th Marines home shortly after Marengo made its unilateral declaration of independence right before we seceded, leaving nothing but the Marengo Militia. Or I suppose it's a National Guard now and larger than when we were there, chasing after Ari Redmon. But I seem to recall the guerrillas being pretty nasty when I briefly served there with the Marine Light Infantry."

"The star system's government has decided to take care of its own security issues rather than depend on the Federation, which is commendable."

Decker chuckled.

"Marengo is a frontier world that would go fully autonomous if it weren't for the Shrehari Empire looming beyond the Rim Sector and the Protectorate Zone criminal organizations, looking for ways of taking over legitimate worlds. If you'll recall, the fine citizens of Marengo are not only ruggedly individualistic and inclined to view independence as an absolute, but they're also almost obnoxiously so. A large faction, even in the government, would prefer if they charted their own course, separate from the Federation. I suppose it results from years of nastiness caused by the Commonwealth and Celeste governments to keep the star system off balance and dependent on others."

"Want to come work with me?" Talyn gave him a sly smile. "Because your assessment is right on target. I always figured you'd make a good senior-level analyst."

"I'll leave the political analysis to my daughter, thank you very much."

"What do we have that we can send to Marengo fast?"

Decker grimaced.

"Nothing that would arrive before or at the same time as Curtis. I suppose we could send the 1st MLI. It's at twenty-four-hour notice to move, and *Gondolier* is in orbit right now. But even at best speed, it would get there several days after *Iolanthe* and Tillman's ship."

"Is Lora Cyone still in command of the 1st?"

He nodded.

"Yes."

"She has experience fighting guerrillas on Marengo."

"True. Alright, I'll send the 1st MLI to give Ghost Squadron some backup, just in case things spin out of control. After all, that's why we brought the six MLI battalions into SOCOM and trained them as Tier Two SOF units. You just alert your agents that my people are on their way."

***

"Lora! How's my favorite light infantry officer?" Decker beamed at the craggy-faced woman with short silver hair when she appeared on his office display.

"Why do I get the feeling you're about to rain on my parade, General, sir?" She replied with a straight face, though merriment danced in her eyes.

She and Decker had been lovers many years earlier before he started working with Hera Talyn, and they still had a soft spot for each other.

"You, my friend, are returning to your past misdeeds. The 1st Battalion is hereby alerted and will ship out aboard *Gondolier* tomorrow at this time, headed for Marengo."

Cyone's eyes widened slightly.

"Marengo? I hadn't heard the rebels there were back in action."

"They're not — yet. But we suspect they will be shortly. Or at least someone will begin something nasty." Decker went on to describe what happened on Garonne, Tillman's involvement, and his heading for Marengo with Ghost Squadron on his tail. "We think Tillman will stir up more trouble than the Marengo National Guard can handle."

"The guerrillas were tough bastards back in the day, something you'd have found out firsthand if you hadn't absconded with Ari Redmon almost as soon as you showed up. You still owe me for going AWOL."

Decker grinned at her.

"It was for a good cause, Lora."

"I know. I've heard a lot about the Black Sword mess from Josh and the others involved. You sure led an interesting life after we said goodbye on Parth."

"And it ain't over yet. I'll send you your orders before sixteen hundred today, but essentially, you'll be under Curtis' command once you arrive."

"Fair enough."

"Have fun, Lora."

A wicked smile spread across her seamed face.

"Oh, I most certainly intend to. This could well be my last deployment as battalion commander. Any idea where I'm going next?"

"Yep. You're coming to SOCOM HQ as one of my staff planners."

Cyone's face twisted into an expression of mock disgust. "What fun!"

"Look at it on the bright side. We'll be working together again."

A wistful air replaced the mock disgust.

"Yet it won't be like before."

"No. But we've both moved on since those days."

— Thirty-Two —

Iolanthe dropped out of FTL halfway to Marengo, near a Federation interstellar subspace array, and queried it for messages, as per standard operating procedures.

"Got one for you, Curtis," Ardross said as Delgado entered the bridge, summoned by the officer of the watch.

"Did you get anything?"

"No." Ardross grinned. "But then, you're the mission commander."

Delgado sat at an unoccupied workstation and decoded the message.

"SOCOM acknowledges we're en route to Marengo, pursuing Tillman. They sent the 1st Battalion, Marine Light Infantry, aboard *Gondolier* to back us up. They should arrive a day or two after we do."

"Are the bosses expecting the sort of trouble Ghost Squadron can't handle alone?"

"They're not telling me much other than the guerrillas have been quiescent since secession but could still be a force in being, nonetheless. Naval Intelligence recently dispatched agents to Marengo to figure out what was happening. We'll contact them — or rather Miko will do so — the moment we're in orbit. I have the node coordinates. But the fact they've sent undercover operatives and now the MLI means they think this might be something more than just a routine op against a bad guy from Celeste."

"Any response required?"

"No. The automatic receipt showing we downloaded the message is enough. You can go FTL anytime you want, and the sooner, the better. Tillman is unlikely to have dropped out of hyperspace."

"Once the drives have cycled and we jump again, I'll push the highest hyperspace bands I can in this ship. But I think we'll still arrive before *Manticore*, even with our brief stop to pick up the mail."

And it turned out that Ardross was right. When *Iolanthe*, once again concealing her true identity as the tramp freighter *Freya*, arrived in Marengo orbit, Tillman's ship was nowhere to be found. Traffic control, operating from the Valeux orbital station, assigned them a parking orbit but asked no questions about their business on Marengo, which suited Ardross just fine.

Once they settled in to wait for *Manticore*, Steiger sent a brief missive to the node indicated in the message from SOCOM, opening a line with her Naval Intelligence colleagues, and waited as well. Twelve hours later, just after she received a reply with instructions for an in-person meeting in Treves, Marengo's capital, Tillman's ship entered orbit.

"Put a bead on *Manticore*, Chief." Ardross took the CIC's command chair and turned his eyes on the primary display which showed the megayacht in her full splendor as she orbited a few thousand kilometers behind *Iolanthe* but at roughly the same altitude. "And keep it there. I want to know about the slightest thing she does, even if it's just venting her sublight drive tubes."

"Aye, aye, sir," Chief Rasmussen replied.

"Sir," the operations petty officer raised his hand. "The shuttle carrying Colonel Delgado, Chief Warrant Officer Nunes, and Chief Warrant Officer Steiger to Treves is departing now."

"Excellent, thanks." Ardross sat back with a contented smile on his face. Everything was proceeding as planned.

For now.

***

Delgado, Nunes, and Steiger, dressed in casual civilian clothes, sat silently in the unmarked shuttle's passenger compartment, each lost in their thoughts. Steiger wasn't thrilled Delgado had decided he and Nunes would accompany her to the meeting with the Naval Intelligence operatives in a hole-in-the-wall diner on the outskirts of Treves. But she conceded it would probably be quicker if he were to speak directly with them rather than rely on Steiger as an intermediary.

The shuttle landed at the executive end of the Treves spaceport, where the wealthy park their air and spacecraft. They found an autotaxi on the other side of the executive terminal and climbed aboard. Steiger gave it the address of the diner, and they sped off.

When they entered the place, which wasn't nearly as cozy as they'd expected, Steiger in the lead, a dark-haired man sitting in a booth with an equally dark-haired woman raised a hand, and Steiger headed for them.

"How are you doing?" She asked, sliding into the booth next to the man.

"Fine," he replied. "I see you brought friends."

"Curtis Delgado and Jake Nunes."

The man cocked an eyebrow at her. "The ghostly Delgado?"

"Yep, and his data man."

"In that case, welcome." He gestured at the remaining seats in the booth. "I'm Valin, and my friend here is Areta. We're from the same outfit as Miko but on the blue side."

"How long have you been here?" Steiger asked.

"Two weeks. Pardon me." Valin pulled out a small, flat object the size of a playing card, thumbed a corner, and then stared intently at its surface for a few seconds. "There. My jammer's activated. No one can understand us now."

Steiger smirked and pulled its twin from her pocket.

"We had coverage all along."

"Well, then," Valin smirked back at her, "Colonel Delgado, a pleasure to make your acquaintance. Your reputation precedes you in black ops circles. I'm Valin Komo, and she's Areta Dorack."

"Likewise. And this is Chief Warrant Officer Jake Nunes, Ghost Squadron's intelligence officer."

Valin Komo nodded at Nunes.

"Pleasure, Jake. Now, I figure you're here because you want to know what's happening, right?"

Delgado grinned at him.

"Can't hide anything from you, Valin. Must be because you're a spook."

He quickly explained about events on Garonne, Tillman's involvement, his sudden departure from Celeste, and his arrival at Marengo, leading to the suspicion he intended to make sure the rebellion here would succeed.

"Are there any reports or rumors about the guerrillas reawakening after being put out of business a few years ago?"

Komo stroked his beard with a thoughtful air.

"It's funny that you ask because that's what we were assigned to investigate here. And we've discovered that no rebels are waiting for the right moment. At least not the homegrown sort. But it seems like a few hundred off-world mercenaries are sitting around, waiting for something."

"No offense, and not that I doubt you, but how did you find out?"

"No offense taken, mate. I'm careful of my sources as well. You see, we've been investigating rumors that an abandoned Marine base a few hundred kilometers south of here, a place called Sinjin, and tens of thousands of hectares surrounding it were bought by a private corporation last year. The purchaser said nothing about the use they'd make of it all, but apparently, several hundred men and women are now living on the old base."

"And how did you come across those rumors?"

"We knew the zone around Sinjin was the locus of the rebels back in the day, and we sniffed around the various towns and villages surrounding the area. We were promptly informed about the enigmatic sale of the abandoned Marine Corps base. From there, we investigated further, but hearing about the several hundred occupants was as far as we got." He grinned. "And then you showed up. It shouldn't be difficult to check on the place from your ship in orbit. We'll give you the coordinates."

"Is the Marengo government interested in what's going on there? Or do they not know or care?"

"No idea. Yet running a large compound full of private military contractors isn't exactly against the law in the Federation."

"Sure. Until they begin operating against any lawful government."

"But until they make an illegal move, you can't do anything against them. Hell, they might not even be interested in creating chaos on Marengo. Sinjin might just be a staging base for an operation in the Protectorate Zone, where PMCs can run as wild as they want."

Delgado nodded.

"True."

"And even if your Tillman visits them, so long as they remain quiet, they're not a target."

The Marine grinned.

"Listen to the special ops spook telling me about restraint."

Komo smiled back.

"As I mentioned, I am aware of your reputation, special ops Marine. You like to get the tangos before they know you're there and don't leave any evidence of your actions."

"That almost sounds like Ghost Squadron's unofficial motto."

"Perhaps, but it might also lead to a happy trigger finger."

Delgado raised both hands in surrender.

"No worries, mate. We'll wait for the mercs to make the first move. I'm not authorized to hit a target without ensuring it's legitimate. But once I determine it is…" Delgado's grin widened, and his eyes took on a manic expression as he drew a thumb across his throat.

"Okay, wise guy," Komo said, chuckling. "What do you want us to look for?"

"Keep sniffing around the place and listen for any signs that there may be movement in the background. We'll put Sinjin under surveillance from orbit and wait."

— Thirty-Three —

"A shuttle departed from *Manticore* and headed toward the surface while you were there," Ardross said as soon as Delgado entered the CIC after returning from Treves. "It landed in a place—"

"That used to be called Marine Base Sinjin." Delgado winked at Ardross as he took his accustomed seat.

"Precisely. You got that from the Naval Intelligence agents?"

"Yep. About a year ago, unknown parties purchased the old base and a large portion of the surrounding area, and now it appears that Sinjin is home to several hundred people. You got a lock on the place?"

"Of course. Chief, bring up the target area."

"Aye, aye, sir."

"I had a few satellites deployed, so we now have continuous surveillance on the target."

"Excellent."

As Delgado watched, the overhead image of what had clearly once been a military installation appeared on the

CIC's primary display. It had been built from an insta-base kit, containers dropped from orbit filled with everything needed to set up a functioning installation in twenty-four hours, the emptied containers serving as building shells. The structures were set in even, orderly rows and columns, with wide streets between them, and the base was surrounded by an earthen berm topped with barbed wire and sensors. A chicane cut through the berm, giving access, while the fields beyond were cleared of vegetation, out to a kilometer, preventing anyone from approaching unseen.

"This is real time?" Delgado asked as he noted the tiny figures of human beings moving about with purpose. Everyone seemed to be wearing a dark uniform of some sort, along with tactical gear, and most of them carried weapons.

"Yes. If you'll look to the base's northwest corner, you'll see the shuttle sitting on the pad. Two people came out of it, one being Tillman, the other a female. Both wore the same uniform and black tactical gear as the base's inhabitants."

Delgado chuckled.

"Tillman's playing dress up, is he? Do we have any idea who the woman is?"

"Not a clue."

"How many life signs are you reading, Chief?"

"Four-hundred and twenty-seven."

Delgado let out a low whistle.

"That's a short battalion. Thank the Almighty SOCOM is sending the 1st MLI. Otherwise, the odds would have been too even for my taste. I prefer having an overwhelming advantage." He shook his head. "You can do a lot of damage with over four hundred trained personnel, even if they are private military contractors. I'll bet there are enough ex-regulars in the ranks to make it a tough proposition for adversaries."

"Such as the Marengo National Guard?" Ardross asked.

"If the folks down there decide to operate in full guerrilla mode, the Marengonians won't know what hit them, at least for the first few attacks. I mean, how many full-timers are in the Guard? A few thousand, with the vast majority being part-time? No, the mercs hold a distinct advantage in the short term."

"And long term?"

"That's up in the air." Delgado made a face. "Unless and until we can find out more about those PMCs, I can't tell you whether they have a chance in hell of keeping the Guard chasing its own tail after they open the ball."

"So now what?"

"We keep watching until they do something illegal. Then, we pounce."

And so, for the next day and a half, the sensors recorded every second of life in the former base and its immediate surroundings, but the only thing they saw were mercenaries training. They'd established an extensive shooting range, several close combat galleries, a lengthy obstacle course, and field problem areas. By every appearance, they could have been regulars. Even Tillman and the woman accompanying him took part.

The Q ship *Gondolier* arrived shortly after that, carrying five hundred troopers of the 1st Battalion, Marine Light Infantry.

"Hey, Lora!" Delgado's trademark grin split his face when Cyone appeared on the CIC's primary display. "How are tricks?"

Smiling back, she said, "Hi Curtis. Tell me you have a target and a plan of attack. I was told by General Decker, in not so many words, just before we left that this was my last kick at some action before I join the staff in Sanctum."

Delgado grimaced theatrically.

"You have my deepest sympathies, buddy. And to answer your question, we're waiting for the supposed opposition to make a move."

He briefed Cyone on the events leading to them orbiting Marengo.

When he finished, she made a face.

"Sounds like this Tillman has a hornet up his ass."

"He certainly has something somewhere, but we wait until the mercs commit an illegal act."

"Let's hope it's not too long. Five hundred of us cooped up in a Q ship gets overly snug at times. And there's only so much parkour you can do before the squids get annoyed." She let out a brief chuckle. "Sinjin, eh? That brings back memories. It was the battalion's main base when I had recon platoon years ago. There are still plenty of folks in the 1st who were with the unit back then, so it's not *terra incognita* for us. Which makes me wonder why we don't simply drop in on them, take Tillman into custody, and warn the mercs that at the slightest illegal act, they'll get put out of business by the Federation Marine Corps. Permanently."

"Don't think I didn't contemplate it, but I get the feeling Tillman owns the PMC, and they could fight to keep him free. Heck, they might even be conditioned for loyalty. It could quickly turn into a bloodbath, and I'd rather not have any of my troopers get killed for the sake of taking the skunk. When they make a move, we'll do what we do best — wallop 'em and vanish. With you here, it seriously reduces the risk of us taking casualties, and that's how I like things."

"Okay. Fair enough. I suppose I'm still influenced by the old MLI thinking — damn the casualties, let's just do it."

Delgado chuckled.

"The MLI has become valuable enough that simply throwing lives away isn't on the menu anymore. And that's how it should be."

Cyone sighed.

"Perhaps my joining the SOCOM staff after this mission is for the best. It's time we relics from another era left command of the MLI to the younger generation who are less imbued with the old ethos of victory at any cost."

"Don't be too hard on yourself, Lora. You've had life experiences most of us couldn't visualize in our worst nightmares, and that shapes a mind's way of thinking."

She gave Delgado a rueful smile.

"Fine. Enough of venturing along that particular path. How will we find out when and where Tillman intends to strike so we can prevent him from doing so?"

"That's the sixty million cred question, isn't it? My intelligence officer is conducting an open-source scan of Marengo, its notables, and upcoming events to form a picture of anything that could attract Tillman's attention. We know his goal is causing havoc, the more, the better, to punish Marengo for the losses he suffered and not coincidentally further destabilize the Rim Sector on behalf of the Commonwealth government, more particularly the *Sécurité Spéciale*. So it'll be something big, perhaps a single strike that'll upend the entire planet."

"With a little over four hundred mercs? Doesn't seem like he's got that much firepower."

"Depends on their quality and the vulnerability of the target."

"And what will they do to escape afterward? They can't take over the government or destroy the entire National Guard and the police. Unless Tillman intends to dispose of them once they've accomplished their mission."

"That's something we don't know just yet, although I'd say Tillman's megayacht is big enough to transport the lot of them, albeit in austere conditions in the cargo bays. They'd just need to hold ground long enough for shuttles to pick them up."

***

Zan Tillman wore a satisfied smile as he watched a platoon of his mercenaries go through their paces in one of the shooting galleries. He and Artemis Ferran wore the same black uniforms as the troopers, including the brimmed field cap, but no tactical harnesses this time.

"Aren't they magnificent, Artemis?" He asked in a relaxed tone. "I'll bet they could measure up to any Federation Special Forces unit."

Ferran, who didn't find the mercs as impressive as her boss did, shrugged.

"Realistically, I wouldn't take that bet, Zan. Don't get me wrong. They're extremely good. Better than the Marengo National Guard full-timers and almost as good as any Marine infantry battalion, but Special Forces, they're not. Nor do they need to be for this mission."

"Oh, I think you take skepticism a bit too far, my dear. All of them are battle-hardened men and women, with most having fought in the Protectorate alongside different organizations in recent years. I should know. I hired every single one myself to create the Varangian Guard as my very own private military unit." The pride in his voice was unmistakable.

Ferran's expression didn't change, although she thought once again that the grandiose name, which was taken from an elite unit of the Byzantine Empire consisting mainly of Norse mercenaries known for their fearlessness in battle, was a bit much. But she couldn't resist needling him.

"Maybe if you'd used them on Garonne, the outcome would have been different."

Tillman gave her a sideways glance.

"Perhaps, but then who would I have used here? There aren't enough unhappy deportees on Marengo to create a critical mass of insurgents, and splitting my Varangians up between both worlds would have been even worse. Once we've taken care of Marengo, I'll redeploy them to Garonne, and this time, President Verrill will lose."

Ferran held her tongue. He'd always had a blind spot where his beloved Varangian Guard was concerned, and nothing she said would change his opinion of them. She supposed Tillman suffered from a touch of hubris, which wasn't surprising, considering he was one of the wealthiest human beings in all creation. So long as his hubris didn't lead to nemesis…

"When will you share your plan for victory with us?"

"In good time, Artemis." Tillman spotted a man approach out of the corner of his eyes. "Ah, Droungarios Meltes. Your troopers are performing magnificently."

Ferran did everything possible to not roll her eyes at Tillman's use of the ancient Byzantine rank for a battalion commander. Meltes, on the other hand, seemed to take it in stride and saluted, a gesture Tillman returned.

"Sir."

Avram Meltes was a former Commonwealth Marine Corps major who got into trouble when he brutalized prisoners his unit had taken during a minor revolt on a Rim Sector world and took early retirement rather than face a court martial. But since he wasn't one to hang up his gun belt, Meltes headed for the Protectorate Zone and joined a

PMC operating there. He quickly gained prominence through his unflinching ruthlessness, and when Tillman created his Varangian Guard, Meltes was at the top of the list as a candidate for commanding officer.

Broad, muscular, with an impassive, square face, short gray hair, and a deep voice, he cut an imposing figure. His dark eyes, however, chilled Ferran to the core every time she gazed into them because there was nothing within, no soul.

But then, that's probably why Tillman got along so well with Meltes. He didn't have a soul either, and Ferran repressed a shiver at the thought of what Tillman could and would do to advance any cause he espoused. She'd seen it often enough during her years as his principal adviser.

"Soon, Droungarios, your people will prove their worth."

"I look forward to it, sir." Meltes' voice was as flat and emotionless as his gaze.

— Thirty-Four —

"What do you have for me, Warrant?" Delgado waved at Nunes to enter his cabin and take the other available chair across the tiny desk from where he sat.

"A few possibilities, sir, but only one that fits. We're assuming Tillman wants to strike at the star system government rather than its economic infrastructure, which is too dispersed for the sort of effect we think he wants. He won't stay here forever and run a guerrilla war, which was likely the mercenaries' initial mission."

Delgado nodded.

"Makes sense."

"The government installations have minimal security these days, what with the insurgents having gone dormant or disappeared altogether. It's mostly the Marengo Gendarmerie, which protects the important elements — the prime minister, the cabinet, the National Assembly, the Supreme Court, and a few others."

"Okay."

"The biggest political event that'll happen this year is the opening of the Fourth National Assembly since independence, which occurs in nine days, seeing as how the elections happened a month ago. Every member of the Assembly will attend, including cabinet members and the prime minister, as well as the Supreme Court justices, the permanent deputy ministers, and the heads of the National Guard and the Gendarmerie. They'll sit in the Assembly's main hall for about an hour or so while the prime minister speaks about his program for the next four years."

Delgado's eyebrows crept up.

"The entire senior leadership of the star system in one confined space? Sounds like a hell of a target for disruption. What are the security arrangements?"

Nunes grimaced.

"There's not much available through open sources. The best I could do was to gather whatever information was available on other openings of the National Assembly, and only the previous one took place after the insurgency subsided and the 14th Marines departed. But based on it, the Gendarmerie will be out in force providing close protection and internal perimeter security while the National Guard will patrol the external perimeter. They'll also deploy aerospace defense domes to protect against any overhead risks. In theory, it should be enough deterrence against anyone wanting to play silly buggers, including insurgents."

"But not a battalion of highly trained mercenaries who probably count a lot of ex-regulars in their ranks."

"No, sir. Especially not if they can approach unnoticed until the last minute, or better yet, infiltrate a few of their people among the spectators — because there is room for them, as well as a giant outdoor display on the National Assembly's front lawn to accommodate those who can't get inside." Nunes hesitated. "Will you warn the Marengo government?"

Delgado frowned in thought.

"What more security can they put on the National Assembly than they will already have if you're right?"

"Not much. But we or the 1st MLI could add to that."

"I'm not sure the Marengonians will want the assistance of Federation Marines, especially since we're only talking about a mere four hundred mercenaries. Based on their experience during the insurgency, they'll discount the threat, notwithstanding the fact these mercs look like a very different breed from the usual kind. If you'll recall the intelligence brief we got from SOCOM, Marengonians are bloody-minded folk who'll figure they can handle it and deny us landing rights. After all, there's a powerful faction within the ruling party who'd have liked full independence from both the Commonwealth and the Federation instead of joining the latter upon secession."

Nunes scoffed.

"Bloody-minded is right. But then, the last Fleet intervention on Marengo didn't go that well, to begin with, the 1st MLI's sterling results notwithstanding. Okay, sir. We keep stumm about being in orbit and continue watching, ready to pounce as necessary."

"And now we need to develop a few contingency plans for the day in question." Delgado climbed to his feet. "We'd better do that in the conference room since we'll need Wash and Metellus."

"There's one thing that still bothers me about the setup below," Nunes said as they headed down the corridor to pick up Major Tesser and Chief Warrant Officer Testo.

"Oh? What's that?"

"Where are the insurgents? They simply faded away after Marengo became a sovereign star system, and yet those insurgents were probably backed by the *Sécurité Spéciale*. If Tillman is acting on their behalf, wouldn't he or they have done something to revive the insurgency? Or did they completely vanish?"

"Good question. Unfortunately, neither I nor Naval Intelligence have any idea."

***

"We will destroy the Marengo National Assembly during the prime minister's speech opening it for the fourth sitting." Tillman gave Ferran and Meltes a faint smile as he raised his wine glass to his lips. "Which will eliminate the entirety of the star system's senior leadership and throw it into the sort of turmoil that hasn't been seen since the Second Migration War."

They were in Tillman's sitting room, part of the VIP suite he occupied on Base Sinjin, a name he'd kept when he bought the installation and the surrounding land.

"And how will we do that, sir?" Meltes asked in his flat tone. "Considering the level of protection it'll get, what with all the notables inside. Unless you're contemplating a suicide mission for my Varangians."

"I wouldn't destroy a fine unit just like that, Droungarios. No, I have plans for the Varangians that don't involve getting them killed." Tillman took another sip of wine, eyes on Meltes while Ferran suppressed a sigh at her employer drawing out his announcement. He had a tendency to do so when he'd come to a momentous decision.

"Then how, sir?"

"Have you ever heard of MHX-19?"

Meltes frowned as he combed through his memory, then his eyes lit up. "You mean Mayhem?"

"Mayhem?"

"It's what we called the stuff in the Corps. Stands for the long version of the name — maximum yield high explosive mixture. Does this mean you have some?"

Tillman nodded with an air of smug satisfaction. "I have a few kilograms, enough to flatten the National Assembly and kill everyone inside."

"How did you get hold of the Mayhem? It's the most controlled substance in the universe. The Fleet doesn't just hand it out to anyone."

"I've had it for a while. Let's just say it came to me via a circuitous route and was part of a larger chunk stolen from a pre-secession Fleet ammunition depot. I suspect most of it was eventually retrieved by Naval Intelligence and used to utterly destroy Amali Island on Pacifica several years ago. The attack killed most of the Coalition members meeting there so they could discuss the latest failure on Cimmeria. Fortunately for me, I wasn't on the island that evening. I had business with ComCorp in Hadley and decided to stay overnight instead of returning and joining the party."

Ferran remembered that day only too well. She and Tillman had left Pacifica aboard *Manticore* only hours after the news of the devastating explosion spread. They wanted to put as many lightyears between themselves and the perpetrators as possible. Ever since the Coalition's virtual elimination, Tillman had kept the Centralists at a distance, preferring to act on his own in the pursuit of centralizing political power on Earth.

"That's quite a story, sir. But I don't understand how you'll plant the Mayhem, so it collapses the National Assembly on everyone's head. They'll be watching every square millimeter of the precinct between now and the end of the opening ceremony. You'll never get a few kilos inside ahead of time."

"No worries. I intend to deliver the MHX-19 while the Assembly is in session. Remember, it doesn't take much of it to scour a square kilometer, so we only need to get those few kilos of the stuff close enough. And I've come up with the ideal solution. Remember, the Marengonians won't be expecting an attack, and that's what I'm counting on." A smile appeared on Tillman's lips as he explained how he'd get the explosives in place.

"And once the star system's government is gone, you'll begin attacking key installations to collapse the planet's infrastructure. We will turn this place into a pit of anarchy where people end up fighting each other for survival."

— Thirty-Five —

When the day of the National Assembly's opening dawned, both Ghost Squadron and the 1st MLI were ready to move. They sat on their respective ship's hangar deck, fully dressed in armor and armed with live ammunition. The shuttle pilots, also dressed for battle, hung around with the Marine troopers, shooting the breeze.

Delgado had briefed everyone on the three contingency plans named Plan Alpha, Bravo, and Charlie. It meant they were ready to launch at ninety seconds notice — the hangar decks' inner airlocks were already shut, and the control room was staffed. Waiting in full armor wasn't the most comfortable thing, but everyone knew the stakes were high.

Something was stirring inside Base Sinjin and had been since the previous evening. The mercenaries moved with greater purpose and a quicker pace. That morning, vehicles had emerged from the hangars, forty-five vans, each capable of carrying at least a section. They looked innocuous from orbit, but something told Delgado they were military-grade under the skin, armored and equipped with hidden weapons stations.

At seven-thirty, local time, the mercenaries, in full fighting order, lined up in front of the vans. Ten minutes later, the tiny figures climbed aboard and they drove out in three packets of fifteen, with five minutes between packets.

"That looks like almost all of them, sir," the sensor chief said over his shoulder at Delgado. "I'm picking up a few life signs in the hangars and the old operations center."

"Any idea whether Tillman was among the troopers who left?"

"Not a clue, sir. If he was in full fig we wouldn't have been able to spot him, and everyone who boarded those vehicles wore armor and helmets."

"We'll have to assume he's in the operations center, then." Delgado took a seat and let his fingers drum on the workstation's surface as he thought.

So far, the mercenaries hadn't broken any laws and for all he knew, they were simply exercising a road move. He couldn't even tell whether they carried live ammunition for their personal and crew served weapons. Still, after a while it became clear they were headed in the direction of Treves rather than sticking to the local roads and Delgado knew he had to make a go no-go decision soon, considering the time it took to reach the surface and deploy.

"What do you reckon, sir?" Nunes asked Delgado as both of them watching the three part convoy wend its way toward Treves at a constant speed and with unvarying intervals between vehicles and packets. Delgado had to admire the discipline they showed. It was professional level. "Do you think we misjudged it and they're just training?"

Delgado shook his head.

"My instincts tell me no, Jake. But I still can't figure out how they'll do it, considering the security around the National Assembly."

They continued observing the convoy in silence until the sensor chief raised his hand

"Sir."

Delgado and the CIC officer of the watch turned their heads toward him in perfect synchronization.

"Yes?" The latter said.

"Something high-powered just lit up in one of the hangars." A red dot appeared over one of the large buildings on the display.

"A shuttle, perhaps?" Delgado asked.

"We should find out any second now, sir. It's moving."

A few heartbeats later, the small boxy shape of a black shuttle emerged. It hovered in place for a moment, then slowly rose, pushed up vertically by its belly thrusters until it reached a height of one hundred meters, after which its upward motion changed to a forward vector, and it accelerated away.

In the direction of Treves.

"Sir, I'm not picking up any life signs aboard the shuttle," the sensor chief said. "It's either being remotely piloted or is under AI control."

"Which makes me wonder what its mission is." Delgado's face settled into a frown. "The National Guard's aerospace defense domes will ensure that shuttle doesn't come near the National Assembly."

"Sir, a second shuttle powered up and is emerging from the hangar. No life signs aboard it either."

Delgado sat up just as Commander Ardross entered the CIC, alerted by the officer of the watch that something was happening below. He took the command chair while the OOW quickly briefed him in a low tone.

"Okay. Let's try this on for size," Delgado said. "The first shuttle is armed with hypervelocity missiles and tasked to take out the aerospace defense domes. Once they're gone, the second is free to attack the National Assembly building."

Ardross nodded.

"Makes eminent sense."

The shuttle lifted off and followed its mate toward the capital but flew nap of the earth instead of a hundred meters above the treetops. "Would you like me to take them out while they're flying over an uninhabited area?"

Delgado considered the proposal briefly and gave a nod.

"You might as well. Since there are no life signs aboard, we can't be accused of wantonly killing people because they might present a threat."

Ardross issued orders to the gunnery chief, who replied, "I already have a lock on both targets, sir, and can shoot whenever you wish."

"Very well. Fire at them, Chief."

Two hypervelocity missiles left *Iolanthe*'s launchers, one from the port side, the other from the starboard side. They accelerated to Mach 9, heading for the two shuttles that were flying at a leisurely speed lest they arrive in Treves too early. Neither of the missiles carried a warhead and relied solely on the force of their impact to destroy the targets, even hardened ones like space shuttles.

Silence settled over the CIC as everyone waited for the moment of impact. The primary display now showed a split image, with the first shuttle on the left and the second on the right. Beneath them were hundreds of square kilometers of untamed, primeval forest, but they'd be coming over the inhabited areas soon.

The first strike, disintegrating the lead shuttle, came as a complete surprise as it turned into a small ball of debris that tumbled to the ground. The second target's destruction, however, left everyone speechless. A blinding flash of light replaced the shuttle, and the display's modulator kicked in to dampen the brightness. When it faded away a few seconds later, both the small spacecraft and any shred of vegetation on the ground for a kilometer had vanished, the earth scoured to the bedrock.

"Holy hell, what was that?" Delgado was the first to regain his voice.

"Checking," the sensor chief replied. The view on the display zoomed out, and the sensor chief replayed the moment of detonation. "It wasn't nuclear. There's no radiation, and the shape of the explosion is wrong."

"Antimatter, then?"

"Possibly, sir. But the visual signature isn't quite right." The chief tapped his chin with an extended index finger for a bit, then said, in a grave tone, "It could have been MHX-19, also known as Mayhem."

"Mayhem?" Both Delgado and Ardross repeated the word simultaneously.

"How the hell would Tillman have got hold of the most restricted explosive compound in the known universe?" The former asked. "As far as I know, it's held only in a handful of munition depots, all of them on OutWorlds and therefore beyond the Commonwealth's reach. Besides, they greatly increased security around the substance after a fair chunk of it went walkabout several years ago. We'd have heard about it if more had gone missing since then. And they would have probably sent us on a recovery mission."

"If this explosion was caused by MHX-19, could it have come from the block that disappeared?" Ardross asked.

Delgado's forehead furrowed in contemplation.

"I don't know, but General Decker and Admiral Talyn might. They were involved in recovering part of it when both worked undercover for Naval Intelligence's Special Operations Division. I've heard rumors around the Regiment they used what they recovered in a hard strike against the nasty people who had it stolen in the first place."

"Let's ask them. In the meantime, it's pretty clear that whoever sent those shuttles intended to cause harm. The force of the explosion would likely have been enough to vaporize the National Assembly and most of the central government precinct, killing thousands of innocent people and throwing the star system into utter chaos. What do you intend?"

Delgado gave Ardross a half smile.

"I figure we now have enough evidence to stop the convoy, seize Sinjin, take everyone into custody, and shoot those who resist."

He stood.

"I'll need to activate Plan Delta."

"We don't have a Plan Delta, sir," Nunes said.

"That's right. Which means drafting it up on the fly because those mercs will know someone destroyed their shuttles. Hell, everyone within two hundred kilometers of the Mayhem explosion is now aware something bad happened." Delgado briefly glanced at Ardross. "I'm taking Ghost Squadron to stop the vehicles and sending 1st MLI to Sinjin as soon as I get my armor on. Be prepared to launch rods from God on call if they fight back."

"Will do, Curtis. Good luck."

"I don't need luck, Keever. I just need to be fast and hit them before they have a chance to think things through. And you should consider boarding *Manticore* for a routine inspection and maintaining control of her until we finish."

***

"What happened?" An alarmed Tillman asked the operations officer as the links to both shuttles vanished, and a faint rumble reached their ears in the base's operations center.

"In my opinion, sir," the man replied after a moment's reflection, "the MHX-19 might have gone off prematurely."

"The shuttles are definitely off the air," the operations noncom said, staring at blank workstation displays. "No carrier signal, nothing."

"What if we simply lost contact? Will they carry out their primary mission?"

The officer shook his head.

"No. If they lose contact with the controller, they'll return to their point of origin. It's a failsafe built into the AIs piloting them. But I think the sound we just heard was the Mayhem exploding over virgin forest."

"Then someone must have shot the shuttles down," Artemis Ferran said.

"It does seem that way."

"*Manticore* would have warned me of any naval unit arriving in Marengo orbit."

"Maybe a Q ship hit them. There are always any number of old freighters up there, and the Federation has a lot of warships disguised as tramps."

Ferran tilted her head as she frowned.

"But that must mean they've got surveillance on Sinjin if they spotted the shuttles quickly enough to blow them up before they reached inhabited areas."

The operations officer nodded.

"Indeed. And it means they've also got a bead on the convoy headed to Treves."

"In that case, we need to leave now," Tillman said.

"Not a particularly good idea. Should we attempt to evacuate, they will pursue us, and we're much more vulnerable out in the open, be it on the ground or in the air. I think we're staying right here for now."

"Do you believe they'll have figured the second shuttle carried a big load of MHX-19 and that it was aimed at the National Assembly in Treves?"

"Most assuredly, sir. I understand Mayhem has a signature distinct from that of an antimatter explosion. That we planned on crashing the shuttle into the Assembly building at a time when the star system's senior leadership was inside is an easy deduction to make once they saw the size of the detonation."

"Then what do you propose?"

The operations officer shrugged.

"Warn the CO that the operation is off and recall the Varangians headed for Treves. Then hope for the best."

"The best being?"

"That if there is a Federation Fleet Q ship in orbit, it'll let us surrender peacefully and leave."

At that moment, Tillman's communicator chimed for attention, and he unclipped it from his best.

"It's *Manticore.* I wonder if they're worried about the explosion." He flicked it on. "Tillman."

"Horner, sir. You asked to be warned if anything unusual happened in orbit."

"Yes," Tillman replied with a hint of irritation in his voice.

"Two freighters just disgorged large shuttles, one of them thirteen, the other fourteen, and they're headed straight toward the settlement zone. None of them are flashing a beacon, nor do they have any markings whatsoever, but they appear armed."

Tillman and the operations officer exchanged a glance.

The latter said, "That's more than a battalion, sir. If each of the shuttles carries a platoon, we're talking seven or eight companies."

"And," Captain Horner continued, "Two more shuttles from one of the ships are approaching us. Their crews intend to board."

— Thirty-Six —

"You will let no one in my ship, Horner."

"I may not have a choice, sir. They've just identified themselves as Federation Navy and have lit the correct beacons."

"Keep them off my ship or find yourself a new berth. Tillman, out."

The operations officer gave his employer a surprised look.

"Um, sir... The Federation Navy can board any ship within Federation space, just like the Commonwealth Navy can in our space."

"*Manticore* is Commonwealth territory and therefore out of bounds to the Federation."

"I figure they won't see it that way, sir. I know how they think. They'll board *Manticore* or destroy her. Either way, she's lost to you."

"Maybe she can fend them off. After all, she is heavily armed."

The officer let out a bark of humorless laughter.

"If two Q ships are in orbit, your yacht won't last more than ninety seconds before turning into a debris cloud. They'll have targeted her when they launched their shuttles and raised shields. No matter how heavily armed *Manticore* is, she can't fight what are effectively two cruisers beneath their disguise."

Tillman's face hardened.

"Then what do you suggest I do?"

"If you want to stay alive, surrender and cooperate with whoever is arriving aboard those shuttles."

"And if I decide we will fight?"

"Then with all due respect, sir, I shall leave the decision to the CO. He'll rule on this matter, not you. Seeing as how it's our lives that will be at risk."

***

"The convoy has split into three at the last intersection, sir, each packet taking a separate route toward Treves' outskirts," Chief Warrant Officer Testo reported. He, Nunes and Sergeant Major Hak sat at consoles in the passenger compartment and ensured contact with the Q ships and the other shuttles and kept updated on the situation below.

"How long before we're in range?"

"Just under five minutes."

Delgado, sitting behind the pilot, stared at the display showing a live aerial view of the three packets, courtesy of the geostationary satellite. After a few moments of thought, he touched the display in three places.

"I've just indicated the intercept points, designated A, B, and C. Get the Erinyes onto point A, the Keres on point B, and the Moirae on point C. They're to land a shuttle at the front and back of the packets, blocking the roadway, weapons hot and aimed at the vehicles. Keep the rest of the craft hovering overhead. Hopefully the mercs will be smart enough to surrender."

"Wilco." A few moments passed, then, "Orders transmitted and acknowledged."

"Thanks." Delgado patted the pilot on the shoulder. "We'll hover overhead as well."

"Aye, aye, sir," the petty officer at the controls replied.

Delgado barely had time to split his display into three views, one for each packet, when the lead shuttles swooped down and landed across the road, thrusters kicking in at the last minute. Their dorsal gun turrets rotated in the direct of the approaching packets. Then, the tail end shuttles dropped down behind the last vehicles, cutting off any hope of retreat.

As the packets ground to a halt, Delgado flicked on the emergency military channel in the hopes of being able to contact the convoy's commander.

"Mercenary commander, this is Lieutenant Colonel Curtis Delgado of the Federation Marine Corps aboard one of the shuttles overhead. Your convoy is under our guns. I suggest you stand down."

A few heartbeats later, a deep voice came over the emergency channel.

"This is Avram Meltes, the commanding officer of the Vangarian Guard PMC. What is your purpose?"

"Thank you for responding. My purpose is to avoid the needless loss of lives. Yours, mainly. And I'm calling so we can negotiate your surrender. As you might have noticed, my shuttles are armed and they're carrying a battalions' worth of Marines. Another battalion is on the way to Base Sinjin as we speak. You have no prospect of resisting us. I also have two starships in orbit ready to drop kinetic penetrators on you and Sinjin at my orders. So, what do you say, Avram Meltes? Are you willing to lay down your weapons, withdraw to your base and await our arrival peacefully, undertaking to offer no resistance and to obey our orders? Whatever mission you had in Treves isn't going to happen. That load of Mayhem destined for the National Assembly exploded, as you might have noticed, thanks to a hypervelocity missile from one of our ships."

"I was wondering about that, but since I received no recall order from my employer—"

"Who is listening," Tillman's angry voice cut in on the frequency.

"Mister Tillman, I presume?" Delgado asked.

"Indeed."

"May I infer you remained at the base?"

Meltes cut off any further words from Tillman, saying, "He's monitoring the mission from the operations center. We will offer no resistance and obey orders, Colonel."

"Excellent. You will return to Base Sinjin by the shortest route, where you will park your vehicles on the parade square and form up in front of them, unarmed. Make sure the people you left behind join you. And please make sure Mister Tillman doesn't go anywhere. I have a particular interest in speaking with him."

"But I will not speak with you," Tillman growled in a loud tone.

"Meltes, if he tries something stupid, your people have my permission to wing him, but try to keep him alive."

"Noted, Colonel."

"My other battalion will land at Sinjin imminently. I suggest you inform your rear party that they're to offer no resistance."

"I'm sure my operations officer is listening to our conversation, Colonel. He'll greet your other battalion and place himself under their orders."

A new voice came over the network. "Received and understood, sir."

"That was him," Meltes said.

"Glad to see you're taking this seriously," Delgado replied. "You wouldn't be former regular service, would you?"

"Commonwealth Marine Corps. I retired from the 5th Regiment as a major ten years ago."

"That explains why you catch on so quickly and why you're not disposed to make some futile gesture of resistance. We'll speak again once I'm on the ground. Now turn your convoy around. We'll accompany you back to Sinjin so no screwing around, please."

"No fears, sir."

"Glad I'm dealing with a professional. Delgado, out."

Tillman, unable to contain himself any longer, exploded.

"You simply gave up. I can't believe the commander of my Varangian Guard bared his throat and gave up."

"The Varangian Guard surrendered to a superior force, Mister Tillman. And you'll obey my operations officer. Otherwise, he'll do as Colonel Delgado suggested and wing you."

"You're a damned traitor, Meltes, and deserve a traitor's death."

"I have no intention of dying needlessly, nor does anyone else around here." When Tillman didn't immediately reply, Meltes said, "It's simple, sir. If I'm correct in my assumptions, they have twice as many troopers as we do. We can try fighting them off, but we'll lose in the end, and many, if not most, of us will become casualties. Those are Federation Marines and since they undoubtedly launched from Q ships, they'll be from their Special Operations Command, meaning Special Forces. No private military corporation can or will stand against them. It would be suicide."

"Dammit, Meltes, I'm your owner. If I decide you fight, you'll do so."

"Sir, you're my employer, not my owner, and as such I have the right to withdraw my services if you threaten the survival of the unit."

"Then I'll have your second in command take over."

Meltes let out another brief burst of laughter.

"No one in the Varangian Guard will obey you. We value our lives more than we value whoever hires us."

"We'll see about that."

Meltes breathed in and let it out again.

"Look, we're mercenaries and suffer from a mercenary's failing — we will always surrender to a stronger force when we have no way of escaping because, as I've said before, we value our skins more than your fate. I can always find employment elsewhere if I'm alive. But your failing is perhaps worse than mine. You forgot I was a mercenary and came to believe I was truly a Varangian Guard of old. Now if you'll excuse me, I need to turn this convoy around."

***

With Ghost Squadron's shuttles shadowing them, the Varangians' vehicles returned to Sinjin in the same orderly manner. When they finally passed through the chicane cutting into the berm, Delgado ordered his craft to land near those who'd brought the MLI down. Its troopers had deployed around the base and guarded a small knot of mercenaries standing in the middle of the parade square.

While Ghost Squadron spread out around the parade square, Meltes had his people park their vans in precise rows, disembark, and form up in three ranks. None of them wore their helmets, something Delgado noted with approval. He raised his visor and sought out Cyone who stood in the middle of the square.

"Did they give you any trouble?"

"Not a bit." She gestured at the three people standing apart from the rest of the mercs. "That's Tillman and his adviser, Artemis Ferran, along with the PMC's operations officer. He had a gun on Tillman until we took over."

They watched the mercenaries settle into their ranks and a man they assumed was Meltes marched up to take position in front of the formation.

"Folks," his voice boomed across the broad, paved space surrounded by one- and two-story buildings, and the various conversations died away almost instantly. "Two battalions of Federation Marines have landed and surrounded us. I have no idea what their intentions are but I've surrendered this unit. This means that the Varangian Guard will be dissolved, and our contracts will be terminated. I ask that you cooperate with the Marines and obey their orders, hoping they'll let us go once they're done here. Whether we'll regain our weapons is up to them."

Then, he pivoted on his heels and Delgado quickly understood he was expected to take over. He walked up to the man and halted a pace in front of him.

"Major Meltes?"

"Yes."

"Colonel Curtis Delgado. Thank you for ensuring every living human being on this base is here. I'd have hated to shoot any holdouts."

"When I give my word, I keep it."

"The second shuttle you sent out was carrying MHX-19?"

"Yes, sir."

"And its target was the National Assembly."

"Indeed, sir. The first shuttle was to take out the aerospace defense domes so the second one could impact the Assembly building."

"How did you get the MHX-19?"

"Mister Tillman brought it with him." Meltes briefly recounted Tillman's explanation of how he came to own the highly restricted explosive.

"Is there any left?"

"I don't know. There could be some in Tillman's private shuttle." Meltes indicated one of the hangars, and Delgado dispatched a section from B Troop, which was nearest him.

"Whose idea was it to bomb the National Assembly?"

"Tillman's. Our mission was to start a guerrilla war against the government, but we were not yet ready to begin operations when Tillman arrived and altered our plans."

"So Tillman is your employer."

"Was. He called us the Varangian Guard, and that's the name under which the unit was listed with the Commonwealth Adjudicating Authority. I dissolved it after we spoke on the radio earlier and quit as leader of the PMC."

"You're aware that won't absolve you from any consequences."

Meltes nodded.

"I'm fully aware and ready to face the music. Sometimes you win, sometimes you lose."

Delgado was developing a grudging respect for the taciturn former Marine and said, "My superiors will decide what happens to you and your people. Tillman, I'm taking with me. He has to answer for the MHX-19 and the plan to bomb the National Assembly as well as actions he's responsible for in another star system. Do you know if *Manticore* can carry your entire unit back to Celeste?"

"I believe so, sir. Tillman said it could serve as our escape should the attack on the National Assembly go wrong."

"Alright. Here's what's going to happen. This base will become an internment camp for your people until my superiors decide what to do with you. I will keep my troopers here until then, standing guard on your unit, weapons depot, and shuttle hangar. Ensure everyone knows they're to obey orders and are confined to barracks between mealtimes. I expect a response from Caledonia within the next thirty-six hours. Who was aware of the MHX-19 attack?"

"Tillman, Ferran, me, my operations officer, and my armorer."

Delgado nodded.

"Okay. Tillman and Ferran, I'm sending up to my ship right away. You and the other two should stand by because you might join them in custody pending trial."

"Understood, sir."

"Dismiss your troopers to their barracks and confine yourself to your quarters."

"Yes, sir."

Shortly after, the section from B Troop returned and reported no MHX-19 aboard Tillman's shuttle. He'd loaded everything he had aboard the craft *Iolanthe* had downed.

— Thirty-Seven —

"Well done, Curtis." Rear Admiral Hera Talyn nodded appreciatively once her husband finished summarizing Delgado's report about the situation on Marengo. "He has your devious mind, Zack. At least that portion you developed after you came back to active duty."

"And he has the potential to become even better than I am." Decker gave her a smile. "What are your thoughts on the disposal of the Varangian Guard?"

"Load them aboard Tillman's ship and send them back to Celeste with their tails between their legs. There's no point in burdening the Federation's military legal system with four hundred additional cases. And since they failed to kill a single citizen of Marengo, we'd have a hard time getting convictions for all except those who were aware of the MHX-19 attack on the National Assembly. And even the latter wouldn't get much of a sentence since it failed."

"Tillman and his adviser?"

A predatory smile lit up Talyn's face.

"They're coming home with Curtis. Since he has them in custody, I really would like my people to conduct in-depth interrogations. They must harbor so many secrets we'd like to uncover — commercial, financial, maybe even political, and military. And the turmoil caused by one of the wealthiest men in the Commonwealth vanishing without a trace will be incalculable, especially if he's being guided by the *Sécurité Spéciale* when it comes to fomenting insurrections in Federation star systems. Perhaps he even knows about some of his peers doing likewise on their home worlds' former colonies."

"What'll you do with Tillman and Ferran once you've squeezed them dry?"

"Probably terminate them. We certainly can't allow either to return home." She dropped the smile and said, "At least we now know what happened to the rest of the MHX-19 we suspected was still floating around in private hands."

"Hopefully, Tillman's stash was the last of it. Can you imagine what would have happened if his scheme had succeeded?"

She nodded.

"Political mayhem and societal collapse on a star system scale. We got away cheaply this time, and mostly due to luck. If the Commonwealth has embarked on a widespread disruption campaign, lighting violent fires on their former colonies, we won't always be this lucky."

Decker shook his head.

"No. But it makes me wonder whether we should deploy SF squadrons on those worlds. It's better than nothing."

"I've heard worse ideas. The Commonwealth is acting. We're reacting mainly because we're still trying to figure out who and what we are. And that puts us at a disadvantage."

"Is that an order?"

"What do you mean? Sending special operations squadrons to vulnerable ex-colonies? I suppose it is."

"Consider it done. I've been mulling over a deployment scheme of that nature anyway since Garonne. It'll take two or three weeks to cover all the Rim Sector's former colonies, which is the most the division can do. But the sovereign star systems should be able to look after themselves anyway. They have strong National Guards as well as resident Army and Marine Corps regiments."

"In that case, please send Ghost Squadron directly to New Oberon from Marengo. This morning's report indicates that the rumblings there have increased alarmingly, more than on the other former colonies, and we have only a Constabulary Group there. The battle group from the 22nd Marines was withdrawn last year."

Decker nodded.

"Sure. But what do you want to do about Tillman and Ferran? I can have *Gondolier* and the 1st MLI take them back to Caledonia, but I'd rather send the 1st off with Curtis, especially if New Oberon is getting closer to an eruption."

"I'll have an aviso meet *Iolanthe* in New Oberon orbit and take both aboard. It'll bring them to us."

A lazy grin spread across Decker's face. "Having access to avisos on call is nice, isn't it?"

She winked at him. "Perk of the job. So long as they're available, and I do believe one is at the moment."

He climbed to his feet. "I'll get the deployment in motion."

"Do you still wish you were out there yourself?" Talyn asked, studying her husband's face, craggier now than when they first met.

Decker shrugged.

"I've become used to my circumstances, so no, not really. We have to grow up someday, don't we?"

***

"No rest for the wicked," Lora Cyone's holographic projection said when Delgado discussed their new orders. She, *Gondolier*'s captain, her battalion second in command, and sergeant major had joined Delgado, Major Tesser, Commander Ardross, Sergeant Major Hak, and Chief Warrant Officer Testo virtually in *Iolanthe*'s conference room.

"It beats sitting around Fort Arnhem wishing something would happen, Lora."

Cyone nodded.

"It sure does. Didn't you carry out a mission on New Oberon back when you were a company commander?"

"Yes. We took out some really nasty human traffickers while looking for Aleksa Kine. There was a Marine Corps battle group from the 22nd Regiment on the planet, but it was withdrawn after secession. However, the Constabulary increased their presence, and now the 74th Constabulary Group, with over fifteen hundred members, is stationed on New Oberon. It also has an embryonic National Guard of about five hundred full-timers and two thousand part-timers based in Fort Lysander. The full-timers are mostly former Army or Marine Corps. However, a few of them are retired Arcadian National Guard who emigrated from Arcadia after secession, preferring to live in the Federation rather than stay in the Commonwealth. The part-timers on the other hand, are mostly local reservists and pretty much useless if an insurgency erupts in the next while."

"And we have no idea what to anticipate regarding enemy action?" *Gondolier*'s captain asked.

Delgado shook his head.

"No. Naval Intelligence has detected signs of something developing on New Oberon, but they lack information about its nature. Since there are no orbital controls as such, pretty much anyone can land unseen and establish one or more bases of operations in the backcountry where no one will find them. And that means the first thing *Iolanthe* and *Gondolier* will do when we arrive is carry out a full scan of the surface."

"What are those indications intelligence picked up?" Cyone asked.

"A recent and unexpected increase in criminality in the towns and cities, and attacks on outlying settlements and farms by roving bands."

"Did Arcadia deport any undesirables when it still owned New Oberon?"

"Yes, although the number was relatively small. Nothing like what Celeste dumped on Garonne. But New Oberon being close to the lawless Shield Sector frontier, I wouldn't be surprised if organized crime groups are making a comeback and looking to take over — with *Sécurité Spéciale* encouragement. They have a long history of using OCGs to do their dirty work. Compounding the problem, the New Oberon government is still relatively weak and unused to running a sovereign star system since the Arcadian colonial administration left rather abruptly after secession. Not that the colonial administration was a paragon of governance and virtue. On the contrary. It was probably one of the most corrupt in the Commonwealth."

Cyone grimaced.

"Nice place."

"Like all the former Home World colonies, it's dysfunctional to a certain extent, but the vast majority of citizens are honest folk who want nothing more than a productive, quiet life."

"It only takes a small percentage to turn a peaceful place into hell."

"And that's what we'll try to prevent. Again."

"Three times during a single deployment must be some kind of record," Commander Ardross said.

"I don't know about that, but I'm sure your ship will need a resupply after we finish on New Oberon."

"We can always call at Starbase 51 if this mission becomes lengthy, but we should be good for a few more weeks."

"Let's hope we can solve New Oberon as fast as we did Garonne and Marengo. If there are no more questions, let's get Meltes' mercenaries aboard *Manticore* and send them back to Celeste or wherever they want to go before we head out to our next destination." Delgado turned to Major Tesser. "Wash, I'll let you take care of the mercs. Meanwhile, I should sit down with Mister Tillman and inform him of his fate."

A few minutes later, Delgado entered *Iolanthe*'s brig and stopped in front of the transparent aluminum door to Tillman's cell. Ferran occupied the one next door, and both looked up at him with expressionless eyes as they sat on their bare bunks. By now, they'd been locked up without speaking to anyone for more than forty-eight hours, their meals delivered automatically via dispensers built into the bulkheads.

Delgado touched controls beside both cell doors, activating two-way voice communication, and said, "I trust you're comfortable."

"And I trust you're aware you've messed with the wrong individual," Tillman replied. "I'll see you on a mortuary slab for this."

A slow grin spread across Delgado's face.

"That's the spirit, Zan. Much better to plot revenge than fall into despondency. But whatever fantasies you harbor, none of them will come to pass. As far as the galaxy is concerned, you, my friend, have become a *desaparecido*, someone who disappeared and will never be seen again. Artemis, perhaps you as well. Still, in a few days, you'll both be boarding an aviso and taken to Caledonia, where Naval Intelligence will interrogate you. Once you've told them everything, you'll either be killed or spend the rest of your lives in anonymous detention, perhaps in a maximum-security penal colony on Parth."

"You can't do that. I am a citizen of the Commonwealth, a prominent one, and I have rights."

"Sorry, Zan. You forfeited those rights when you armed the deportees on Garonne and encouraged them to massacre innocent civilians. And you sealed your fate by attempting to murder an entire star system's leadership with that MHX-19 bomb. By the way, simple possession of the explosive is a serious criminal offense in itself."

Tillman gave Delgado a contemptuous look.

"So that's what your precious Federation has become — a society not ruled by law but by might makes right."

Delgado chuckled.

"And the Commonwealth is pure? Hell, it's been using the might makes right principle for decades. I shudder to think what it would have degenerated into by now had Grand Admiral Kowalski not declared the Armed Forces the fourth branch of government and removed it from political control. The rule of law in the Commonwealth has become increasingly incidental since the Federation seceded now that the OutWorlds are no longer moderating the central government's baneful influence over human affairs. Yet that's neither here nor there. I simply wanted you to know about your fate. As for you, Artemis, your crimes might well be considered less than those of your boss and your future could be brighter than his. But determining that is beyond my pay grade. I'm just a Federation Marine Corps lieutenant colonel. Try to enjoy your enforced rest. I doubt we will speak again. Goodbye."

With that, Delgado turned on his heels and left after shutting down the voice communicators, leaving the two prisoners in an enforced silence that marked the beginning of their preparation for interrogation.

When Major Tesser reported on loading the former Varangian Guard aboard *Manticore*, he said, "I suspect Avram Meltes and *Manticore*'s captain won't be reporting back to whoever will run Tillman's conglomerate now that he's disappeared."

"Oh? Do tell."

"Meltes asked me whether we cared if they headed for the Protectorate and set themselves up as a PMC there."

"And what did you say?"

"I told him as long as they left Federation space and never returned, we wouldn't give a damn what they did."

— Thirty-Eight —

"Zan Tillman and his mercenaries vanished from Marengo."

Andreas Bauchan frowned at his chief of staff, who'd taken a chair across from Bauchan's desk at the latter's invitation.

"What?"

"As you might recall, our agents arranged to supply the mercenaries' base with food and made weekly deliveries. During their latest visit, a few days ago, they found the base abandoned."

"And we're sure Tillman was there?"

"Yes, sir. Our agents spotted him during their previous visit. Now, there is no trace of him or anyone else, and the Marengo government is still in the dark about the mercenary unit's existence. However, a massive explosion that scoured a square kilometer of old growth forest to the bedrock between the base and Treves on the day of the National Assembly's opening has left them mystified.

"Really?" Bauchan sat back and stroked his chin with his right hand. "Could Tillman have decided to eliminate the star system's senior leadership in one stroke instead of going with the original plan of starting a new insurgency? If so, why did he and his people vanish?"

"No idea. Tillman's ship, the *Manticore*, has also disappeared."

"Curioser and curioser," Bauchan murmured as his mind parsed the possibilities. "I think perhaps the Federation was onto Tillman all along and stopped his attempt, then made him disappear. What do you figure, Edouard?"

"We know the head of the Federation Naval Intelligence's Special Operations Division, Rear Admiral Hera Talyn, and her husband, the deputy commander for operations of their Marine Corps' 1st Special Forces Division, are as capable as they come. Some would even call them preternaturally lucky, and they've trained the sort of field operators who are scarily good. So yes, I think the Federation Fleet's SOCOM now holds Tillman, which means we'll never hear from him, his mercenaries, or his ship again. Everyone and everything will simply have vanished."

"And we can scratch Marengo from the list of star systems that'll descend into chaos."

"What worries me, sir, is Talyn and her people realizing there's a pattern developing on former Home World colonies and taking action to stop our people before they can strike."

"Which one is next on the list to flare up?"

"New Oberon. The organized crime group we engaged should be very close to opening their insurgency against the government." Metivier hesitated for a fraction of a second. "Will you report the failure on Marengo and Tillman's disappearance to the SecGen?"

"No. He already worries that the Commonwealth hasn't much time left before the Federation takes overt steps against us. Telling the SecGen about our failures might just push him into doing something unexpected and drastic, which we can ill afford."

— Thirty-Nine —

The aviso *Nirah* had already arrived in New Oberon orbit when *Iolanthe* and *Gondolier* dropped out of FTL at the planet's hyperlimit, and Commander Ardross hailed her the moment she was spotted by the sensor chief.

"I understand you carry two prisoners who are urgently needed by Naval Intelligence on Caledonia," the lieutenant in command said once they'd established a link.

"Indeed, we do," Ardross replied. "Shall I send a shuttle, or will you send yours?"

"I'll send mine. I suspect yours will be a tight fit on my hangar deck. Possibly too tight."

"Understood. We'll enter orbit a few kilometers behind you at the same altitude. Once we're stable, I'll let you know."

"Fine."

"*Iolanthe*, out."

Delgado watched the prisoner transfer from *Iolanthe*'s hangar deck control room, wanting to see the evil that Tillman represented leave without revealing himself. But the latter looked like a small, defeated individual, as did Artemis Ferran, after so long in what was essentially solitary confinement, with an actual human being silently looking into their cells three times a day, the sole extent of human contact for days on end.

When *Nirah*'s shuttle slipped through the force field keeping *Iolanthe*'s atmosphere in, and the space doors closed, he wandered off to the wardroom and a cup of hot coffee, black, without sweetener, the way he figured it should be drunk.

Delgado found Rolf Painter sitting at a corner table, cradling a mug in his hands, and joined him.

"Hey, Skipper. We got rid of Tillman and his adviser?"

"Yep."

"Good." Painter took a sip. "How do you figure this one will roll out?"

"No idea just yet. We'll need to wait until *Iolanthe* and *Gondolier* complete the surface scan to look for any hinky sites where bad guys might be hiding."

"Do you think the old Hogue estate is back in use by the cartels?"

"Could be, although we left it full of holes, remember? And what with the corruption in the colonial administration, it'll have sat empty all this time."

"True. New Oberon isn't one of the nicer frontier worlds, is it?"

"No. And to think it's named after the fairy king from one of the most famous ancient plays in the English language. Talk about miscasting. Although I understand the new government, which was installed after the secession, is making some strides in cleaning the place up, But it'll take time, even without the cartels returning to use the place as their base of operations."

Painter's reply died stillborn when the public address system came to life.

"Colonel Delgado, please come to the CIC."

Delgado gave Painter a grin and downed the rest of his coffee.

"They must have preliminary results of the surface scan for me to look at."

Painter raised his mug in salute.

"Have fun and find us some juicy targets to hit. Marengo was a bit of a disappointment in the end."

"You're a bloodthirsty bastard, Rolf."

"Yep. But then, so are you, Skipper."

Delgado sketched a salute and left the wardroom. When he entered the CIC, the officer of the watch turned to him.

"We concentrated the first pass on the settlement area and found three places of interest, including the old Hogue place you identified for us on the New Oberon charts."

"Really?"

Delgado took a seat at his accustomed workstation and called up the link to the sensor files. He studied the video recordings one by one, then sat back. Chief Warrant Officer Nunes, who had joined him in the CIC, was looking at them himself. When Nunes was done, he turned toward his commanding officer.

"Interesting, sir. Someone is living in the Hogue estate, and they fixed much of the damage you caused a few years ago."

"And since the Hogue family lost its holdings on New Oberon, you have to wonder who the new inhabitants are. Could it have been the government taking possession and selling it?"

"Or squatters might be residing there now."

"That looks like a lot of squatters, though. The sensors picked up almost two hundred life signs on an estate that produces nothing."

"So the cartels could be back."

"Yup. We'll have to send a recon team. What did you think of the other two sites?"

Nunes grimaced. "There's clearly something off with both. Too many people concentrated in isolated camps beyond the settled area and no visible purpose for either of them."

"Recon teams for them as well, then."

"I'd say so, sir."

"What size and who?"

"A squad for each site should be enough, and I'd task the Erinyes. They're the best at infiltration missions."

"Done. I'd like the recon teams to insert in," Delgado called up the local time in the New Oberon settlement zone, "thirteen hours when it's the middle of the night down there. They'll observe the targets for forty-eight hours, then extract."

"I'll work with Metellus and Rolf to prepare the patrol plan and the orders. We should be able to backbrief you in four hours."

"Thanks, Jake."

And as promised, four hours later, Delgado, Nunes, Testo, and Painter met in the conference room to discuss the upcoming operation.

"I've decided to send a section each from A, B, and D Troops," Painter said after Testo briefed Delgado on the insertion and extraction parts of the mission. "Lanny Greaves, One-One-Alpha, Raldy Rezal, One-Two-Charlie and Osmin Sberna, One-Four-Alpha. The first two are going for the woodland camps, designated Targets Black and Crimson, and Sberna for the old Hogue place, designated Target Azure. They'll be bringing drones with them."

Delgado nodded.

"Good choices, especially Sberna. His target will be more challenging than the others. Gentlemen, thank you. I approve the plan. Rolf, you may issue the orders to your people and get them to start preparing."

***

Staff Sergeant Osmin Sberna gave his seven troopers a last once-over before they boarded their shuttle, confirming they carried their assigned weapons and gear, including four small recon drones and base units. They wore black armor and helmets, with the visors raised, and carried carbines and holstered blasters.

Nearby, the sergeants commanding the sections from A and B Troops were doing the same while Rolf Painter and his troop leaders watched from the hangar deck control room. Finally, the three sergeants signaled they were ready, and their sections climbed aboard the assigned shuttlecraft.

Once they'd crossed the force field and were through the open space doors, Delgado and Painter headed to the CIC, from where they would monitor the respective landings.

"You know," Corporal Leroy Taggart, Sberna's wingman, said to no one in particular once the shuttle began spiraling into New Oberon's atmosphere, "this kind of feels like déja vu all over again."

"What do you mean?" Lance Corporal Carlo Torres asked.

"Us, headed to the old Hogue estate on New Oberon, like before."

"Yeah, except we're going on a recon, not a strike, so it might be déja vu but not all over again, right?"

"Meh. Close enough for memories."

Torres shook his head, chuckling.

"If you say so, buddy."

The shuttles split up as they neared the ground, each headed for its particular landing zone, flying nap of the earth. Sberna's eventually landed on an old logging road below the crest of a tall hill overlooking the Hogue estate and shouldn't have been visible from the target. The Marines jogged down the aft ramp, dispersed in a rough semi-circle, knelt, and waited for the small spacecraft to lift off again. They stayed in position for a good five minutes afterward, listening and looking into the darkness through their night vision visors.

Finally, satisfied that nothing other than the creatures of the forest moved around in their immediate vicinity, Sberna stood up, and the others followed suit. They headed up the hill through sparse undergrowth to where a small clearing should give them a direct line of sight to their target.

The moment they reached the treeline, they saw lights marking the estate across the shallow valley and spread out, taking up a defensive posture. At Sberna's signal, Lance Corporal Guillermo Coronadas, who carried one of the protective cases holding a drone, unclipped it from his harness and withdrew the palm-sized aircraft. After checking it was still good to go, he mated its video feed to his helmet visor, then linked it with the satellite in geosynchronous orbit deployed by *Iolanthe* a few hours earlier. Less than a minute later, he received confirmation that the video feed was being received by the Q ship's CIC. Then, he launched the drone toward the target.

The tiny thing vanished from view almost immediately. Yet Coronadas and Sberna saw what it picked up projected on the inside of their helmet visors, while the Marines in *Iolanthe*'s CIC could observe on the primary display.

Someone had recently patched up the estate and restored power and perimeter security. Armed guards, villainous-looking men and women wearing civilian clothes and carrying older model carbines, the sort available on the civilian market, patrolled inside the perimeter.

They had the wild appearance of cartel toughs from beyond the frontier, merciless and deadly.

"That definitely isn't an honest establishment," Chief Warrant Officer Nunes commented as he watched the feed from the surface on the CIC's primary display.

"No, it isn't," Delgado replied. "Not if the outbuildings are being used as barracks again for the same sort of subhuman scum we cleaned out last time."

"That's what the life sign readings are telling us, sir — fifty warm bodies per building."

They watched as the drone made a few more passes over the estate before it turned back to the hilltop clearing and Lance Corporal Coronadas' outstretched hand.

"One-one-alpha just launched their drone over Target Black," the sensor chief said.

Target Black was an old logging camp dozens of kilometers from the nearest habitation. Just over a hundred life signs were spread out among dilapidated dormitory buildings and the camp was surrounded by a new fence topped with barbed wire.

The drone spotted the same sort of rough individuals armed in a similar fashion as those at the Hogue estate patrolling the perimeter, a sign they likely belonged to the same organization.

Next came the feed from the drone overflying Target Crimson, an abandoned mine on the other side of the settlement area from Target Black. It also sported a new perimeter fence protecting the hundred odd life signs within and patrolled by virtual clones of the Targets Black and Azure guards.

"They're obviously up to no good, sir," Nunes said once the feed from Target Crimson faded away.

"I know that, and you know that, but there's no law against a hundred or more close friends squatting in abandoned buildings and carrying civilian pattern weapons. Well, perhaps the squatting part might be questionable, but it would be for local authorities to roust them if they cared. And out here on the frontier, they generally don't."

"So what do we do, sir? A preventative strike?"

"No." Delgado shook his head. "We wait until they make a move, just like on Garonne and Marengo."

"Except this time, we're not dealing with disciplined private military contractors or psychotic deportees, but vicious yet highly organized criminals. A completely different sort of animal."

"And because they're vicious, they'll venture out to commit criminal acts sooner rather than later, especially if the *Sécurité Spéciale* is masterminding their actions on New Oberon. Besides, they need to profit from their activities here, and the only way is carrying out their instructions and plundering the civilian population."

— Forty —

The drones ventured back out over the targets just after daybreak and lingered longer this time. And what they transmitted back to their controllers and *Iolanthe* was rather revealing — weapons practice, unarmed combat bouts, and groups hunched over three-dimensional projections of built-up areas discussing how best to attack them. It seemed a little too disciplined for Delgado's taste, proving that the people down there belonged to a long-established organized crime group whose plans might well include overthrowing the shaky New Oberon government and setting themselves up as rulers.

Delgado discussed the matter with Cyone, who'd been watching the drone feeds on a repeater from *Iolanthe*'s CIC, and she agreed.

"Jake Nunes could be right about a preventative strike, Curtis. We have clear evidence they're up to no good."

"Sirs," Nunes said in an urgent voice. "You have to see this from Target Azure."

The drone feed showed five naked bodies, three females and two males, all of them young, being carried out of a barracks building. Every one of them had signs of severe physical abuse — bruises, cuts, puncture wounds, and blood streaks everywhere, especially in the groin area.

"Do we have any teenagers reported missing on New Oberon?" Delgado asked in a soft tone that masked his growing rage.

"Wait one, sir." A few minutes passed while they watched the bodies being tossed into an open pit behind the estate and the pit filled in by an excavator dumping loose dirt into the hole. "There are fifteen missing underage children reported to the Constabulary in the last six weeks. Based on the facial imaging of the five we just saw, they disappeared from five different parts of the capital, Titania, over the last two weeks while they were away from home in the evening. Their disappearances coincided with violent criminal activities, mainly break-ins and looting of commercial establishments. The police and Constabulary are utterly mystified as to why they vanished."

"Typical short-sightedness. Do you have sufficient cause for preventative strikes now, Curtis?" Cyone asked.

"Yes, I do." Delgado sounded grimmer than ever. "How would you like to take out Targets Black and Crimson while I wipe out Target Azure?"

"It would be a pleasure."

"Then start planning. We should get together in six hours to discuss our respective plans and finalize them. I'd like to strike in the early hours of tomorrow morning before the depraved animals get a chance at taking more kids to use up and kill."

"Will do. Cyone, out."

Delgado stared at the blank workstation display in front of him without seeing anything. His mind seethed with rage at seeing those young bodies, half-destroyed, being tossed into the earth like they were no more than garbage. And yet, he knew how badly the cartels treated their playthings. He'd witnessed almost the very same thing in this place. Then, he caught a hold of his emotions and shut them down. He had a mission to accomplish, and that mission would eliminate the vile individuals who committed this outrage.

He worked with Testo and Nunes to develop his plan of attack, and it bore eerie resemblances to the one General Decker had used a few years earlier on the same target when he commanded Ghost Squadron and Delgado had Erinye Company.

"Why mess with perfection, right?" Testo said when Delgado remarked on it. "The general is still the best tactician I've ever met."

"True. Well, I think we have what we need. Now I speak with Lora, and we synchronize our attack timetables."

***

At twenty-two hundred hours, Delgado strode into the hangar deck, where his company commanders, troop leaders, and squadron staff awaited their orders. The traffic control display above the control room door showed a live overhead view of the Hogue estate, suitably enhanced to banish the darkness. Ghost Squadron's leaders stood in a semi-circle in front of it, falling silent almost immediately.

"You're probably wondering why I called you together at this ungodly hour."

Delgado wore his trademark grin as he spoke the traditional joke, one that was already ancient when the first humans left Earth to travel among the stars.

"Nah, Skipper. We're aware of your quirks," Rolf Painter replied.

"By now, everyone has heard about the victims our recon team's drone spotted." They nodded silently. "It looks like the cartels are back on New Oberon and just as vile as the last time we cleaned out this nest of degeneracy. They may or may not be trafficking humans into the badlands beyond the frontier — we can't tell. But it seems that they're just as bad as the Saqqas."

Delgado caught Aleksa Kine and Miko Steiger's gaze and held it briefly. The former had been undercover with the Saqqa Cartel, and after being found out, she ended up trafficked to an alien world herself as a slave, as had the latter. Ghost Squadron rescued both in a daring raid when then Lieutenant Colonel Zack Decker still commanded it.

"There are two-hundred and twenty-four of them in the old Hogue estate, and they're using the same buildings as barracks." While Delgado spoke, Testo touched the controls on a pad in his hand, and the four outbuildings identified as such lit up with a red glow on the display.

"The recon team hasn't been able to identify any air defenses or fixed gun emplacements, meaning it's likely the largest weapons they have are the crew-served automatic cannon we saw then train with, and those appear to be stored in the armory when not in use. But that doesn't mean we'll simply drop in on them and say hello."

"This is my concept of operations." The view on the display zoomed out. "Our shuttles will drop to the deck well beyond visual and ground sensor range and split into two groups, one which will come at the estate from the east and one from the west. Both elements will land within the perimeter simultaneously, and the shuttles will sweep the area with fire while we disembark. Moirae Company will clear the two eastern-most barracks and Keres the two western-most. Erinye Company will secure the landing zone and act as a reserve. We don't know if they're holding any more captives, so take care when you clear the buildings. But do not take any prisoners."

Delgado let his eyes roam over the assembly, trying to find any signs of reticence, but they were inured to killing beings they barely recognized as human.

"Once we've eliminated the cartel members, we climb back aboard the shuttles, take off, and make a few strafing runs to destroy the estate thoroughly before returning to Iolanthe." Any questions about my concept?"

Captain QD Vinn raised his hand.

"I'm getting a sense of events repeating. Isn't that the same way we did it under General Decker?"

"Yep. As Metellus said, why mess with perfection?"

"You got that right, Skipper."

"Right, people, my orders."

For the next fifteen minutes, Delgado went through the execution of the operation and the timetable, along with details on what the 1st MLI would be doing concurrently.

Upon finishing, he asked, "Any questions?"

When no one raised a hand, Delgado said, "Going once, going twice, gone. You may now brief your people."

As one, they came to attention and filed out of the hangar in silence, each of them digesting their part in the mission and mentally drawing up the orders for their respective companies and troops. Delgado returned to his quarters and checked his gear one last time before stretching out on his cot and attempting to read a trashy novel by way of distraction. He had no other tasks until H-hour, and despite his efforts, his thoughts continuously returned to the plan he had presented, attempting to find flaws and worrying about overlooked details.

He chuckled to himself. Oh, the joys of command. Only three hours to go before they launched.

And four hours before they put paid to the latest cartel intruders on New Oberon.

But as the military wisdom goes, no plan survives contact with the enemy. Shortly after midnight, Titania time, the CIC urgently called Delgado.

— Forty-One —

"What's up?" Delgado immediately headed toward his workstation and sat facing the CIC primary display.

It showed three separate satellite views, one of each target, and all were teeming with humans busily doing something. But what that was he couldn't tell.

"Someone seems to have kicked a proverbial anthill, sir. Every single life sign in the three locations is active."

"Get the recon teams to send their drones."

"Already done, sir," the sensor chief said. "We should receive feeds momentarily. I'll put them on the portside secondary displays."

Delgado's mind was furiously racing through alternatives since his original plan had just been tossed out of the nearest airlock. He punched his communicator and put it on send to all.

"Ghost Squadron and shuttle pilots, suit up and report to the hangar deck. We're going as soon as possible." Next, he shifted his focus to the signals petty officer. "Get me Colonel Cyone."

"Yes, sir. Wait one."

Less than a minute later, Cyone's face materialized on Delgado's workstation screen.

"You're launching now, aren't you?" She asked before he could say a word.

"Yes. They're plotting something major tonight, and whatever that is, we need to forestall it."

"That's what I figured. *Gondolier*'s CIC has been monitoring the same feeds as *Iolanthe's,* and I got called. I'll see that my people load and our shuttles launch stat."

"We'll have to strike the targets hard and fast. Strafe them with the shuttles just before landing on top of them. No creeping up and trying to jump the assholes by stealth."

"Roger that."

"See you on the other side, Lora."

"Cheers." Her face faded away, and the sensor chief said, "Recon drones on secondaries, sir."

Delgado glanced at the first one, covering Target Azure. Shadowy human figures were moving about with purpose while large ground vehicles, primarily old box vans, were driven out of a dilapidated hangar. Groups of twenty were slowly coalescing beside each van, all armed, while heavy, crew-served weapons appeared through the door of the structure they'd baptized the armory, carried by their handlers. The feeds from Targets Black and Crimson showed very similar activities, albeit with fewer vehicles and humans.

"Okay. Keep me apprised of everything that's going on. I've got to get aboard my shuttle."

"I'll link your shuttle into the satellite feed, sir," the sensor chief said. "That way, you can see everything as it occurs."

"Excellent. Thanks, Chief."

"De nada, sir. Good luck."

Delgado gave him a wolfish smile.

"We don't need luck, Chief. We need to arrive on time and on target."

As he left the CIC, he encountered Commander Ardross, who was heading toward it.

Delgado didn't break stride.

"Hi, Keever. Bye, Keever.

"I understand your plans have been upset."

"As in, flushed down the toilet," Delgado said over his shoulder. "The OOW will tell you about it."

He passed by his quarters to don his armor and pick up his weapons, and when he entered the hangar deck, Delgado was gratified to see he was the last one to arrive. His officers, warrant officers and command sergeants were waiting for him by his assigned shuttle, helmet visors raised while the troopers were already aboard their craft, armor fully buttoned up.

"A minor change of plans, Skipper?" Major Tesser asked as Delgado joined the cluster.

"The old plans are no longer valid. Our tangos are preparing what seems like massive road moves. We still don't know where, but there can be only one destination."

"Yeah. Titania," Chief Warrant Officer Testo said.

"As soon as we finish here, we'll link into the satellite and observe events happening on the ground in real-time. The 1st MLI should be ready to launch as well. We'll keep the same groups as our targets, but beyond that, I need a few minutes to figure out the next steps and that will depend on what the enemy is doing when we get near. Ideally, we'll do one pass overhead with the shuttles shooting at everything they have, then land right in the middle of the target."

Delgado went on to quickly assign landing spots for each of the companies, blipping them from his helmet visor's heads-up display to those of his people.

"I'll call you over the squadron push if that plan changes. Any questions? No? Please remember to brief your pilots. Mount up."

They quickly dispersed, and Delgado signaled the hangar deck petty officer in his control room that he could shut the inner airlock and open the space doors. Then, he climbed aboard the command shuttle and settled in behind the pilot as the aft ramp lifted. A red light began to strobe, signaling that the space doors were opening, leaving nothing but the thin film of the force field between the deck and space.

The thirteen shuttles crossed the force field one by one, then dropped away from *Iolanthe* as they formed into a vee. Delgado could barely make out the twin formations that emerged from *Gondolier*'s shadow a few kilometers ahead of them. Still, he counted eighteen in two groups of nine, meaning on this occasion, the entirety of the 1st MLI was on its way. And in record time.

Delgado tapped the petty officer at the controls on the shoulder. "Let's get there as quick as possible."

"How hard do you want me to redline it?"

"Right up to the outer safety limits, PO. We must get there before they leave."

"Right. Hang on, sir."

"Skipper, the bastards are putting vehicles into convoy formation," Testo said from the passenger compartment. "Though most of them are still screwing around instead of forming up, ready to embark."

Delgado touched the display to his right, and the split image of the targets appeared, each labeled with its name. He felt the shuttle shake as it entered the atmosphere at a steep angle, heading downward faster than he'd ever experienced.

"How long until we splash down on the target, PO?"

"Fifteen minutes, sir."

"Let's hope they screw around for at least that long."

Delgado kept a tense watch on the display, silently willing the cartelistas to delay climbing aboard their vehicles.

"Five minutes, sir," the pilot interrupted Delgado's anxious thoughts. He pointed at the primary display in front of him. "You can see the target."

Delgado looked up and was surprised to note the amount of artificial illumination emanating from the old Hogue estate. It hadn't been evident in the satellite views, but now that he was watching it live as they swooped down, he could tell they'd strung up a lot of lights, as if they didn't care who noticed their occupation of the site.

"Ghost Lead to Ghost flight, arm all weapons." The pilot's voice sounded over the radio as he touched his controls, activating and deploying the gun pods on either side of the shuttle and readying the missiles in their launchers in the shuttle's belly.

The pilot watched as each of the craft automatically sent the ready signal over the permanent link between all of them.

"We're good to go, sir. One pass shooting up everything we see and then land on top of them. Assigning targets."

The Hogue estate grew on the primary display as the shuttles lined up for a pass that would take them a few dozen meters over the heads of the cartelistas. They still hadn't noticed the rapidly approaching flight even though they should be able to hear the whine of the thrusters by now. Complacency, Delgado figured. The cartelistas still figured they weren't under threat on New Oberon. But then, he noticed several of them look up at the sky in the direction of their approach and a few even raised their weapons.

Yet it was too late. At a command from the pilot, the targeting sensor's grid overlay the live view and with a faint rumble from beneath their feet, small missiles leap from their launchers and sped towards the line of vans. They struck a few seconds later, joined by those of the other twelve shuttles and the vehicles erupted in balls of fire.

Delgado barely had time to note the hits when the four-barreled guns on either side stitched the clusters of cartelistas with a steady stream of plasma, throwing them over.

Then, they were past and entering a sharp turn as the shuttle braked hard. Delgado's craft rose by a hundred meters as it shed the last of its forward velocity and went into a hover. He watched his companies land in their assigned spots while the center of the compound burned merrily, flames throwing dancing shadows on the dilapidated building walls.

The shuttles disgorged their cargo of armored troopers who immediately dispersed, some covering the piles of dead and dying cartelistas, others headed for the buildings assigned to them under the original plan.

Just then, Cyone called.

"What's the news, Lora?"

"Art and I have taken our targets." Art Knowlton was the 1st MLI's second in command who had been assigned target Crimson along with half of the battalion. "The only survivors are half a dozen who were hunkered down in reinforced operations rooms at each site. They're obviously not cartel, so I've got them shackled and loaded aboard my shuttles in case you want to take them with us."

"Excellent. My folks are still clearing the site, but it doesn't look like there are many survivors down there."

"There are a dozen life signs concentrated in the main house, sir," Chief Warrant Officer Testo said. "Perhaps another operations room?"

"Get Moirae Company to clear it, Warrant."

— Forty-Two —

Lucius Farnes, Moirae Company's commander led his troops into the main house a few minutes later, while the other companies were walking among the downed cartelistas, administering mercy shots to those who still breathed.

It was over within moments, most of the dozen surrendering, although a few fired back before they could be disarmed, their shots winging the Marines on point, and they getting killed in return.

Delgado had his shuttle land and joined Captain Farnes in what looked like a makeshift operations center. The nine surviving tangos knelt with their hands joined on the tops of their heads, eyes cast downward. Delgado noticed that they didn't resemble the cartelistas Ghost Squadron killed.

He raised his visor as he studied the prisoners.

"Who's the leader among you?"

No one replied.

"We can do this the easy way or the hard way. The hard way involves field interrogation techniques they don't actually teach at the Naval Intelligence School, but which are extremely effective."

One of them looked up in surprise.

"You're Federation Fleet?"

"Yes, we are. By the way, we destroyed your three columns without any honest citizen on this planet being the wiser." Delgado stepped up to where the man knelt. "And you are?"

He compressed his lips and shook his head, indicating he wouldn't say anything else.

"It's going to be field interrogation, then." Delgado glanced over his shoulder at Chief Warrant Officer Nunes. "You want to do the honors?"

"Absolutely, sir. It'll be a pleasure to wring the neck of an asshole who thinks sending cartel psychopaths to attack a colonial capital and massacre who knows how many innocents is a great idea."

Nunes walked to the kneeling man, grabbed him by the front of his tunic, and lifted him effortlessly to his feet. Then, he shoved him hard against the corner of a metal table, causing the man to grunt in pain as he bent over. He grabbed the back of the man's head, and slammed it down, face first. This time, the man let loose a howl of pain.

"Are you ready to talk with me?" Delgado asked in a conversational tone. "Or do I let Jake here beat you up some more? I know he'll gleefully kill you with his bare hands for what you tried to do on this world. Only he'll do it slowly to extend your pain and his pleasure."

"If you're regular Fleet, you can't treat prisoners this way," the man finally mumbled around a broken nose and swelling lips.

"Who'll know, sunshine? You wouldn't be the first we rough up because he refuses to talk."

"I can't tell you anything because I've been conditioned. We all have, so you can beat me to death if you like, but you won't get a thing."

Delgado's eyebrows shot up.

"Does that mean you're Commonwealth government operatives? Private sector organizations rarely condition their folks."

"What if we are? Will you treat us as proper prisoners?"

"If you're Commonwealth, that changes things, and we will take you into custody for processing rather than have you join the cartelistas in the Great Void. But it also means you're announcing the Commonwealth government is committing hostile acts on a Federation world, which will trigger retaliation. You sure you want to take that road?"

"I have no choice. If you try to interrogate me, I'll likely have a fatal heart attack. If I don't answer your questions, you'll end up killing me, and I'm not ready to die just yet."

"Then who are you, and who do you work for?"

"We work for a security agency whose head reports directly to the Secretary General of the Commonwealth."

A wolfish grin spread across Delgado's face.

"The infamous *Sécurité Spéciale*, organizing an uprising by cartel members on a Federation world. What you've done can almost be construed as an act of war. Hell, perhaps my government will see it as such. Okay, funny man. You and your people are my prisoners. I'll let more experienced interrogators deal with you once we return to Caledonia. Do you, perchance, have operatives at the other two sites used by the cartelistas?"

The man nodded.

"Yes. Half a dozen at each."

Delgado turned away as he activated his radio.

"Light Niner, this is Ghost Niner."

"Light Niner," Cyone replied almost at once.

"Be advised the people you've captured are Commonwealth government operatives. Treat them as prisoners of war."

"Wilco."

"Ghost Niner, out." Delgado turned back to the man who'd been speaking. "And what do we call you?"

"Trevin Margos."

"Not your real name, of course. Are you the leader?"

"No, and yes."

"Very well, Mister Margos. As you can see, field interrogation the way we practice it gives us results, seeing as how we now know what you are." Delgado winked at him. "I'll transfer you and your people to my shuttles and take you with me when we leave. Sadly, none of your tame cartelistas survived. We'll just leave them for predators to snack on. I doubt anyone on this world will come looking." Delgado glanced at Farnes. "Cuff 'em and load 'em, Lucius."

While Erinye Company picked up its recon teams, Delgado ordered a final strike against all three sites to destroy them utterly and was satisfied they'd left nothing more than ruins behind them.

The first hint of dawn appeared over the distant horizon as the shuttles reached into the sky and Delgado allowed himself a smile of satisfaction as he felt the adrenaline drain away and post-mission fatigue settle in. He still had the hot wash to conduct before he could take a nap, but at least he'd have time for a shower and a bite to eat while his and Lora's company commanders conducted their own hot washes.

***

"Did you want the prisoners transferred to *Iolanthe*?" Cyone asked when she and her officers materialized as holograms in the Q ship's conference room.

"No. Since we won't even attempt interrogations, they're fine aboard *Gondolier*."

"Good. That means we can leave."

"Yep. Hang on while I tell Keever."

Delgado got Ardross on his communicator and informed him he could take their tiny flotilla out to New Oberon's hyperlimit and jump on the first leg back home.

And no one below even knew they'd had two Q ships in orbit, let alone a Special Forces squadron and a light infantry battalion eliminating some four hundred cartelistas bent on overthrowing the government. Fat, dumb, and happy, Sergeant Major Hak called them when Delgado remarked on it. Just like civilians ought to be.

The nine surviving *Sécurité Spéciale* agents picked up by Ghost Squadron languished in *Iolanthe*'s brig just like Tillman and Ferran had, but Delgado felt no pity for them. They were professionals who'd lost and would suffer the full consequences of their defeat, though he wondered how hard Naval Intelligence would try to turn them. This human spy versus spy seemed rather new to his eyes, something that had only developed since the Federation seceded. But in truth, the *Sécurité Spéciale* and Naval Intelligence had been at war for a long time, longer even than General Decker and Admiral Talyn's days in the field, though Delgado was unaware of it.

After completing the hot wash — no surprises were raised by the company commanders in both units — Delgado visited his lightly wounded in the ship's sickbay. All were in good spirits and as one of them said, annoyed with themselves for not having ducked in time.

He then finalized his report for SOCOM and had the signals petty officer add it to the subspace communications queue. He then slipped into his bunk, turned off the lights, and fell into the deep sleep of the successful commander. He didn't even wake for the jump warning, let alone the fleeting nausea of the jump itself. When Delgado woke, *Iolanthe* was in hyperspace and about to drop out of FTL at the heliopause.

He wandered over to the wardroom and swallowed a breakfast sandwich and a cup of coffee in splendid isolation since he was halfway through a watch, and the ship's officers were elsewhere. Afterward, he changed into physical training gear and spent a good hour and a half in the ship's gym, working out the rest of the adrenaline dregs from the previous day's mission. Delgado felt quite proud of himself when he returned to his quarters totally at ease with the decisions he'd made and looking forward to a stint back at home and time with Saga.

— Forty-Three —

"They admitted to being *Sécurité Spéciale*?" Talyn chuckled. "The agency must not have the best morale in the galaxy these days. There was a time when they'd have stonewalled to the death."

Decker shrugged.

"Curtis and his people can be persuasive using the most primitive methods. But I suspect the people they sent to New Oberon were of the more disposable sort, not hardcore operatives. It's conceivable that the Commonwealth is running out of qualified agents to recruit these days.

"Perhaps." Talyn nodded. "What worries me is that a fair number of the honorable senators on Wyvern, upon hearing of this outrage against the sovereign and independent Federation, will see it as a *casus belli* to trigger a war between us and the Commonwealth. And we aren't quite ready yet."

"Then we keep it under wraps, just like Garonne and Marengo. Hell, based on Curtis' report, the good citizens of New Oberon never even knew the cartels were back with a vengeance. At best, they'll puzzle over why criminality took a sudden nosedive and carry on with their lives. Maybe some hardy explorer will stumble across the ruins one day but won't ever find out we saved them."

"It'll suck to be the explorer. Okay. We'll deny the New Oberon operation really happened, let alone the *Sécurité Spéciale* was involved. It'll keep the hotheads in the Senate from erupting. But we'll interrogate the operatives Curtis captured. Maybe we can convince a few to turn double agents, especially if they understand that going back to Earth after their plan's total failure might not be ideal for their ongoing well-being.

"Still, taking twenty-one of their agents out of circulation isn't a small thing."

"Sure, but the Almighty knows how many others are out there, plotting mischief on our frontier worlds."

"Hopefully, the squadrons I deployed will catch them before they can do too much harm. But we need to send the Commonwealth a warning that the games they're playing must stop."

Talyn raised an eyebrow.

"What do you suggest?"

"Once you've squeezed the *Sécurité Spéciale* dry, execute them, load them aboard a tramp freighter set on automatic pilot, and send it to Earth."

"Too bloodthirsty and not spectacular enough. Pass."

"In that case, I'll let you figure it out, Admiral. I've got more immediate concerns." Decker climbed to his feet and blew a kiss at his spouse. "See you when we get home."

***

"We haven't received the daily update from the assistance team on New Oberon for five days running now, sir," Edouard Metivier said after taking a chair across from Bauchan's desk. "As a result, I asked our resident agent to check up on them."

"And?"

"I just received his report. He found the OCG members dead from plasma wounds and their vehicles destroyed along with all three sites, which suffered major structural damage. The resident found no trace of our team, save for three bodies inside the Hogue estate's main house. The state of decomposition indicated they'd died three to four days earlier."

Bauchan sat back and sighed.

"Meaning the Federation Fleet intervened again, and they took all but three of our operatives alive. What are the chances the Federation finds out they're *Sécurité Spéciale*?"

Metivier grimaced.

"Considering they're new hires from the Armed Forces and National Guards and not long-service agents with ingrained loyalty to the agency, I'd say the Federation knows by now."

"It's possible that our fast-tracked recruiting and training program was a mistake."

"We had no other way of increasing numbers to provide cadres for the organizations we're hiring in the Federation. And we still must rely on unsupervised private sector sources like Tillman. The entire disruption program is too much, too fast, sir."

"Speaking of Tillman, anything new about him?"

Metivier shook his head.

"He's vanished just as surely as the New Oberon assistance team."

"I'm starting to regret launching Operation Shambles at the request of the SecGen. The damned Federation seems to be several steps ahead of us so far, no doubt thanks to Admiral Talyn's superlative intelligence network." Bauchan climbed to his feet and walked over to the windows. "You know, considering the problems we've had in the last two to three years, I wouldn't be surprised if Britta Trulson was one of Talyn's operatives, considering she vanished without a trace the day the OutWorlds seceded and formed the Federation, her work on Earth done."

Metivier, who'd always felt his boss' close relationship with the tall, handsome Cimmerian had been unwise, didn't say a word.

"But that's neither here nor there. What do you recommend going forward regarding Operation Shambles?"

"I'd end it, sir. One failure is happenstance, and two are coincidence, but three failures in a row mean the enemy has blown the operation. Since they likely know about our involvement by now, we can expect retaliation, and the more we persist, the worse any reprisals will be."

Bauchan turned to face Metivier and studied him for a few heartbeats.

"Very well. Call off the rest of the operation."

"Will you brief the SecGen?"

"Do I have a choice? He ordered me to disrupt the Federation."

"Better you than me, sir. The SecGen will not be happy."

"He'll be even less happy when the Federation retaliates."

— Forty-Four —

"Hail the conquering hero!" Brigadier General Zack Decker stuck out his hand after returning Delgado's salute. "Congratulations, Curtis. I couldn't have done better myself."

He'd made the trip to Fort Arnhem especially so he could greet his old squadron and the 1st MLI after a satisfyingly successful mission, even though the sun had barely peeked over the eastern horizon when the shuttles from *Iolanthe* and *Gondolier* landed. The *Sécurité Spéciale* prisoners had been taken directly to Sanctum, where they would enjoy new quarters in the base's detention center.

"I'm sure you could have, sir. But it is gratifying to come back with all my and Lora's people alive while the bad guys are either dead or gone for good."

"That's because of your excellent leadership."

"And because our troopers are the best in the known galaxy, bar none."

"You're stood down for the next three weeks, and I know a certain captain expects you to show up at her apartment in Sanctum once you've completed your after-action items."

Delgado's grin widened.

"And you don't mind, sir?"

"You're both consenting adults. Besides, you remind me of what I could have been if I'd stayed on the straight and narrow as a command sergeant. Which means I'd be glad to call you son if Saga and you decide to tie the knot." Decker cocked an eyebrow at Delgado. "Which I hope is in your future, Curtis. I know Saga would be delighted beyond belief because it's clear to Hera and me, if to no one else, that she loves you deeply."

An air of embarrassment settled over Delgado's features.

"And I love her just as much," he replied in a soft tone.

In that case, set a date, reserve the Fort Arnhem chapel, and book the Pegasus Club for a reception that'll outdo Hera's and mine."

Delgado snapped to attention.

"Yes, sir!"

Lora Cyone approached them and saluted Decker before he shook her hand as enthusiastically as he had Delgado's.

"Was your last mission as commanding officer of the 1st MLI satisfactory?"

Cyone grinned back at Decker.

"I suppose it was."

"Good, because after the three weeks of vacation I'm laying on you and your battalion, you'll hold a change of command ceremony and report to me in Sanctum."

"Must I?"

"You've had a longer career in the field than many, Lora. It's time to pay the staff piper."

"I guess it is." Cyone, noticing Delgado's goofy grin for the first time, gave him a suspicious glance. "Why do you suddenly look like you're walking on air, Curtis?"

"That's because the moment he gets to Sanctum later today, he will ask my daughter to marry him."

Cyone let out an exaggerated sigh.

"Finally, he came to his senses."

"With a little prodding from me."

"Well, that's the end of the 'will he, won't he' speculation around this place, and I, for one, am relieved."

Delgado frowned at her.

"Was I providing entertainment to all of you?"

"Look, we've known for a long time you were sweet on Captain Decker, and she was sweet on you."

"And here I thought we hid it well."

Cyone started laughing.

"Oh, Curtis. You two couldn't hide a thing."

"At least keep it quiet until I ask her and hopefully get a yes."

"That, I'll do for you. But once she agrees, you will let the regimental families know so we can prepare the wedding of the millennium."

"What if we decide to elope?"

"Then Ghost Squadron will hunt you down," Decker growled. "And they will find you."

Movement in the corner of his eyes caught Decker's attention, and he turned in time to see an aircar, now grounded, drive up to where his was parked. It bore the markings of the Joint Base Sanctum motor pool, and he briefly wondered who was joining them unannounced. Then, Captain Saga Decker, wearing her black Marine Corps uniform, stepped out and walked toward them.

She saluted her father and said, "Why didn't you ask me to join you, Dad?"

"Because I figured you needed your beauty sleep."

Saga narrowed an eye at her father in mock anger, then turned her attention to Curtis Delgado, and a smile of pure happiness appeared on her face, though she wasn't aware of it.

"That was quite the mission you ran, Curtis. But I'm glad you're home safe and sound."

Delgado, who wore a goofy smile of his own, replied, "You know I'll always come back."

"I should hope so."

Decker exchanged a significant glance with Delgado and gestured toward his daughter, resulting in the latter's smile being replaced by a grave expression.

"Saga, I know this isn't the most romantic setting, and I was going to wait until I joined you in Sanctum before asking, but—"

"Yes," she interrupted him. "I will marry you, you big lummox."

Decker let out a whoop of joy, which attracted the attention of every last Marine forming up in three ranks on the parade square as Saga and Curtis Delgado embraced, though it was a bit awkward because he still wore his armor.

"Attention, everyone," Lora Cyone's voice boomed across the square. "Lieutenant Colonel Curtis Delgado has asked Captain Saga Decker to marry him, and she said yes."

The ensuing cheers were so deafening that they could almost be heard back in Sanctum, and the officers and command noncoms from both units approached the couple to congratulate them. As they shook hands with Curtis and Saga, Decker Senior beamed at his daughter and soon-to-be son-in-law.

Lora Cyone noticed the moisture in the corner of his eyes. She winked at him, and he winked back. Everything was well in Zack Decker's world, even if the clouds of war were gathering on the horizon. But now was a joyous occasion, and she watched him bask in the moment, marveling once again at the difference between the man he was now and the one she met long ago on an alien world. And she knew he hadn't finished scaling the heights of military fame.

***

Talyn entered the interrogation room in the dungeons of Fleet HQ, Joint Base Sanctum, Caledonia, and stopped to study the seated man whose manacles were attached to the steel staple in the middle of the bare metal table in front of him.

He, looking ragged, almost manic, with an unkempt beard and hair sticking out in every direction, glanced up at her expressionlessly, then stared at the far wall again.

"Mister Tillman, I'm Rear Admiral Hera Talyn. I head the Federation Armed Forces Naval Intelligence Special Operations Division."

"And?" Tillman replied in a voice made rough through disuse.

"You demanded to see someone with stars on their collar, so here I am. But not to listen to any complaints about your treatment. No, I'm here to interrogate you."

Tillman let out a brief bark of humorless laughter before licking his lips. "As I told your minions several times, I've been conditioned against interrogation and can't reveal a damn thing I don't want to."

"And our tests proved it." Talyn walked around Tillman, running the tips of her fingers on the nape of his neck before taking the chair across from him. "But there are a few people in the known galaxy who can break through any conditioning, provided they don't care about the subject's condition when they're done. I'm one of them. Now shall we begin?"

She stared into Tillman's eyes, and after a few seconds, they widened, and he began to scream as if the demons of hell were looking for his missing soul. Perhaps they were. But then he talked. A lot. If he wasn't quite sane anymore at the end, it didn't matter. Zan Tillman died of cardiac arrest soon afterward.

And Hera Talyn, who could have been a Sister of the Void if she'd had a soul herself, walked away somewhat unsteadily but satisfied Tillman's death served a greater purpose.

Her ability to enter another's mind in such a fashion was one of the few secrets she'd always kept from her spouse and everyone else. Talyn had never let another person watch her break conditioning during interrogation and she never would because she feared what might happen to her if the talent became known to others. She'd turned the recording equipment in the cell off before entering and would write out her report the moment she returned to her office. It wasn't as if the results of her interrogation would be used in a court of law, now that Tillman had merged with the Infinite Void.

But Talyn wouldn't get involved in the interrogation of the twenty-one *Sécurité Spéciale* agents Ghost Squadron had brought back, nor that of Artemis Ferran. None of them were worth the horrendous expenditure of psychic energy she incurred whenever she broke someone's conditioning. At best, her officers would turn them. At worst, they'd exile them to Parth, not as prisoners but as citizens who could never leave the planet.

***

"Due to the failures, I've aborted Operation Shambles." Bauchan stood before Secretary General Brodrick Brüggemann's desk while the latter stared out the windows at a gray Lake Geneva beneath a leaden sky as he listened to his spy chief's report.

"How many worlds were you targeting?"

"Eight former colonies, sir."

"And because you failed on three, you're abandoning the other five? Why?"

"Because those three were the most promising. If they didn't succeed under the circumstances, the remainder had no chance."

Bauchan had no choice but to give Brüggemann a rationale he could accept, even if it wasn't the complete truth. Simply stating that the Federation was always one step ahead of them because their Naval Intelligence and Special Forces were vastly superior to the Commonwealth's wouldn't have helped. In fact, it might have made the SecGen's increasingly short temper snap, and Bauchan wasn't ready to be shown the door just yet.

Brüggemann turned to face Bauchan and the latter noticed his superior seemed to have suddenly aged by decades. His drawn features were pale and his eyes no longer had the fire he knew so well. Only his voice remained strong and steady.

"And what do you propose instead of Operation Shambles? I will not let the Federation build up its strength in peace. They must pay for splitting humanity in two."

"I have no alternatives to propose right now, sir. We may consider relaunching Operation Shambles under fresh parameters with different approaches. The Federation is stronger than we are, albeit preoccupied by restive frontiers, which we don't have, and bringing the fight to them must be from the perspective of the weak."

"And that is?"

"Maybe we could promote and finance direct terrorism on their principal worlds."

"Well, then, get to it."

"Yes, sir."

Bauchan left a brooding Brüggemann to contemplate Lake Geneva again as he returned to his office. Sponsoring acts of terror in the Federation's most densely populated star systems would without a doubt lead to open retaliation. And that meant war. One the Commonwealth wasn't ready for and perhaps would never be.

But, he had his orders and would carry them out.

Once he was alone, Brüggemann let out a heartfelt sigh as he collapsed into his chair. The end of his tenure as Secretary General of the Commonwealth couldn't come soon enough. Thanks to the shock of the OutWorlds seceding, his health had gone downhill over the last two years from worry, though he'd sworn his doctor to secrecy. And it was getting harder and harder to keep up the facade. Perhaps he should simply resign early and hand the reins over to the Deputy SecGen for the remainder of his term. That way, he might regain some of what he'd lost and live just a little longer.

It was an idea worth pursuing.

His executive assistant poked her head through the open office door.

"The Secretary of Transportation is here for his appointment, sir."

Brüggemann repressed another sigh, put on the best poker face he had left and gestured at her to send him in. There would be no rest for the wicked.

— Forty-Five —

At fifteen hundred hours, the strains of Wagner's Bridal Chorus from Lohengrin heralding the wedding party's arrival filled the Fort Arnhem chapel and the base beyond. Due to limited seating in the chapel, most of the 1st Special Forces Regiment, and the 1st and 2nd Battalions, Marine Light Infantry Regiment members formed orderly rows outside, watching on a giant display.

Inside, the bride and groom, both wearing full-dress Marine Corps uniforms with medals, badges, and devices, entered from the vestry and slowly marched down the aisle while everyone stood and watched. Five officers and five command sergeants carrying sheathed swords escorted them. Behind the pair walked Brigadier General Zachary Thomas Decker, father of the bride, and Rear Admiral Hera Talyn, standing in for the groom's long-departed mother.

The best man, Sergeant Major Emery Hak, and the matron of honor, Commissioner Caelin Morrow, stood beside the altar, both beaming at the approaching couple.

Like everyone else, they were in their finest uniforms, although Commissioner Morrow made a splash of Constabulary gray among the sea of Marine Corps black interspersed with Navy blue.

The honor guard spread out on both sides of the chapel and stood stiffly at attention while Lieutenant Colonel Curtis Delgado and Captain Saga Decker walked up to the waiting officiant.

Zack Decker and Hera Talyn joined the spectators in the filled pews, among them Major General James Martinson, the Commander of the 1st Special Forces Division, Colonel Josh Bayliss, the commanding officers of the Marine Light Infantry Battalions and the Pathfinder School, and Lieutenant Colonel Lora Cyone, now the G3 Operations at divisional HQ.

The music died away, and the officiant, a Marine Corps major of the Chaplain Branch, raised both hands. "Please sit."

"Dearly beloved," he continued, "we have gathered here today to witness the union of Saga Decker and Curtis Delgado under the aegis of the Almighty in the Infinite Void. Curtis and Saga have written their own vows, and we will momentarily hear them. But first, I must ask if anyone in the assembly opposes this union."

When no one raised a voice, he nodded.

"Then we may go ahead. Saga?"

The soon-to-be-wed faced each other, and the younger Decker took Delgado's right hand in hers.

"Curtis, I vow to love and honor you for the rest of my life and into eternity." The elder Decker, wiping away a tear, was impressed with the strength and steadiness of his daughter's voice. "Today marks the beginning of the rest of our lives, but we will henceforth face the future together, and I couldn't be happier. I love you, Curtis, with all my heart and soul."

Zack noticed Josh Bayliss knuckle the corner of his eyes. He'd known Saga since she was a wee little baby and had seen Zack suffer when her mother left him and took their daughter away. But he'd also been there as father and daughter found each other again, and Saga chose her father's career path rather than her mother's, making Zack so proud of her.

Even Hera Talyn's eyes held a tear or two, which told Zack his spouse wasn't quite as soulless as she made out to be.

"Saga, I vow to love and honor you for the rest of my life and into eternity itself. Today, we become one and will embark on a new future together until the Almighty calls us into the Infinite Void. And I couldn't be happier either. I love you with all my heart and soul, Saga, and I always will."

"The rings?" The officiant held out his hand, and Hak, then Morrow, deposited small gold bands in it. He offered the rings to the happy couple, and one at a time, Saga first, they slipped a ring on the finger of the other.

"I now pronounce you wed in the eyes of the Almighty and humanity."

A spontaneous cheer arose outside as Curtis Delgado leaned over to kiss Saga Decker, and the attendees inside the chapel picked it up until the sound was so deafening it made any further words by the officiant die stillborn. He waited patiently until the applause died away, then smiled at the couple.

"May your life together be filled with happiness."

Major Washburn Tesser, who commanded the honor guard, gave the order to march off and, once outside, on the path leading from the chapel door to the street, had the two rows face each other and draw swords.

They formed an arch, sword tips touching, beneath which the newlyweds would march as they headed for the open sedan chairs carried by Marines to take them to their temporary quarters. Competition among Ghost Squadron members for the honor had been fierce.

And to the strains of Felix Mendelssohn's Wedding March from A Midsummer Night's Dream, the couple, grinning like they'd won the biggest prize in the universe, marched down the aisle. They passed through the vestibule and beneath the arch of swords to the roaring applause of several hundred Marines who'd witnessed the ceremony on the big screen. General Decker, Admiral Talyn, and then the rest of the attendees, in order of rank, followed them, all passing beneath the arch.

Delgado and Saga Decker climbed aboard their respective chairs, which were hoisted onto the shoulders of their porters. With Ghost Squadron spontaneously forming a guard around them, they were slowly marched across the base to the visiting officers' block so they could change into mess uniform for the reception, which was due to begin at seventeen hundred hours. This was, after all, a military wedding in the traditional style, especially since both the bride and groom were Federation Marine Corps officers.

That evening, the Pegasus Club witnessed the biggest party since Zack Decker and Hera Talyn had tied the knot at Fort Arnhem. Some claimed it was larger, yet no one paid attention.

The place was filled with people in their finery doing their best to celebrate the wedding of two highly respected officers in proper Marine fashion. No one even gave thought to the idea the Club would collapse under the weight of the merriment.

Near midnight, Curtis and Saga slipped away with a pair of glasses and a bottle of champagne and climbed the hill behind the Club to sit in the aptly named Observation Post's gazebo, as her father had done with Talyn on their night.

"How do you feel?" Curtis asked as they sat facing the Fort and its bright lights.

"Elated, but at the same time a little sad my mother didn't even bother sending a congratulatory message."

He poured some champagne into their glasses and raised his.

"To hell with her. If you hadn't decided to follow in your father's footsteps, we wouldn't have met, and the greatest love story in human history would have never been."

Saga, feeling a little lightheaded and maybe more than a little drunk, giggled.

"The greatest love story in human history? I'll settle for a lifetime together, and perhaps we can make little Curtises and little Sagas along the way."

"Or little Zacks and Heras. But you're right. To a lifetime together."

They both drank and settled back on the bench, sighing contently. Then Curtis noticed a crowd forming at the foot of the small hill.

"Uh-oh. If this is what I think it is, we're about to be serenaded. Just like we did to your father and Hera a few years ago."

"Let's hope they can still sing as well as they did back then."

General Decker moved to the front of the throng and raised both arms. When he dropped them, everyone present burst into the same heavily modified and rather lewd version of Blood Upon the Risers they'd sung at the previous Decker family wedding, but this time Curtis and Saga were in the Observation Post while her father and Talyn stood among the guests singing lustily. When they came to the chorus, the newlyweds were roaring with laughter. Then, they joined in.

Once the last notes died away, Curtis and Saga kissed long and hard to deafening cheers before saluting the crowd with raised and, more importantly, refilled glasses.

Suddenly, a rocket cut through the night air and burst into a flower of sparks, followed by many more as the sounds of whooshing and popping reached their ears.

A final tribute to cap off a day when the Special Forces family had come together to celebrate the union of a pair of budding legends.

And the Pegasus Club still stood undamaged the next day.

About the Author

Eric Thomson is the pen name of a retired Canadian soldier who spent more time in uniform than he expected, both in the Regular Army and the Army Reserve. He spent his Regular Army career in the Infantry and his Reserve service in the Armoured Corps.

Eric has been a voracious reader of science fiction, military fiction, and history all his life. Several years ago, he put fingers to keyboard and started writing his own military sci-fi, with a definite space opera slant, using many of his own experiences as a soldier for inspiration.

When he's not writing fiction, Eric indulges in his other passions: photography, hiking, and scuba diving, all of which he shares with his wife.

Join Eric Thomson at http://www.thomsonfiction.ca/

Where, you'll find news about upcoming books and more information about the universe in which his heroes fight for humanity's survival.

Read his blog at https://blog.thomsonfiction.ca.

If you enjoyed this book, please consider leaving a review with your favorite online retailer to help others discover it.

Also by Eric Thomson

Siobhan Dunmoore

No Honor in Death (Siobhan Dunmoore Book 1)
The Path of Duty (Siobhan Dunmoore Book 2)
Like Stars in Heaven (Siobhan Dunmoore Book 3)
Victory's Bright Dawn (Siobhan Dunmoore Book 4)
Without Mercy (Siobhan Dunmoore Book 5)
When the Guns Roar (Siobhan Dunmoore Book 6)
A Dark and Dirty War (Siobhan Dunmoore Book 7)
On Stormy Seas (Siobhan Dunmoore Book 8)
The Final Shore (Siobhan Dunmoore Book 9)

Decker's War

Death Comes But Once (Decker's War Book 1)
Cold Comfort (Decker's War Book 2)
Fatal Blade (Decker's War Book 3)
Howling Stars (Decker's War Book 4)
Black Sword (Decker's War Book 5)
No Remorse (Decker's War Book 6)
Hard Strike (Decker's War Book 7)

Constabulary Casefiles

The Warrior's Knife
A Colonial Murder
The Dirty and the Dead
A Peril So Dire

Ghost Squadron

We Dare - Ghost Squadron No. 1
Deadly Intent - Ghost Squadron No. 2

Die Like the Rest – Ghost Squadron No. 3
Fear No Darkness – Ghost Squadron No. 4
Violent Fires – Ghost Squadron No. 5

Ashes of Empire
Imperial Sunset (Ashes of Empire 1)
Imperial Twilight (Ashes of Empire 2)
Imperial Night (Ashes of Empire 3)
Imperial Echoes (Ashes of Empire 4)
Imperial Ghosts (Ashes of Empire 5)
Imperial Dawn (Ashes of Empire 6)

Printed in Great Britain
by Amazon

55890298R10205